RECKLESS OBSESSION

by

Dai Henley

Published by New Generation Publishing in 2018

Copyright © Dai Henley 2017

First Edition

www.newgeneration-publishing.com

 New Generation Publishing

ACKNOWLEDGEMENTS

Writing *Reckless Obsession* required a great deal of help. I am eternally grateful to the following:

Brian Challis

Cornerstones Literary Consultancy

Hannah Duffy

Rod Ellaway

Hampshire Writers' Society

Colin House

Di Ingram

Barbara Large

Brendan McCusker

Barbara Needham

Dave Rees

Alan Reynolds

Alun Richards

Paul and Marilyn Stallard

Susan Swalwell

Dee Waterman

A special mention must go to my wife, Lorraine, for her unswerving support and for putting up with the vagaries of living with a crime writer.

OTHER BOOKS BY DAI HENLEY

B Positive!
This is not a celebrity memoir. Nor is it a tear-jerking, depressing journal - it's quite the opposite. This is the inspirational story of someone determined to succeed in business, sport and life. It encompasses the dramatic changes in the social, technological and economic fortunes of the country from the end of WW11 to the present day. With great resolve and spirit, the writer tackles everything thrown at him with positivity and enthusiasm. It's not a coincidence that his blood type is B Positive.

Blazing Obsession
What would you do if your wife or husband and your two children were murdered in an arson attack and the killer got away with it on a technicality? And the 800 year-old law of double jeopardy means he can't be tried again.

Grief-stricken James Hamilton, a successful and wealthy entrepreneur, is incensed with the judge and disillusioned with the legal system. Together with his wife's best friend and a canny private investigator he plans the perfect retribution.

Is anything perfect?

For more details, sample chapters, reviews and links please visit: www.daihenley.co.uk

CHAPTER ONE

Tuesday 20th February 2001

Detective Chief Inspector Andy Flood would never get used to waking up with a cold, empty space by his side. He stumbled to the bathroom, trying not to make a noise and wake up his daughters.

His mother, who'd moved in after his wife's murder, would wake the girls later, give them breakfast, take them to school and pick them up in the afternoon.

He shaved, dressed and left home as the sun rose to drive to his office at Southwark Police Station. He took his customary route, driving his beloved Honda through a little used B-road close to Greenwich Park. Sunlight dappled through skeleton trees, melting the sheen of frost on the tarmac.

Flood thought about the overwhelming number of live cases filling his in-tray, giving him less time to work on a particular closed case; the one closest to his heart. His deliberations were interrupted when he spotted a Ford Focus smashed into a tree fifty yards ahead.

'What the fuck… just what I need.'

The severely crumpled bonnet and shattered windscreen confirmed a severe collision. Smoke poured from the engine and flames flickered underneath the car.

The Honda skidded to a halt as Flood slammed his foot on the brakes. Pulling his mobile from his pocket, he called the emergency services as he dashed towards the driver's door.

A young woman's head lay slumped against the headrest. Blood poured from a deep gash on the bridge of her nose. It dribbled down her mouth and chin onto her white blouse turning it crimson. Her lips moved, trying to say something.

He yanked the driver's door handle. It didn't budge. The impact had jammed the door. He noticed the bonnet's paintwork bubbling in the intense heat, like stew in a cauldron.

On his fifth adrenaline-fuelled tug, the door gave way.

Leaning in, he noticed smoke pouring through the air vents. The acrid smell of burning tyres and plastic caught in his nostrils and throat.

Flood shouted, 'Can you hear me?' The woman gave the slightest of nods. He reached over her body to grab a coat lying on the passenger seat and used it to apply pressure to the head wound still oozing blood. Realising he had little time, he unfastened her seatbelt, gently eased her out and placed her limp body on the grass verge. Her eyes rolled upwards.

He put his lips close to her ear. 'C'mon, stay with me. Help's on the way.'

A minute later, he flinched, as the car exploded, shooting flames and white-hot metal fragments skywards. Lying over the woman's body to protect her, Flood felt the shards land on the back of his jacket. He stood and shook them off but not before they'd scorched his skin.

As he knelt down again, he heard the sound of increasingly strident sirens followed by screeching brakes as an ambulance and a fire engine arrived. He put his lips close to her ear again. 'Hang on. You'll be OK now.'

The paramedics took over as Flood explained that he was a police officer. They applied a dressing to her gaping wound and checked her for other injuries. When they'd set up a drip and applied an oxygen mask, they lifted her onto a stretcher. As they manoeuvred her into the ambulance, one of the paramedics turned to Flood.

'Did you know there's a bullet wound in her chest?'

'What? I assumed the blood on her blouse came from the head injury.'

'No. I'm certain,' the paramedic said, as he jumped into the back of the ambulance as it roared away, sirens blaring.

Flood called his sergeant. 'Tom, I've got a car crash and shooting incident. I need a Crime Scene Manager with the team here, urgently. I'll secure the area until they arrive. We're on Cripps Hill, two hundred yards short of the junction with the A206.'

Turning to the car wreck being damped down by the firemen, he added, 'Better organise a low-loader. Forensics and the Traffic Unit will need to check out the wreck.'

*

When Flood arrived at the police station, he walked up the stairs feeling blisters stinging his hands and back. He entered the toilets and peered into the mirror. Grimy streaks ran down the side of his face. Looking more closely, he noticed the tips of his hair and eyelashes were singed. After running his hands under the cold tap, he cleaned himself up as best he could and returned downstairs.

When he reached his office, Flood typed out notes on what he'd witnessed in case they may prove useful later. The image of the woman's blood-covered face and body never strayed far from his mind. He asked DS Tom Jordan several times for an update on the investigation.

'Sorry, Guv. Nothing to report. We're working flat out to reconstruct what happened.' Later that afternoon, Superintendent John Fox put his head around Flood's office door.

'Just heard about your victim. She didn't make it, I'm afraid.'

Flood grimaced as he looked up at his boss. 'I'm not surprised. Do we know who she is?'

'Her name's Jenny Cahill. Ring any bells?'

'Should it?'

'She's one of us. An authorised firearms officer. Recently acquitted at the Old Bailey for fatally shooting a major villain, Terry Connor.'

CHAPTER TWO

Tuesday 20th February 2001

By the time Flood arrived home that evening, everyone had gone to bed. He went straight to his study, as he'd done every night for the past eighteen months.

Back then, he'd taken one heck of a chance. He'd photocopied the case notes relating to his wife's murder, stuffed them into his briefcase and brought them home from the station. Flood never forgave the police for relegating the investigation to cold case status after two and a half years due to the absence of new leads.

It should have been straightforward. Two months before her murder, Flood had been responsible for putting away a notorious gang leader. He suspected that the gang had taken revenge by fatally mowing down his wife as she cycled to work.

The case notes now lay strewn across the desk and floor of his study. He attempted to make sense of them, looking for inconsistencies in the hundreds of statements taken at the time of the murder.

A whiteboard, similar to the one in the Major Incident Room at the station, took up a wall of his study. Yellow Post-it notes with scribbled comments written on them together with mug shots of suspects covered most of the surface. Laser-straight, colour-coded marker pen lines connected each one.

He stood, ripped off one of the stickers, screwed it up and threw it in the general direction of the wastepaper basket. 'Another bloody dead end,' he muttered.

After two hours, he stopped. He placed his thumb and forefinger on the bridge of his nose and closed his stinging eyes, bringing them temporary relief. Opening them, he glanced at the clock on the wall. It showed 1.30 am.

Flood left his study and locked the door behind him. The room was strictly off-limits to his mother and daughters.

Especially his daughters, seven-year-old Pippa and nine-year-old Gemma. He climbed the stairs. Before going to the bathroom, he looked in on their bedrooms. He kissed the top of their heads as they lay sleeping and whispered, 'Sweet dreams, princess,' to each of them.

*

Superintendent Fox buzzed Flood as soon as he arrived at the station early the next morning. He asked him to come to his office, a goldfish bowl stuck in the middle of a huge open plan admin centre on the first floor.

The big fish sat behind his desk, papers and files neatly stacked to one side. Flood tapped the door. Fox waved him in. 'Take a seat.' He indicated one opposite him.

'Andy, I want you to be the lead officer on the Jenny Cahill case.'

'You must be joking, Boss. You know how many live investigations I'm involved in.'

Fox leaned forward. 'We're talking about the cold-blooded murder of a police officer. The case is bound to be high profile. You know what the media's like. Love a good cop killing.'

'Yeah, I know but...'

'Andy, you're my best detective. I want you to give this case top priority. I'll reallocate your current caseload, OK? Give you whatever resources you need. I want this sorted before I feel the heat from above. Understand?'

'You're the boss.'

'You start immediately.' Fox stood, signifying an end to the meeting. 'Let me know if you need anything else.'

*

By the afternoon, Fox had transferred Detective Sergeant Laura Miles and two extra Detective Constables to Flood's team. The experienced DS had worked with Flood before. Her face reminded him of Agnetha from *Abba,* the one with the

5

square jaw line, impossibly grey-green eyes and light blonde hair. She even spoke with the merest hint of an accent. It all fell into place once she'd told him her mother was Scandinavian.

Laura had helped Flood settle in after he'd been promoted from DI in Hampshire to DCI at the Met. Several disgruntled, long-serving officers resented his promotion from the sticks.

Once, he'd overheard a conversation in the station's local watering hole, The Ship Inn, as he sat hidden behind a pillar talking to a DC. He heard an officer say, 'I can't believe the Met would promote a turnip from Hampshire. The most he's probably had to deal with is a bloody stolen bike.'

Laura had turned on them.

'Have you seen his record? For starters, he's got three Chief Constable's commendations for courage and dedication. He's sorted out more villains than both of you will in the rest of your careers put together. Lay off him.'

'Ooh, get you! Got the hots for him, have you?'

'Piss off.'

He'd smiled to himself. He liked her attitude.

*

Flood arranged the first meeting of his twenty-strong team in the Major Incident Room later that day. The Crime Scene Manager had already attached the known information about the case onto the whiteboards, including head and shoulder shots of Jenny Cahill and Terry Connor. He'd added photos of the crime scene from different angles showing the burnt-out car and a detailed road map of the area.

The room, humming with chit-chat, fell silent when Flood strode in carrying a file. Placing it in front of him, he opened it, removed his jacket, loosened his tie and rolled up his shirt sleeves.

'OK, listen up, everybody. Yesterday, one of our own was gunned down on a road near Greenwich Park in broad daylight. I witnessed what appeared to be a car accident. Except it wasn't. The car crashed after the driver, an

6

authorised firearms officer with the Met, Jenny Cahill, had been shot.' He turned to the whiteboard and tapped her photo. 'She died from her injuries at the hospital.'

Several officers groaned. One spat out, 'Bastards.'

He paused before continuing. 'A month ago, a judge acquitted Jenny of killing Terry Connor, a leading member of an organised gang, The Goshawks.' He pointed at Connor's photo.

'They're so-called because this particular bird of prey is extremely territorial. It possesses a ferocious attitude and razor-sharp talons. I'm told Attila the Hun wore its image on his helmet. The gang had the motivation; retaliation for her acquittal. If we don't sort this out, every villain in London will think we're a soft target.'

He looked down at the file containing a checklist he'd prepared and allocated routine jobs to several DCs: checking CCTV coverage, preparing and distributing hand-outs seeking eye witnesses and conducting further searches at the crime scene.

Flood tapped the photo of Terry Connor again, and turned to DS Collins.

'Bob, I want you to work with the Intelligence team. Prepare a detailed report on this guy. I want information on his links with other members of The Goshawks. In particular, the leader. Check out what the PNC and HOLMES have to say.'

The Police National Computer database and The Home Office Large Major Enquiry System had proved useful in many of Flood's investigations. Except the one that mattered most to him; finding his wife's killer.

He turned to DS Martin, the area forensics officer. 'Jim, I want information about the gun and ammo used. Talk to the Collision Investigation Unit about what's left of the car. They'll have set up a reconstruction by now. I suspect another car's involved. We could be looking for more than one person of interest.' DS Martin made a note in his notebook.

Flood continued: 'I've applied for a warrant to conduct a search of Jenny's house. DS Miles and I will interview her husband, Martin Cahill, also a firearms officer, later today. He

7

can tell us about Jenny's background. Any questions?'

'Yes, sir.' DC Tyler, an ambitious twenty-four-year-old officer on the graduate fast-track programme, put up his hand. 'As Martin Cahill is also a firearms officer, do you think that could be a factor in this case?'

'Could be,' Flood replied. 'I'll assess that when I interview him. Anything else?'

The room remained silent. 'OK. I want you to check and double-check your contacts. I don't care how tenuous the links to the gang are. Note down everything. I want maximum effort. We didn't come into this line of work for an easy life. Let's meet again, 10.00 am tomorrow morning, see what we've got.'

The meeting broke up amid a babble of animated conversations.

The search warrant Flood requested came through at 5.00 pm. He decided to visit Cahill immediately.

*

The Cahills lived in a semi-detached house on a modern estate in Lewisham, south east London. Flood and Laura took with them two DCs in a separate car to conduct the search. All four huddled in the porch, seeking protection as the temperature rapidly dropped below freezing. The lights from the hallway reflected on a myriad of nodding daffodils surrounding the neat front lawn.

Flood rang the doorbell. On the second ring, the door opened. Cahill's large, muscular frame, highlighted by a white T-shirt stretched over his barrel chest, filled the doorway. He wore the haunted, unshaven expression of someone in deep shock. Flood noticed that his watery eyes had trouble focussing on the officers for more than a few seconds at a time. He recognised Cahill's symptoms, remembering his own dark turmoil four years previously.

After introducing himself, Laura and the DCs, he continued: 'We're sorry for your loss. I know it's only twenty-four hours since your wife died but you know how these things work. We'll be as quick as we can. Our absolute priority is to discover who did this.'

Cahill mumbled, 'I hope you do.'

'We have a warrant from the magistrates to search your house and take away anything we think may help us in our inquiries. My DCs will carry out the search. May we come in?'

Cahill shrugged his shoulders and slouched back into the dining room without a word. Flood and Laura followed. The DCs pulled on their latex gloves and began their search in the study and living room.

Flood usually adopted his ABC approach at initial interviews: Assume nothing. Believe no one. Check everything. Under these circumstances, he decided to start more sympathetically.

'May we sit down?' Cahill waved at the chairs surrounding a glass dining table as he flopped down opposite Flood and Laura.

Flood asked. 'When did you see your wife last?'

'On the morning of the shooting. I waved to her as she left early in her car. She had to attend a meeting at the Deptford station.'

'She didn't need her uniform?'

'No. These days she helps out recruiting civilian staff.'

'What did you do that morning?'

'I had a day off. Our shifts often don't match. I visited my mother in Walworth.'

'Can you give us her address?' Laura readied her pen.

'Are you saying I didn't go?'

'No. This a matter of routine, as you will know.'

He mumbled the address. Laura wrote it down in her pocket book.

He added, 'I'm not sure how much she'll remember. She's got early-onset Alzheimer's.'

'What about the trial when the jury acquitted your wife? Did you go? See anything which might help the investigation?'

'Of course I went. Every day. I was there when the jury

gave their verdict. Bloody tough time for her. And me. We couldn't believe the coroner issued a verdict of unlawful killing. Connor was a bloody gangster! The CPS had no option but to charge her with murder. She could have been put away for a long time if she'd been found guilty. It really fucked up our lives.'

Cahill looked out of the window and turned back to Flood.

'Thank God the jury used their common sense. I couldn't believe Jenny still wanted to work for the Met. They took her back. She couldn't do firearms any more. Been doing admin stuff ever since.'

'Anybody react particularly badly when the judge acquitted her?'

'Only the usual stuff. A few lowlifes cursed the judge and Jenny. The police offered us a Witness Protection Programme. Jenny wanted to take it up. I talked her out of it. I told her, our lives would never be the same again. We'd have to move away, lose contact with our friends, family, everyone. If I'd agreed, none of this would have happened, would it?' Cahill leaned forward and put his head in his hands.

Flood continued: 'I know how painful this must be for you. What can you tell us about Jenny?'

'What do you want to know?'

'I assume she had friends, work colleagues, family? Can you think of any of them who might have wanted to harm Jenny?'

'She had loads of friends. You're not seriously thinking one of them did it, are you?'

'You know we can't rule anything out at this stage of the investigation. Can you provide us with contact details of her closest friends, colleagues in the Force?'

'I suppose so.'

'You can give DS Miles the details before we leave. Did she have any family?'

'Only her mum and dad. They live in Northampton.'

'Do you have their address?'

'Yes.' Laura noted it down.

'Had Jenny spoken to you about anyone she may have

upset?' For the first time, Cahill focussed his eyes on Flood.

'No. No one. Everyone loved Jenny.'

'Can you describe your relationship?'

Cahill glared at Flood. 'What's that got to do with anything? Isn't it obvious what's happened?'

'No, not obvious at all. We need to—'

Cahill cut in, raising his voice. 'My wife was acquitted of killing a scum-bag gangster. His gang wouldn't like that, would they? Obviously, they took their revenge. And you're asking me how I got on with my *late* wife!' Cahill shook his head.

Flood responded, 'I understand your anger. I know how you must feel.'

'*How* do you know how I feel?' Cahill spat the words at Flood. A fleck of spittle hit his cheek. Laura glared at Cahill. Flood thought, *a lot more than you realise.* He wiped the spit off his cheek with the back of his hand. He decided to ditch his sympathetic approach.

'You know better than anybody that this is standard police work. We have to investigate everything. Including talking to husbands of dead wives. Now, tell me about your relationship with your wife.'

Cahill closed his eyes and let out an exaggerated breath. 'We met at the firearms training academy three years ago. We'd both recently divorced. I suppose we both felt a bit needy. We hit it off, got married. Moved here two years ago. We had a great relationship. That good enough?'

'OK. That's helpful.' Flood stood. 'I'll see how the search is progressing. I'll leave you with DS Miles. She'll note down the details of your wife's contacts.'

Before Flood had a chance to leave the room, one of the DCs entered the dining room carrying two laptops, one under each arm. He set them down on the table and nodded to Flood, saying, 'We'll be here for a while.'

Flood turned to Cahill. 'I assume one of these is yours and the other your wife's?'

Cahill nodded. 'Mine's the *Apple Mac*.' The DC made a note.

He asked Cahill, 'We didn't find your wife's mobile phone here. Would she have taken it with her?'

'She's never without it. It's normally in her handbag. I'm sure she had it with her when she left home yesterday morning...' Cahill struggled to finish the sentence as he fought to hold back his tears.

Flood moved towards the door. 'I'll take a look around.' It wasn't that he doubted the thoroughness of the DCs' work. He believed that seeing how victims lived made him feel more *connected* to them. It put flesh and bones on people.

He began upstairs in the master bedroom. Erotic prints adorned a puce-coloured wall. A full-length mirror covered the wall opposite. Fake animal skins covered the large king-size bed. Very *adult,* he thought.

He pulled on a pair of latex gloves before checking through the wardrobe and drawers. Jenny's clothes outnumbered Martin's significantly. Brightly-coloured dresses and tops together with a whole cupboard full of pairs of fashionable high-heel shoes.

In one of the drawers, he scrabbled around Cahill's pristine, folded shirts to discover a three-quarter-empty bottle of *Grey Goose* vodka and three unopened silver foil blister packs with the words *500mg Paracetamol* stamped on them. A plastic box of *tictacs* lay close by. Instinctively, he took a photo of the drawer's contents on his digital compact camera which he always carried with him when he visited scenes of crime. It had proved useful in the past.

The other bedroom had been turned into a gym. Sets of dumbbells of different weights sat on a frame. A bench replaced a bed. A running machine faced a window looking out on to the front garden. Flood imagined Jenny and Martin working out together.

He went downstairs to the living room. On one wall, a montage of photos showed them on their wedding day. Flood found it difficult to reconcile the pictures of the happy couple with what he'd seen of them: Jenny, a beaming, blonde beauty and Martin a handsome, dark-haired, smiling, thirty-something-year-old.

On another wall, two 'Best in Class' silver-framed shooting certificates hung next to each other. Martin and Jenny Cahill's names had been written in a fancy script next to the Metropolitan Police red seal. He took another photo.

Heavy rock CDs and videos competed with historical paperback novels by Phillipa Gregory and Antonia Fraser on the bookshelves. A heap of bodybuilding magazines sat on another shelf.

*

'What do you want to do now?' Laura asked Flood as they got back into the car in frosty darkness, leaving the DCs to continue their search.

'I think we should go and visit Mrs Cahill. What's the post code?'

Laura checked her pocketbook and read it out. Flood punched the details into his Satnav and started up the car. It meant another late night. He'd miss his kids' bedtime… again.

CHAPTER THREE

Tuesday 20th February 2001

As he drove, Flood turned to Laura. 'What did you make of Cahill?'

'He's difficult to fathom. He seems convinced that the gang did it.'

'Did you think his grief appeared genuine?'

'If it wasn't, he's a seriously good actor. I mean, give the guy a break. A nasty piece of work has wiped out his wife.'

'I expected more shock, more denial so soon after Jenny's death. Isn't that the classic way people handle grief?'

'I know for a fact people handle it in different ways.'

'Sounds like you know something about it. Have you ever suffered grief?'

'Yes. I have. I know you have, too. It must have been awful for you and your family when your wife was murdered. It's a cold case now, isn't it?'

Flood glared at her. 'How did you know about that?'

'Everybody in the station knows. You know what the Met's jungle telegraph is like.'

Flood stared out of the car's windscreen. 'I've never discussed that part of my life with anyone. I'm still working on the case in my own time'

'I think you should talk about it. It's good for you. How did you meet?'

Flood sighed. He considered how much of his bottled-up emotions he wanted to share with Laura. Keeping his eyes directly on the road ahead, he said, 'I met Georgina ten years ago. She was a nurse.'

'A nurse? How come?'

'I had to interview a suspect in hospital. She had to make sure I didn't upset him, make his condition worse. As if I would.'

He looked at Laura momentarily before facing the road

ahead. 'She really got me. Understood me. Liked the fact that I wanted to sort out the bad guys. Saw it as a crusade. She didn't complain once about my job. Unlike my previous girlfriends. With them, the job always got in the way.'

'You've got two young daughters haven't you? How are they coping?'

'It's tough. My mother lives with us. She helps a lot.'

'What about you?'

'Me? I get by. The thing about being married and a copper is, no matter what crap you face, you can go home and cuddle up to the warm body of your wife, forget about the shitty day you've just had. Coppers who have that can't possibly understand what it's like to be suddenly single.' Flood couldn't stop the words tumbling out.

'I can't believe I've told you all this stuff! You know the right questions to ask, don't you?'

Laura smiled. 'I'll take that as a compliment, shall I?' Flood smiled back.

After a short pause, Laura asked, 'Do you think Cahill's involved in some way?'

'The evidence points to someone shooting Jenny Cahill as she drove her car, just like Connor. I'm thinking; is it a copycat killing by the gang? Or did someone else set it up to appear like one?'

'How do you figure that?'

'Remember what DC Tyler said at the meeting? Cahill's an experienced firearms officer and a good shot. I spotted his shooting certificate on his living room wall. And his alibi? Visiting his mother who suffers from Alzheimer's. Bit convenient, don't you think?'

Laura screwed up her face. 'We'll soon find out about that.'

*

Walworth's High Street, The Old Kent Road, consisted mainly of fast food outlets, charity shops and Asian greengrocers.

Reynolds Close ran parallel with the high street, just a few steps away from the shops. Flood found a parking space close to Mrs Cahill's terraced house. They pulled on their coats for protection against the chilly evening.

The house was in darkness. As Flood pushed the doorbell, he noticed a curtain twitching in next door's lighted window. Receiving no reply, he stepped back to look up at the bedroom windows as Laura peered through the letterbox.

'She's not in.' A trim, silver-haired woman stood in the doorway of the house next door.

'Can I help you?'

Flood responded, 'We're looking for Mrs Cahill.'

'She's in hospital. Who are you?'

'We're police officers.' Flood and Laura produced their warrant cards and flashed them at her. 'I'm DCI Flood and this is DS Miles.'

'Oh, my goodness! Is everything alright?'

Laura asked, 'Can we come in?'

'Yes, of course. Please. Please.' The neighbour opened the front door fully and waved them inside.

Laura continued: 'You are?'

'Mrs Cross. Betty Cross. I'm very friendly with Elizabeth.'

'Elizabeth Cahill?'

'Yes.'

'Can you tell us what happened, Betty. You don't mind if I call you Betty?'

'No, of course not. It was quite a shock. I usually pop in to see Elizabeth about ten o'clock every morning for a coffee and a chat, make sure she's OK. When I called yesterday, she didn't come to the door so I went back to get the spare key she gave me and went inside.'

Flood interjected. 'That was definitely yesterday morning?'

'Yes. It was a good job I did go in. She'd collapsed in the kitchen.' Betty put her hands to her mouth recalling the scene. 'I was shocked to see her lying on the floor, so limp, trying to say something. I called 999. I didn't know what else to do. They told me how to do CPR. I'd never done it before. She didn't respond. Fortunately, the ambulance came very quickly.' Betty looked close to tears.

'Is she still in hospital?'

'Yes. They took her to St Thomas's on Westminster Bridge. I called them last night and today. They say she had a heart attack. It's serious. She's still in intensive care.' She shed a tear which she flicked away with the back of a finger.

Flood leant forward. 'Did Mrs Cahill ever mention her son Martin?'

'Yes. I thought I should try to get hold of him but she never gave me his number and I don't know where he lives. Silly really. He ought to be told what's happened.'

'We'll make sure he knows. Thank you, Betty. You've been most helpful.'

As Flood and Laura walked back to his car, he said, 'Be interesting to see what Cahill has to say now. Let's visit him again tomorrow.'

*

Flood turned the key in the lock to his front door and pushed it open. His mother, Stella, stood with her arms crossed in the hallway as he stepped inside.

'About time! You've missed their bedtime... again.' She flicked her head up toward the girls' bedrooms. 'You might catch them before they go to sleep.'

'I know! I know! Heard it all before.'

Flood flung his briefcase on the floor and brushed past his mother after giving her a cursory air kiss. He removed his jacket, hung it up, and climbed the stairs, two at a time, to Pippa's room. He watched her tiny body gently rise and fall in a peaceful sleep. He gently brushed her newly-washed and dried silky hair with the back of his hand before kissing her on her forehead and silently closing the door.

He opened Gemma's bedroom door. As she saw him, she put down the latest Harry Potter book, *The Chamber of Secrets,* to which she'd become addicted. Her smile widened as she held out her arms. 'Daddy! Daddy! Hug! Hug!'

He sat on her bed, cuddled her and kissed her on the cheek. 'You should be asleep, young lady.'

'I know. Did you catch any bad men today, Daddy?'

17

'Yep. Locked them all up too. You're safe now.'

'Is Nana cross with you again? I heard her shouting at you.'

'No. She's a bit upset, that's all. How did you get on at school today?'

'Good. Mrs Timpson says I'm very creative. Look, I made this.' A collage of different materials representing a map of the world lay on her bed. She picked it up and displayed it.

'That's excellent,' said Flood inspecting it closely. 'I think Mrs Timpson's right.' He spent more time with her before kissing her forehead and stroking her hair. He'd made a habit of treating both girls the same ever since they'd been born. It made life easier.

'Goodnight, Gem. Sleep tight.'

As he went down the stairs, he vowed to make more time for his girls. By the time he'd reached the bottom, he remembered he'd made a similar vow many times and not fulfilled it.

Flood strolled into the kitchen and smelt burning. His mother reached inside the oven. Her glasses misted over as she pulled out a dried-up chicken casserole. She took off her oven gloves and asked, 'Do you want a drink?'

'Don't worry, I'll get it.' He opened a bottle of Merlot and poured himself a large glass.

As Flood tucked into his dinner, his mother sat opposite him still wearing her apron. She watched him eat, holding her head in the cups of her hands.

'Sorry about the burnt dinner,' she said.

'It's fine.'

'I don't know why I'm apologising. I never know when you're coming in. I can't remember the last time we all sat down to eat a meal together. Your father would turn in his grave if he saw the way this family carries on now.'

'Mum, do you know how many times you've said that? Is it to make me feel guilty? Because if it is, you've succeeded.'

He put his knife and fork down either side of his plate and sighed. 'You've no idea what my job's like. It's full-on. Perhaps I shouldn't have had a family.' He glowered at his mother before picking up his cutlery, piercing a small piece of chicken with his fork and jabbing it into his mouth.

His mother frowned, wrinkling her forehead. 'How can you say that? The girls are lovely. All they need is time with their daddy. Besides, it's not *just* the job, is it?'

'What do you mean?'

'You know what I mean. This extra stuff you're doing to find out who killed Georgina. That's over four years ago, for goodness sake. I know it's a terrible thing to have happened but you've got to let go. Do you want to be known as a neglectful father?'

She waved a hand in the air. 'I know you love all this... this police work, but can't you see it's destroying you... and your relationship with the girls? They're growing up fast. Next thing you know, they'll be teenagers, going to university. Is that what you want? To be so distant from them, they won't care about you?'

'Of course not.'

She raised her voice. 'And what about me? Since Georgina died and I moved in, I've devoted my life to looking after your family. I do everything.' She counted each task with her fingers. 'Preparing and cooking the meals, washing, ironing, and shopping. And goodness knows what else.'

Flood opened his mouth to say he appreciated everything she'd done. Before he could utter the words, she lowered her voice back to normal.

'Listen, I don't want a prize but I'm not getting any younger. I'm in my seventies, for God's sake! You're going to have to put in a bit more time with the girls.'

She sat back in her chair. 'Have you remembered it's Parents' Day at the school in two weeks? Don't miss it like last time.'

'I won't.'

'You said that before.'

Flood raised his voice. 'OK. OK. I've got it.'

'It's your choice. I think you need to think about the future. Not try to put right the problems of the past. It's selfish. It's not fair on me or the girls. There. I've said my piece. It's up to you.' She stood, picked up Flood's plate and cutlery and carried them to the kitchen. 'I suppose you're off to your study now, *as usual*?'

He wanted to say more. No point. His mother always had the last word. After topping up his wine glass, he picked up his briefcase and walked to his study. He unlocked it, pulled down a file from the shelf above his desk and fired up his laptop.

Two hours and several glasses of Merlot later, he gave up, having made no progress whatsoever. He slammed down the lid of his laptop with a thud.

His conscience troubled him as he trudged upstairs to bed, festered by his mother's comments. He decided to take Pippa and Gemma to school the next morning. Give his mother a break. He'd still have time to take charge of the 10.00 am review meeting.

CHAPTER FOUR

Thursday 22nd February 2001

'*I* want to sit in front with Daddy,' Pippa said, as they made their way to the Honda.

'No, me. Me, Daddy. I'm the oldest!' Gemma always used this as a reason to get one over her sister.

Flood, carrying the booster seats he'd taken from his mother's car, said, 'Stop it, you two. I'm putting you both in the back seats. Tell you what; I'll be your personal chauffeur for the day.'

Pippa immediately poked her tongue out at Gemma. Flood spotted her. 'Don't do that, Pippa. I bet you don't behave like this when Nana takes you to school.'

The girls settled down into their seats as Flood started the car. Speaking with an exaggerated American accent, he drawled, 'Fasten your seatbelts please. We're about to take off. Our destination is Disneyland. We'll be there in fifteen minutes.'

Both girls shouted out, 'Wicked!' They'd never been, but a few of their friends had. Flood promised them he'd take them one day.

He drawled again, 'Here on the left is the famous Alice in Wonderland ride. Around the next corner, they're holding the Mad Hatter's Tea Party. You're both invited. Hold onto your teacups!' The girls giggled as the tour took in the other attractions.

They chuckled even more when Flood, putting on his well-practised Donald Duck voice, said, 'Join me, folks! We're off to meet Mickey, Minnie and Pluto. We're going for a paddle in the lake!'

When they reached the school, Gemma said, 'I wish you could take us every day, Daddy.'

'Me too,' Pippa chimed in.

'I can't promise. We'll see. Be good today, eh? My spies

are out. I'll know if you misbehave.' He wound down the window. The girls got out of the car and kissed him through the opening. He watched them skip to the entrance as they joined in excited chatter with the other girls. Before they disappeared, they turned and waved, broad grins illuminating their faces.

The warm glow in Flood's body slowly evaporated as he headed to his office to review progress on the Jenny Cahill case. His team had discovered that CCTV didn't exist on such a minor road. No eye witnesses had come forward either. A landscape gardener working in a garden three hundred yards away, despite the early hour, said he'd heard three loud bangs on the morning of the crash. He'd assumed the noise came from a car backfiring.

Scene of Crime Officers had scoured the area for over four hours. Two inches of snow falling immediately after the incident didn't help. They'd discovered nothing out of the ordinary. A charred, battered oak tree didn't amount to much.

Flood asked DS Bob Collins, 'Have you heard from Intelligence yet?'

'I pushed them hard. They've given me some preliminary information and promised a detailed report by tomorrow: gang members' names further down the food chain, that sort of stuff. We know Tommy Lidgate is The Goshawks leader. Intel established that Terry Connor became his right-hand man after we'd banged up Lidgate's son Barry, three years ago.'

'Any more details on the Connor shooting and Jenny's acquittal?'

Collins flicked over several pages of his notebook before replying.

'Yes. Intel got a tip-off that two of the gang – Harry Lewis, the driver, and Terry Connor, the shooter – were on their way to eliminate a member of a rival gang who'd crossed them. Our informant said they'd be tooled up.

'The firearms unit intercepted them. As Jenny Cahill and two other officers pulled ahead of their car, she alleged that Connor, sitting in the passenger seat, aimed a gun at her. At her trial, she swore on oath that she had no choice. Jenny believed that she and her colleagues' lives were in danger. She got her shot away before Connor's. It proved fatal. The Met's guidelines for opening fire are the strictest in the world. The CPS decided she had a case to answer. They charged her with murder.'

Flood sensed the room falling silent and noticed a couple of officers shaking their heads. Collins continued: 'Naturally, the prosecuting barrister tried to prove that Connor didn't aim a gun at her despite the fact that a fully-loaded .38mm Smith and Wesson lay in the road close to the front passenger door. The case revolved around how it got there. The defence alleged that Connor dropped it, not wanting to be caught in possession of a firearm. The prosecutor claimed Connor dropped it after being shot by Jenny. The jury had to decide whose testimony to believe; Harry Lewis, who backed Connor or the other two firearms officers who backed Jenny's version. The jury believed her.'

Several officers muttered, 'Good.'

'Thanks, Bob.'

Flood turned to DS Jim Martin, the forensics officer. 'Jim, did you find out about the ammo used in Jenny Cahill's murder?'

Martin put on his glasses to read from his notes. 'The firearms and forensics teams made this case a top priority. The good news is that they found three bullets inside the car. Two missed the target, both found embedded in the rear seat frame. Forensics found the fatal bullet lodged in the driver's seat-frame after passing through Jenny's body. The shooter used 9mm jacketed hollow points, powerful enough to penetrate the car's windscreen. The firearms guys and the Collision Unit have produced a detailed reconstruction.'

He walked to the front of the room, rolled out a drawing and stuck it to another whiteboard. It showed the outline of a side-facing car marked 'Jenny's car'. He'd drawn a red line from the passenger side window of another car in front.

'The fact that Jenny's vehicle crashed suggests that someone fired the bullets while she was driving. Allowing a margin for deflection through the windscreen and the angle of the bullets embedded in Jenny's car, it most likely suggests that the shooter fired the gun from the window of a moving car in front.'

He ran his finger along the red line joining the cars. 'Forensics have already confirmed that the shooter used a Beretta M9. They're commonly used by criminals. You can buy one for under a grand. The cartridges would either have been discharged in the car or into the road. When we arrived, we closed it off and conducted a thorough search. We found nothing. Can't do much now the road's been reopened.'

'How important is finding the cartridges, Jim?' Flood asked.

'It's more about the bullet. We need to match the striations and scratches on the bullet to a specific 9mm Beretta with the same characteristics. It's as definitive as a fingerprint. Find the gun and it's possible we'll find the owner.'

'Good,' said Flood. 'Any questions?'

DC Tyler spoke again. 'What you've shown in the reconstruction suggests that the shooter is travelling in a car, leaning out of the passenger window. He gets a full frontal fatal shot away which pierces the windscreen *and* Jenny in a moving car. The gunman must be a bloody good shot.'

'Correct,' Jim said. 'Or he got lucky. It happens. The reconstruction proves it's possible.'

Laura glanced up from her notebook. 'So we're looking for the shooter and an accomplice driving the car.'

Flood turned to her. 'It looks that way.'

He detailed one of the DCs to specifically check the PNC files for members of all London gangs with a history of drive-by shootings. Flood continued: 'DS Miles and I interviewed Martin Cahill yesterday. He gave his mother as an alibi. We visited her house last night.'

He explained the outcome. 'It looks like Martin Cahill lied to us about his whereabouts at the time of the shooting. We'll interview him again this afternoon to clarify his movements.'

DC Tyler asked, 'Did the search of Cahill's house throw up anything useful?'

'No, it didn't. The techies are checking out their computers.

We've since found buckles, presumably part of Jenny's handbag, plus a burnt-out mobile and SIM card at the crime scene. Martin Cahill gave us the name of her service provider and DC Smith is following them up. We'll have to wait for the call records. Anything else?'

Collins put up his hand. 'Intel told me there's a suspicion that The Goshawks gang have Met Police officers on their payroll. No hard facts yet.'

'Just what we need,' Flood groaned, as he closed his file. 'The solution to this case isn't going to drop out of the sky into our laps. Check your sources of information again. Shake down your contacts, no matter how small-fry they are. I want all of them visited. Somebody will know something. All leave is cancelled until we get a result. We'll get together again tomorrow morning. Thanks for your hard work so far.'

*

In the afternoon, Flood and Laura drove out to Lewisham to interview Martin Cahill again. DC 'smart-arse' Tyler's comments about the accuracy of the fatal gunshot stuck in Flood's brain.

They grabbed sandwiches and ate them in the car as Flood drove through yet another snow flurry. The car's wipers whined under the strain of clearing the windscreen.

Flood turned to Laura, 'How are things with you now?'

Three months earlier whilst on a surveillance job, she'd confided that she'd recently divorced her husband, Richard. They'd been married for twenty-five years.

'No change. Rich is still an arsehole! I chucked him out more times than the cat before we finally split up. One night, I even packed his suitcase. Left it outside the house. He'd promised me so many times he'd mend his ways. In the end, I couldn't handle it.'

'Why is he like that?'

'He can't hold down a job because of his drinking.'

'Sounds like you gave him every chance.'

'I did. I still feel guilty, though. He depends on me. You'd think, wouldn't you, that being a grandfather of a lovely four-year-old girl, he'd want to enjoy time with her.'

'Yes. I would.'

Laura gazed out of the front window. 'He's spoilt what should be a happy time for us. When he's drunk, he doesn't give a toss. He becomes obnoxious.' Flood didn't know how to respond.

After a short silence, Laura said, 'Anyway, enough about me. Any progress on finding Georgina's killer?'

'No. Afraid not. Nothing's changed. My mother's been giving me a hard time, too. Wants me to spend more time with my girls. I want to. God knows, I want to. It's impossible. I give a hundred per cent to the day job *and* I'm still working on Georgina's case. It's driving me mad.'

'Must be hell. It's unfinished business for you, isn't it?'

'The thing is… I *know* I'm a bad father. I can't help it. The girls don't understand why I'm so obsessed. They will one day, I'm sure.'

*

Snowflakes stuck to their coats as they made their way from the car to Cahill's front door. The daffodils looked a sorry bunch this time. Pods of snow had collected in their heads forcing them to bow down towards the ground. Flood rang the bell. The door swung open to reveal Cahill wearing the same clothes he'd worn twenty-four hours earlier. He clutched a can of lager to his chest.

Flood said, 'We've got a few discrepancies we'd like to clear up. Shouldn't take long. Can we come in?'

Cahill shrugged, took a swig from the can and turned into the dining room. Flood and Laura followed him. They sat in the same chairs as before.

Flood said, 'I'll get straight to the point. You said you went to visit your mother on the day someone murdered your wife. Is that correct?'

Cahill slurred, 'Yes.'

'Did you visit her at her home?'

'Yes.'

'You're sure?'

'Are you saying I didn't go?' Flood ignored the question.

'We visited your mother's house last night. You obviously aren't aware of the fact that she had a heart attack on the morning of your alleged visit. A neighbour told us she found her collapsed in the kitchen. She called the ambulance and they took her to A&E. She's still in Intensive Care. What do you have to say to that?'

Cahill, looking stunned, exclaimed, 'I can't believe it. How is she?'

'We've been told that she's holding her own.'

'Surely someone would have told me what happened.'

'The neighbour who found her didn't have your contact details and your mother's in no fit state to talk.' Flood stood. 'I'd like you to come to the station with us. We'll do everything we can to sort this out quickly. You're not under arrest but we need to clear up this matter.'

'I want to go to the hospital, see my mother.'

'Maybe afterwards.'

Cahill shook his head, stood and walked towards the front door. He reached for his jacket hanging on a hook next to it and pulled it on. 'OK, let's get this over with.'

At the station, Laura took Cahill into an interview room and left him there. She arranged for a cup of coffee to be sent in. Flood went to his office to check on developments.

The searches of Martin and Jenny's computers had revealed nothing helpful. DC Smith had chased up the call logs from the Cahills' mobile phone providers. Reams of print-outs covered his desk.

'How's it going?' Flood enquired, peering over the DC's shoulder.

'It's taking forever, Boss. I'm only about halfway through. Nothing to report yet.'

'OK. Keep at it.'

Flood let Cahill stew for a further half-hour in the interview room to sober up. As he and Laura entered, Cahill remained seated, fiddling with an empty paper coffee cup.

They sat opposite him. Flood said, 'We've checked once again with the hospital. They've categorically confirmed that your mother was admitted at ten thirty on the morning of Tuesday 20th February. She's still there, being kept under observation at St Thomas's ICU.'

Flood and Laura stared intently at Cahill, remaining silent. Thirty seconds passed. Cahill breathed deeply. 'OK. I didn't go to see my mother.'

'Where *did* you go?' asked Flood.

Another silence ensued. 'Look, this is bloody difficult. If I tell you where I went, I need you to treat the information confidentially, right?'

'You know I can't guarantee that. I'll do what I can. Now, where were you at the time of your wife's murder?'

CHAPTER FIVE

Thursday 22nd February 2001

Cahill took a deep breath before replying. Flood realised he did this often.

'I've been seeing someone. It's been going on for six months. I spent the whole morning with her. We had a lot to discuss.'

'Can she vouch for the fact that you spent time together at the time someone murdered your wife?'

Cahill appeared close to tears. He hung his head and nodded.

'Who is she? Where does she live?'

He whimpered, 'If this gets out, I'm screwed. I don't want her dragged into it. Her father's well-known. Can you imagine what the tabloids will make of it? Please treat carefully what I'm about to say.'

'Her name?'

'Katie.'

'Katie who?'

'Katie Brunswick.'

Laura butted in. 'Is she related to Michael Brunswick, the MP?'

'His daughter. I met her at a Tory party fund-raising function. She works as a research assistant for her old man. She's young, pretty. I couldn't take my eyes off her.'

Shifting in his chair, he mumbled, 'This is so embarrassing!'

'Where does she live?' Cahill paused before giving Flood an address in Westminster. Laura scribbled it in her notebook.

Flood stood. 'We'll go there, check it out.' He stared down at Cahill. 'I don't appreciate being lied to. You could have saved us a lot of time if you'd told us the truth in the first place.'

Cahill shrugged. 'Can I go now? I need to see my mother.'

'Yes. We'll be in touch once we've spoken to your girlfriend.'

*

Flood drove Laura back to Southwark Police Station through the late afternoon traffic, slowed by the continuing snow flurries. He stopped at traffic lights shortly after leaving Cahill's house. He said, 'I told you I wasn't convinced about Cahill's story.'

'You did. Do you want me to go and see Katie Brunswick now? It's not far from where I live.'

'Good idea. I'll drop you back at the station to pick up your car.'

When they arrived, Flood went straight to his office and asked DS Collins whether he'd received the file from the Intelligence team.

'It's just arrived. I'll bring it through.'

Collins entered Flood's office waving the file. 'This makes interesting reading, Boss.'

He flicked through to the back of the file, opened an A3-size document showing an organisation chart and flattened it out on Flood's desk using the palms of his hands. He turned it round so Flood could see it and walked around the desk and stood next to him.

'Tommy Lidgate's gang, The Goshawks, suffered a blow when a jury found Barry Lidgate, his son, guilty of attempted murder three years ago. Barry had slashed a rival gang member's throat, practically severing his head.'

'Charming.'

'The judge sentenced him to a minimum of twenty years.'

'Doesn't seem enough.'

Collins pointed to the chart. 'You know about Terry Connor. He's the guy Jenny Cahill shot. He took Barry's place as Tommy's right-hand man. So they've lost two of their top guys. There's another Lidgate, Vinnie, Barry's son, Tommy's grandson, aged twenty-one.' Collins pointed to the chart again. 'He's moved closer to the top of the hierarchy. He's got a number of convictions for violent behaviour.'

'Seems to run in the family.'

'Another key member is Robbie Barlow. He heads up the drug-running side of the firm. He joined the gang a couple of years ago. Intel informs us that although he's believed to be dealing in significant quantities of Class A drugs, his only convictions are for Class B stuff.'

He flicked over the pages one at a time until he reached a section showing photographs of suspected gang members.

'We've got these shots of Vinnie Lidgate but only this one for Barlow, which isn't particularly good.' He pointed them out in turn.

'Any photos of Tommy Lidgate?'

Collins turned over another page. 'We've only got two. He's notoriously shy when it comes to being photographed. There's his prison photo which is fifteen years old. He served five years for GBH. He's managed to avoid convictions ever since by intimidating the shit out of witnesses. The other one is this holiday snap, taken in Spain a couple of years ago.' Collins stabbed a finger at a photo portraying a middle-aged, greying man with a paunch hanging over the side of his shorts.

'Tommy Lidgate's big time. Intel is well aware of him. There's a detailed profile in the file.'

He turned to another page. 'Drug-trafficking is their main source of income. They're allegedly bringing in large shipments from Mexican cartels via France. Intel tell me there's nowhere near enough evidence to convict.'

Flood shook his head. 'How many times have we heard that?'

Collins continued: 'It gets worse. They've been linked to at least five violent gangland murders, typically informants and rival criminals. After the gang torture their rivals, they shoot them in the back of the head and leave their trademark; a crude 'G', carved into their victim's back. It's a sign: don't fuck with The Goshawks. Witnesses are *persuaded* not to testify against them. It's all in the file. Lidgate appears untouchable.'

'So far,' muttered Flood.

'The file also contains the profiles of Vinnie Lidgate and

31

Robbie Barlow.'

'Good work, Bob. Put whatever you can on the board. I'll get the team to focus on putting pressure on these individuals. I'll organise a surveillance operation, make sure members of the gang know about it. Let's haul them in for questioning; let them know we're serious about getting justice for Jenny.'

Collins nodded.

'They may be afraid of Tommy Lidgate but by the time we've finished with them, I want them to fear us more.'

When DS Collins left his office, Flood turned back to the file and read the summary of the profiles. Tommy Lidgate had been involved with gangs since the age of fourteen, working his way up the criminal ladder, starting with minor drug dealing. The offender profile confirmed him as a deeply unpleasant, arrogant person, prepared to sanction intimidation and violence to protect his fiefdom. He rarely used violence himself these days, relying on his henchmen to carry out his orders.

Flood read with disappointment that Anti-Corruption Command had produced a report six months previously suggesting that Thomas Lidgate had been shielded from prosecution by a network of corrupt police officers. An internal investigation had taken place but no charges made.

Flood never understood why corrupt individuals joined the police force. Surely the whole reason you signed up was to ensure the bad guys got banged up. Not be swayed by a brown envelope containing used fifty-pound notes.

He flicked through Vinnie Lidgate and Robbie Barlow's profiles. They confirmed what he'd already learnt: Vinnie had a taste for sadistic, violent behaviour and Barlow had quickly risen to be The Goshawks drug-dealer-in-chief.

*

As Flood packed his briefcase, hoping to get home before his girls went to bed, his mobile rang.

'It's me, Boss.' Laura's voice sounded strained. 'I'm at Katie Brunswick's flat. I can't get a reply. I peered in through the window the best I could. All appears fine. I hung around for an hour, spoke to her neighbours. They say they haven't seen her for the last two days.'

'Interesting. Do any of them have a spare key?'

'I thought of that. No, they haven't. But I remembered Cahill saying she worked for her father, the MP. I called his office in Westminster.'

'And?'

'He's still at the Commons. His PA said she'd get a message to him to call me urgently. I'm still here, waiting.'

'Get him to meet you on site. Hopefully, he's got a spare key.'

'Sure.'

'I'm leaving for home now. Call me as soon as you have something.'

*

Pippa and Gemma rushed to the front door to welcome Flood. As they entered the kitchen, his mother turned, continuing to stir a saucepan of tomato sauce. 'You're just in time. It's so rare for us all to sit down together for a family meal.' Flood ignored the implicit sarcasm as he kissed her on the cheek.

He enjoyed hearing the girls' news as they tucked into their dinner. He discovered a lot too: the names of their best friends, who'd fallen out, who'd been naughty.

'Do you actually *learn* anything from the teachers at school?' Flood teased.

'Of course we do, Daddy. My favourite's Miss Blenkinsop,' Pippa said.

'And mine's Miss Jones.' Gemma would not be outdone.

The shrill ringtone of Flood's mobile resting on the sideboard cut into the conversation. Flood glanced at his mother who gave him a disapproving glare, as if to say, *I dare you!*

He left the table, picked up his mobile and, noticing the caller's name, turned to his daughters and said, 'Sorry, girls, this is important.'

Stella glowered at him, muttering, 'It's *always* important.'

As he walked to his study, his mobile pressed tightly to his ear, Flood heard Laura say, 'Katie Brunswick's father came over within the hour with a spare key to her flat. Everything appears fine. All her clothes are in the wardrobes and drawers. Her bathroom stuff's still here. On the night before Jenny's murder, her father said Katie had called in sick and wouldn't be coming in to work the next morning. Nothing to worry about, she'd said. Her father said it had happened many times before. He's concerned for her. He said she's a troubled person.'

'So it's possible she did meet Cahill that morning? Why has she disappeared?'

'Maybe he tipped her off about the possibility of the media having a field day if news of the affair leaked out and she's gone to ground.'

Flood hesitated before saying, 'I think Martin Cahill has got some explaining to do. Go to his place. Bring him to the station. I'll meet you there within the hour.'

Flood walked back into the kitchen/diner, put on his jacket, leaned over his daughters and kissed their heads. 'Sorry, girls. I've got to go back to work.'

Both girls groaned. 'Tell you what? I'll take you to school again tomorrow, OK?' Flood nodded at his mother hoping the gesture would appease her. 'Now you be good for Nana.'

'You haven't finished your dinner, Daddy,' said Pippa.

'Keep it warm. I'll have it later.'

Flood's mother shook her head. Retracing his steps out of the kitchen, he scooped his car keys from a hook inside the front door and closed it behind him.

*

Laura glanced up from her computer as Flood entered the Major Incident Room at just after nine o'clock.

'Hi, Boss. Cahill's in interview room four.'

'Good. Let's see what he has to say for himself.'

As Flood and Miles entered the room, Cahill stood. 'I know

you're only doing your job but shouldn't you lot be out looking for the shit who killed my wife?'

'I can assure you that is precisely what we're doing. Once you've answered our questions you're free to go. Please sit.'

Cahill did so. Flood and Laura sat opposite him. Flood continued: 'The reason for this interview is to run through your alibi again. First you told us you spent time with your mother at the time of the shooting. Then you admitted you'd lied to us to protect your girlfriend and spent the morning with her. DS Miles visited Katie Brunswick's flat earlier today. She's not there. Her father and her neighbours confirm that she hasn't been seen for the last two days. Can you confirm the last time you had contact with her?'

'I've told you. We had a lot to discuss. I last met her on the morning of the shooting.'

'Where did you meet?'

'It's tucked away, a spot close to one of the entrances to Epping Forest. Obviously, we didn't want to run the risk of being seen together.'

'Epping Forest? That's a long way from where you both live.'

'Her family used to own a house in Loughton. They brought her up there. She told me she loves the forest, feels a special affinity with the place. Used to go horse-riding there as a kid. She told me she practically lived at the equestrian centre nearby.'

'How did you get to Epping Forest?'

'We drove in separate cars. It took me over an hour to get there.'

'What time did you meet?'

'About nine in the morning. After I parked, I walked to her car and we sat talking.'

'Can we be absolutely clear about this? You've not spoken to her or called her since then?'

'No, I haven't.'

'You said you had a lot to discuss with her. What, exactly?'

'This is so embarrassing.' Cahill stared at the floor then looked up at Flood. 'I wanted to end our relationship. She's bad news. She'd become totally obsessed with me. I fell for it. Flattered, I suppose. You know how it is.'

'No, Martin. Tell me how it is?'

'I became besotted with her, too. She turned me on. It took me a while but I recognised she suffered severe mood swings and bouts of depression. She's insanely jealous. She couldn't bear the thought of me going back to sleep with Jenny. I spent the whole morning trying to let her down lightly. She wouldn't have it, went berserk, shouting, crying, trying to scratch my eyes out. She's seriously unbalanced.'

'I think we've got the point,' Flood interjected.

'You don't understand. I knew from what she told me about previous boyfriends that she'd have difficulty in dealing with rejection. I'd tried ending the relationship before. I had to back off, hope she'd eventually see reason. Instead, she hounded me. Sent twenty or thirty texts a day. Here, you can check for yourself.' Cahill pulled out his mobile from his trouser pocket. He threw it across the table in Flood's direction.

Laura picked it up. 'We'll keep this for a while. I'll make sure you get a receipt.'

Cahill stared down at his feet. 'There's something else. Before I realised what she was like, I stupidly allowed her to film us having sex together. She got off on that sort of thing. She threatened to send it to Jenny... and to my mother, for God's sake! As if that wasn't enough, she said she'd send them an email telling them about our fantastic sex life.' He leant forward and put his head in his hands. 'How stupid am I?'

Flood said, 'Pretty stupid. Carry on.'

Cahill looked up. 'I pleaded with her. Pointed out that if the press got hold of this, it would seriously affect my marriage and her father's career. She said she didn't give a toss; only wanted me.' He bowed his head again, shaking it from side to side.

'Did you leave together?'

'No. I felt I'd said as much as I could. I left her in her car, walked back to mine and drove home.'

'What state was she in when you left her?'

'I thought she'd eventually calmed down. She gave me a final hug. I asked her if she felt OK. She said, yes. Trouble is, she's so unpredictable. Mentioned committing suicide a few times.'

'What time did you leave her?'

'About midday.'

'You spent *three hours* talking in her car?'

'You've no idea what she's like. It took me all that time to get her to calm down, going through all the reasons our future relationship wouldn't work. She wouldn't accept that I wanted out.'

'Obviously not.'

'As I drove closer to home, I turned on my mobile. I had four missed calls. That's when I learnt about the shooting. Your guys had been trying to get hold of me. I went straight to the hospital to see Jenny. Six hours later, she died.'

His bulky frame shuddered. He reached inside his trouser pocket, retrieved a handkerchief and wiped his eyes.

Flood waited until Cahill had finished. 'OK. Give us a few moments. We'll see if there's any more news about her whereabouts.'

He and Laura returned to the Investigation Room and asked those members of his team still working late whether they'd made any progress. Several officers shook their heads. Dejected, Flood walked along the corridor to his office and asked Laura to join him.

As she sat down, Flood said, 'What do you think?'

'I'm not sure.'

Flood stroked his chin. 'There's something not right about this, is there? His only motive to kill Jenny as far as we know is to be with Katie. But, he has a motive to get rid of her if she's as unbalanced as he's led us to believe. Yet she's the only person able to provide him with an alibi for Jenny's murder.'

'Surely he wouldn't want to go off with Katie?'

'You're assuming he's told us the truth. Remember, he's already lied to us about using his mother as his alibi. He wouldn't know that would backfire on him. He's relying on

Katie now.'

'But she could destroy him if news of the affair and the sex tape got out.'

Flood rested his elbows on his desk. 'Did you ever see the film, *Fatal Attraction?*'

'Yes, why?'

'It's one of my favourite movies. Assuming Cahill's telling the truth, Katie Brunswick sounds like the bunny-boiler. Remember? When the girlfriend got rejected by Dan Gallagher, played by Michael Douglas, she put one of the family pets, a cute bunny rabbit, in a saucepan and boiled the poor bugger to death.'

Laura grimaced at recalling the scene. 'Ooh! Yes, I do remember. Some scary bitch. Hell hath no fury, eh? You don't think Katie had anything to do with Jenny's shooting, do you? If she's as unbalanced as Cahill says, she'd have a motive, wouldn't she?'

'She would. But it looks like a crack shot killed Jenny. Let's not dismiss the idea, though.'

Flood sat forward in his chair. 'Katie holds the key. She's been missing for two days and given her mental state, I think the level of risk is enough to get a search organised at Epping Forest. I'll talk to Foxy first thing in the morning.'

'OK.'

'Can you follow up her mobile phone provider? If she's turned on her mobile , maybe they can pinpoint its location.'

Laura made a note. She continued scribbling as Flood gave her a list of further tasks.

'Circulate her photo to all stations as a Missing Persons alert. Check with all the London hospitals too. Check out her medical records, talk to her father, see if Cahill's telling the truth about her state of mind.

'Oh, and get the analysts to check out any CCTV following the route from Cahill's home to Epping Forest and back. It may tell us something.'

Laura flicked over the pages of her notebook forward and backwards. When she found what she was looking for, she said, 'I'm trying to get a fix on the timing. He said he met her at nine. It would take at least an hour to get from his place in Lewisham to Epping Forest so he would have to leave at eight at the latest. That's roughly the same time you spotted Jenny's car crashed against a tree near Greenwich. It's at least an hour's drive from Lewisham to Greenwich at that time on a Monday morning. He can't be in two places at the same time.'

'And your point is?'

'My point is, could Cahill have used a hit man?'

'My gut feeling is he didn't. He strikes me as someone who deals with things himself. It's worth checking his emails and phone messages, though. Especially his claim to receiving loads of texts from Katie.'

'You think we should release him?'

'We've no choice. All we've got is a hypothesis, which is that he killed Jenny and made it appear like a gangland revenge killing so he could be with Katie Brunswick.'

Laura shook her head. 'I don't buy that.'

Flood grimaced. 'Let him go. We'll need something more concrete to detain him.'

CHAPTER SIX

Friday 23rd February 2001

Flood arrived back home just after midnight. Everyone had gone to bed. He didn't feel up to working on his cold case. Instead, he poured himself a can of London Pride, his favourite beer, and placed a Leonard Cohen CD in the player in the sitting room. Since Georgina's death, he often wallowed in his favourite melancholic music. Here in the privacy of his own company he could let go, not bothering to put on a brave face to the outside world.

He woke with a start and checked his watch. It showed 2.15 am. The house felt chilly. The central heating had gone off long ago. Granules of frost stuck to the outside of the windows as he climbed the stairs. Remembering his promise to take the girls to school in the morning, he set his alarm for 7.30 am.

After breakfast, Flood scraped the ice off the windscreen of his car, dropped his girls off at school and drove to Southwark Police Station in time for the morning review meeting.

He entered the Major Incident Room, which hummed with the sound of officers engaged in conversations in person and on landlines. Others stared intently at their computer screens and made notes. It never ceased to amaze Flood the amount of legwork undertaken in a major enquiry, all of which had to be documented and filed creating enough paperwork to fill a builder's skip.

Laura, who always seemed to be on duty since joining his team, flashed him a smile. It cheered Flood. That and those sparkling grey-green eyes. Flood learnt that both features disguised an inner toughness. He recalled a case they'd worked on shortly after he'd joined the Met. They'd tracked down and cornered an armed robber. He'd lunged at Laura with a six-inch knife, causing a deep wound in her shoulder. Before Flood could react, she'd skilfully disarmed her assailant and used her good arm to bang his face against the shutters of a shop window. The impact broke his nose. Then, she'd cuffed him.

Laura stood and waved a file. 'Boss, before the meeting starts, I've got something for you. How about this! I got one of the DCs to talk to members of Jenny's firearms unit. They told him that rumours are rife about her seeing a fellow officer, a Carl Russell. Although the car explosion destroyed Jenny's mobile, the service provider provided call logs showing that they'd contacted each other half-a-dozen times a day over the last three months. No question about it. They were definitely in a relationship.'

Flood raised his eyebrows. 'I wonder if Cahill knew?'

Laura shrugged, as if to say, *I don't know.*

Flood asked, 'Any news on Katie?'

'Yes. We've accessed her medical records. It confirms what her father said. She's been on medication for the last eight years for borderline personality disorder.'

'So Cahill's actually told the truth for once. That's a first. By the way, Foxy's authorised a search of the area at first light tomorrow morning, starting from where Cahill says he last saw Katie in Epping Forest. Any news from Missing Persons?'

'Absolutely nothing.'

'OK. Let's start the meeting. You can report what you've told me. I want to know if we've got anywhere with the other line of enquiry. Heard anything?'

'No, I haven't. I've stuck with the Cahill option. DS Collins is investigating the gangland connection.'

After Flood had updated the team, he asked them whether they'd heard from their informants. Several officers shuffled their feet. They glanced at each other or down to the floor.

'Well?' Flood challenged.

DS Collins spoke. 'Sorry, Boss. Every snout we know has clammed up. None of them wants anything to do with the killing of a copper. They're terrified of possible repercussions. It suggests a gangland hit but we can't be sure.'

Flood tapped his fingers on the desk in frustration. 'Unless we get more evidence, we can't arrest Cahill or any of The

Goshawks gang. Come on! For Christ's sake, it's been three days now and we've got absolutely zilch!'

He stomped towards the door and said over his shoulder, 'We'll meet same time tomorrow. I hope you'll have more for me by then.' He added, 'Laura, come to my office.'

As they both sat down, Flood said, 'I think it's highly possible that Cahill knew about Jenny's affair. If so, that's his motive. If his alibi can't be proved, he would have the opportunity.'

'Do you want me to arrest him?'

'Not yet. Bring him in this afternoon. He knows the ropes but suggest that he may need legal representation. That should add more pressure.'

*

Before they entered the interview room, Laura updated Flood. 'Cahill's told us the truth about Katie's text messages. Look, there are hundreds of them.' She turned a print-out of the texts towards him. Flood scanned them:

> *Can't go on living without you.*
> *If u dump me, i'll top myself.*
> *You'll be the one responsible if i kill myself.*

The texts grew more hostile when Cahill didn't reply:

> *You think ure so fucking special. Hope u rot in hell.*
> *Spose you're with that bitch of a wife.*
> *Didn't realise u were such a prick.*

Then there'd be a change of tone before reverting to type:

> *Sorry I didn't mean what i said.*
> *i'll do anything for you.*
> *please please lets carry on the way we are.*

Flood turned the print-out back towards Laura. 'Interesting.'

'We haven't located the sex tapes yet and we are struggling to find anything conclusive on CCTV. It's a big job. We need another day to trace Cahill's journey from his home to Epping

Forest.'

Laura and Flood entered the interview room at 3.30 pm. Cahill and the duty solicitor, whose bulging case lay on the chair next to him, were already seated. Cahill's hulking physique dominated the room.

The solicitor, an urbane, silver-haired man dressed in a pinstripe suit introduced himself and handed over a business card to each of them showing his name; Adrian Scholes.

Cahill leant forward towards Flood. 'I can't believe you're wasting all this time on me. What are you doing to find my wife's killer?'

'We're pulling out all the stops, believe me.' Flood turned to Scholes. 'Your client is free to leave at any time. Although he hasn't been cautioned, I believe it's in both parties' interests if we record this interview.' Scholes nodded his acceptance.

Flood turned on the tape machine and faced Cahill. 'We're following up two lines of enquiry. Either a criminal gang gunned down your wife in revenge for her acquittal, or someone else was involved and made it look like a gangland hit. My officers are investigating both lines thoroughly.'

Cahill sat back in his chair. 'If you think that someone else was me, you're badly mistaken.'

Flood opened his file. He flicked over a page, scanned it and said, 'Let's start with Katie Brunswick. You said she's your alibi but she's missing. We can't confirm your trip to Epping Forest. CCTV so far, is inconclusive. Do you still maintain you went there?'

'Yes.'

'She's been missing now for nearly three days. Do you have any idea where she might have gone after your meeting?'

'No. I don't.'

'You see, this is our dilemma. Katie's the only person who can give you an alibi.' Flood couldn't resist adding, 'That's after you lied to us about visiting your mother.'

'I've told why I lied.'

Flood continued: 'Once Katie alibis you, you're off the hook. Her disappearance is *inconvenient,* to say the least.'

'I don't know what else to say.'

'You could tell us the truth. We've confirmed your mobile contained a huge number of texts from her, most of them threatening all kinds of stuff, including suicide. Perhaps you thought she'd carry out her threat to send the sex tape to your wife and your mother. In which case, you'd have to silence Katie, wouldn't you, to protect your marriage?'

Cahill opened his mouth to retaliate. Before he could do so, Scholes interjected, thrusting his face forward. 'Are you accusing Mr Cahill of having something to do with Katie Brunswick's disappearance? Because if you are, you'll need to provide evidence. It appears to me you're on a fishing trip.'

'I agree it's only one hypothesis, but until we find Katie Brunswick it's entirely plausible. Mr Cahill has a strong motive and was possibly the last person to see her alive.'

Flood turned to Cahill. 'Do you know where she is?'

'I've no idea. I left her sitting in her car at Epping Forest on Tuesday morning. She's a free agent. She could have taken off anywhere.'

Flood continued: 'OK. Let's talk about your wife. Tell me again about your relationship?'

'I've told you before. Why are you asking me the same bloody questions?'

'Did you have access to your wife's mobile phone?'

'No. Why do you want to know?'

Flood opened a file in front of him and turned over to a specific page. 'We've obtained Jenny's call logs from her service provider up to the time of the incident. From these, our technical team retrieved a substantial number of text messages. We've analysed them in detail. It appears your wife was having a relationship with another police officer.'

'Don't be so stupid! I'd have known.'

'Would you like to know who it is?'

'Who?'

'Carl Russell.'

'Carl Russell?' Cahill sniggered and threw his head back in contempt. 'She'd never go with Russell. That wanker?'

Flood turned the file round so Cahill and Scholes could

read the log sheets together. He pointed at them. 'All those calls and text messages marked with a yellow highlighter are to and from Carl Russell. Copies of the most explicit texts sent between them are also shown.'

Cahill and Scholes sat close together, peering at each page as Flood turned them over.

He allowed them a minute to read a selection of the texts. 'I think you'll agree that there can be no doubt about the nature of the relationship. What we're thinking is that if you knew about your wife's affair with Russell, you'd be angry enough and motivated enough to do something about it. And, as we speak, you don't have an alibi. What do you say to that?'

Scholes leaned forward, his eyes narrowing. 'But you can't *prove* Mr Cahill knew about the affair.'

'No. Not yet. That's another line of enquiry we're prioritising. We have officers talking to Martin and Jenny's work colleagues as we speak.' Flood turned to Cahill. 'This is what we have, Martin. Someone good with a firearm killed Jenny. You're good with a firearm. Your wife's having an affair. Your alibi is not yet corroborated.'

Cahill spurted out, 'I've never heard anything so fucking stupid.'

Flood ignored him. 'If we obtain evidence to suggest that you *did* know about Jenny's affair, you'd have a clear motive.'

Cahill's muscular body shook. He hissed, 'I didn't know about the affair, I swear. I still can't believe it. Carl Russell?'

'We've only got your word that you met Katie Brunswick on the day of the shooting. We need to find her urgently, talk to her.'

Scholes raised his eyebrows. 'Until then?'

'We'd like your client to be available for interview at short notice if we discover further evidence. He's free to go.' Flood reached for the audio switch. 'I'm terminating this interview at 6.30 pm on Friday 23rd February 2001.'

*

'What are you thinking now?' Flood asked Laura once they'd

45

left the interview room.

'If Cahill did know about Jenny's affair, he covered it well.'

'He did. He's a cool character. Where the bloody hell is Katie? We need to find her.'

Flood continued: 'I don't know about you, Laura, I could do with a drink. Fancy joining me at The Ship Inn?'

The pub, a regular haunt for off-duty police officers, was less than a hundred yards from Southwark Police Station. They went there to celebrate successful prosecutions or to unwind after a particularly stressful shift. The officers' unofficial ruling prohibited discussing cases. Flood didn't always obey the rule.

Laura replied, 'Sure. See you there. I need to freshen up. A large G&T would hit the spot. Thanks.'

*

Two DCs propped up the empty bar at one end of the saloon and nodded an acknowledgement to Flood as he entered. He nodded back and ordered the drinks. When they arrived, he placed them on a table furthest away from the counter. Not wanting to get involved in a discussion, he ambled over to one of several brightly-lit, flashing one-arm-bandits. Flood always thought they looked out of place in a Victorian pub. He idly pumped several tokens into the slot, hit 'Play' and watched the fruit symbols spin.

Five minutes later, he spotted Laura gliding through the entrance. He pulled back a chair for her before sitting on the one opposite.

'I didn't know you played slot machines,' she said.

'I don't usually. I didn't want to talk to them.' He flicked his head in the general direction of the bar. 'I just wanted to speak to you.'

She'd renewed her make-up and fixed her hair. He inhaled the increasingly familiar aura of her freshly-applied perfume.

She leant forward and raised her glass. 'Cheers.' Flood returned the salutation. Placing her glass on the table, she said,

'So, how's the family?'

'I'm in the doghouse with my mother. She still thinks I'm working too hard.' Flood took a sip of his pint of Best. 'Mind you, I spend more time on bloody paperwork than investigating these days. Talk about arsehole-covering. Foxy wants to know each time I have a pee. Sometimes, I hate the Met. All I want to do is to sort out the bad guys.'

Laura put her head to one side, a smile crossing her face. 'You sound like Victor Meldrew.'

'Do I?'

Laura picked up her glass, held it with both hands and leaned towards him. 'No. You don't really. I think it's because you're so dedicated. On that subject, dare I ask? Any more developments in the cold case?'

Flood stared down at his beer and shook his head. 'Absolutely nothing.'

'I don't think you'll ever be happy until you solve the case.'

He blurted out, 'What bloody well gets me is how the Met can accept the fact that a copper's wife is murdered by some gutless thug and then put it on the back burner. Knowing whoever killed her is still out there is destroying me.'

She shook her head. 'I can't begin to know how that must feel.'

She fiddled with her glass for a moment before saying, 'I think your mother's right. Perhaps you should let it go. I can see it's getting to you. The longer it goes on the angrier and more upset you'll get.'

'I can't let it go, Laura. I can't.'

She looked at her watch, finished her G&T and stood. 'I must be going. Thanks for the drink. My round next time.'

Flood stood too. 'Please don't go yet.' He reached for her hand and squeezed it tightly. Their eyes locked together in an intensive stare. Flood wanted to kiss her, hug her, tell her how much he wanted her. But not here.

She gently withdrew her hand. 'I'd love to stay but I promised my daughter I'd drop in to see her. I want to see my granddaughter, too. I've probably missed her bed-time already.' As she reached the door, she turned and waved.

He imagined what she might be like in bed and considered asking her out but something always held him back. He'd hate it if she rejected him. It didn't seem fair on his memory of Georgina, either. And anyway, the Met had made it clear that they didn't approve of such relationships within the Force. Flood stared after her, transfixed, craving the physical contact he desperately missed. He finished off his pint, ordered another and put his last token into the one-armed-bandit. The three cherries in a row eluded him once more.

CHAPTER SEVEN

Saturday 24ᵗʰ February 2001

Within a minute of arriving in his office the next morning, Superintendent Fox barged in without knocking and slumped down in the chair opposite Flood. He didn't usually do Saturdays.

'I've had the Borough Commander on the phone in a right strop. Michael Brunswick, the MP, has given him a hard time. He wants to know why we haven't found his daughter. He's demanding more action. I told him about the search and that we've registered her as a missing person. What else can I tell him?'

Flood grunted, 'Not much. We've interviewed Martin Cahill. We still haven't established his alibi. Katie going missing doesn't look good for him but that's all we've got.'

'For Christ sake, Andy! I'm under real pressure here. I want your team to know that. The media are expecting a statement. I want to be able to say something positive. Understood?' Fox pushed back his chair and strode out of the office. Flood stared after him and shook his head.

He spent the rest of the day checking with every member of his team making sure they hadn't missed an important clue. As they'd all worked through their lunch breaks, Flood sent out a DC to collect pizzas for his team. As he devoured the last mouthful, Laura tapped on the glass door to his office, looking excited. He waved her in.

'We've found Katie Brunswick!'

Flood wiped his face with a paper napkin and motioned Laura to sit. 'At last! And?'

'She's dead. Dog handlers found her body on the other side of High Beech, a remote part of Epping Forest.'

'Shit!' Flood grimaced.

He stood and gulped down the remains of his coffee from a paper cup. He snatched his coat hanging behind his office door and slung it over his shoulders. 'Let's go before it gets too dark. I want to see this for myself.'

The main road running through the forest to Loughton, the closest town, had been cleared of snow which lay in dirty slush piles in the gutter. They passed numerous entrances and bridle paths to the forest before Flood eventually spotted two squad cars, their blue lights flashing, parked in front of three white vans at a secluded spot close to a path. He parked behind them.

A bitterly cold, thick mist hung in the air as Flood and Laura flashed their warrant cards at a burly constable guarding the wooded entrance. 'Sir, Ma'am, we're treating this as a potential crime scene. You'll have to gear up accordingly.'

He pointed to a bag in the back of one of the police vans containing light-blue forensic suits, shoes and gloves. Once they'd complied, he said, 'Follow the tape on this side. You'll find the team about half a mile up this narrow path. Take care. The ground's frozen hard. It's a bit slippery.'

Sprigs of frost-covered bramble, still with painful thorns, occasionally sprung into their faces as they made their way along the path. Their breaths billowed out of their mouths, adding to the mist, which dampened the sound of their footfall.

As they got closer, Flood recognised the Senior Investigating Officer, DI Fuller, despite his forensic gear. He worked out of the Loughton station. They'd taken several courses together at the Police College and struck up a friendship. They'd exchanged Christmas cards ever since. Fuller knew about Georgina.

After Flood introduced Laura, he said, 'How's the family, Harry? Your boy still having trials for Chelsea?'

'No. Didn't come to anything. He'll have to get a proper job, like mine.' Fuller smiled at his own joke.

'Call this a proper job?' Flood gestured with his arms. Fuller shrugged.

'I've been expecting you. I understand the victim is a key witness in one of your cases.'

'Yes, she is. We're talking to a suspect. We've a ton of circumstantial but short on the hard stuff. What's your take on this?'

Fuller nodded back in the direction they'd come. 'There's a red VW Golf parked close to the entrance. It's registered to Kate Brunswick. It had been driven over a little-used track. I've got SOCOs working on it. It looks like she left her car and made her way here on foot. Come and see for yourself.'

Fuller pointed towards a white tent twenty yards away, lit from the inside. They walked over wooden slatted boards to the entrance. Fuller raised the flaps of the tent, allowing them to observe the scene. 'This is how the dogs found her.'

A photographer emerged from the tent. He nodded at Fuller and brushed past them. 'I'm going back to get the photos developed. They'll be on your desk later.'

The detectives stared at Katie's frost-covered, fully-clothed body lying face down. Both her arms were wrapped around a heavy branch of a fallen oak tree. Flood could just see that a pair of handcuffs held her wrists tightly together.

'What's with the handcuffs, Harry?' he asked.

'At first, I thought she'd died from hypothermia or exposure. The temperature hasn't been above freezing for days. When I noticed the cuffs, I declared it a crime scene just to be on the safe side. I've got other SOCOs searching the area for clues. I've called the pathologist. He's on his way.'

'Good. I'm sure that was the right decision.'

Fuller continued: 'You won't believe this. The handcuffs are Hyatts − standard police issue. I've taken a note of the serial number. It'll need matching to police records.' Fuller reached for his notebook, tore off a page and passed it to Laura who shot a glance at Flood.

Fuller continued: 'Hopefully, I can give you a preliminary indication of what we think might have happened by tomorrow. We'll have to wait for the results of the post-mortem and coroner's inquest to get the full story.'

'Thanks, Harry. Did you find her mobile phone?'

'Yes. It's in an evidence bag. She'd switched it off. You can take it with you for analysis.'

Laura moved a few yards away from Flood and Fuller and held her mobile up to her ear. Then she stamped her feet in frustration and shouted, 'Bugger!'

The detectives stared at her. She looked up and explained, 'I'm trying to call the firearms unit. I can't get a bloody signal here. I'll go back to the car.'

'I'll come with you. Harry, can you call me as soon as you've got something I can use?'

'Sure.'

*

Back in the car, Flood turned to Laura. 'So, you think the cuffs belong to Cahill?'

'I'll tell you when this piece of crap they call a mobile phone actually responds.' She smacked it against the dashboard and put it to her ear. She repeated the action three times before exclaiming, 'At last!'

After requesting the information, she turned to Flood. 'If they are Cahill's cuffs, surely the dumbest cop in the world wouldn't be stupid enough to use them at a crime scene, would he? Always assuming this *is* a crime scene.'

'One thing's for sure. Katie can't confirm Cahill's alibi. I can't wait to hear what he's got to say about that. Get him back in with his duty brief tonight.'

Flood drove back to the police station as fast as the icy conditions allowed. As they reached Borough High Street, Laura's mobile bleeped. 'I hope this is what I think it is.'

She picked it up and listened intently. She finished the call with, 'Thanks for getting the info to me so quickly. It's been a great help.'

She turned to Flood and told him the result of her enquiry.

*

Cahill and Scholes were already seated in the interview room as Flood and Laura entered. She loaded the audio machine with fresh tapes and switched it on.

Flood said, 'I'll come straight to the point, Martin. We've found Katie Brunswick.'

52

Cahill's face brightened up. 'Thank goodness! That means my alibi can be proved.'

Laura and Flood stared at him. Flood said, 'Don't you want to know how she is?'

'Is she alright?'

'Where are the handcuffs issued to you by the Met on the 10th of July 1999?'

Scholes raised his eyebrows. Cahill said, 'What are you talking about?'

'It's a simple question.'

'I assume they're where they usually are; in my police locker with the rest of my kit.'

'Would it surprise you to know that we found a pair of handcuffs in Epping Forest earlier today? The serial number corresponds with the serial number of the handcuffs originally issued to you.'

Cahill put his hands to each side of his head and bowed down towards the table.

'Well?'

Cahill whispered, 'This is so embarrassing.'

'What is?'

Cahill looked up to the ceiling, as if seeking divine inspiration. 'Katie and I used to mess about with them. She's heavily into bondage, domination, that sort of thing.'

'How did you explain the absence of the handcuffs to your sergeant?'

'They often go walkabout. We sometimes take a bunch of them on a big raid in case we have to make multiple arrests. We lend them to other officers. You know how it is. Suspects often go to different stations for processing.'

'How come she had them?' Laura asked. Cahill looked down then back to Flood.

'A few weeks ago she asked if she could keep them. *A memento of our relationship*, she'd said. I agreed. I told my sergeant they'd been used by another copper on a recent raid and he hadn't returned them. He issued me with another pair. Happens all the time.'

Laura continued: 'You're telling me Katie Brunswick

possessed a pair of Met Police handcuffs?'

'I know it sounds stupid, but yes. Ask her. She'll confirm it.'

Flood said, 'We can't ask her.'

'What do you mean, *you can't ask her?*'

'She's dead.'

Cahill's eyes opened wide as saucers. 'Dead? No! You're joking!' He covered his face with both hands. Taking them away, he said, 'Are you sure it's her?'

'We found Katie earlier today handcuffed with a set of *your* cuffs to a branch of a fallen tree, roughly half-a-mile from where you say you last saw her in Epping Forest. It looks like she'd been there for several days. Was it one of your games that went wrong?'

Flood noticed the blood visibly drain from Cahill's face. He tried to speak. His lips moved but nothing came out. He looked sideways at Scholes, who studiously scribbled in his notebook, avoiding Cahill's gaze.

'We're undertaking a forensic search of the area from where Katie parked her car to where we found her as a matter of priority. We'll be looking for footprints, fingerprints and clothes' fibres. We'll compare them with your samples.'

'I told you I went there. You'll find loads of evidence but I can assure you I had nothing to do with Katie's or Jenny's death.'

Flood eyeballed Cahill. 'This is your problem, Martin. If you were with Katie Brunswick in Epping Forest, you'll need to explain the circumstances of her death. If you weren't with her, you'll need to tell us exactly where you were at the time of your wife's murder.'

Cahill again looked at Scholes for support. He cautioned, 'You don't have to answer that but it will look bad if you don't.'

Flood leaned towards Cahill. 'I suggest you think very hard about the position you're in. If there's something you want to tell us about your involvement with either Jenny or Katie's deaths, now would be a good time.'

Cahill blurted out, 'I can't tell you anything else.'

After a short pause, Flood said, 'On the basis that your alibi can't be proved and that there is a clear motive, we're arresting you on suspicion of the murder of Jenny Cahill.'

Cahill leapt to his feet. Until now, he'd maintained an unflappable approach to everything Flood had thrown at him.

'You can't arrest me. I'm a serving police officer, for Christ's sake!'

Laura read him the caution as Cahill stood and turned round in a circle clutching his head. Flood added, 'You'll be released on police bail while we obtain more evidence.'

Cahill looked down at Scholes. 'Do something!'

Scholes shrugged and gazed back at Cahill as if to say, *there's nothing I can do.*

CHAPTER EIGHT

Sunday/Monday 25th February 2001

Flood hadn't been in his office for more than a few minutes the next morning when his phone rang.

'Yes?'

Gill, the station's receptionist, said, 'I've got someone on the phone. Insists on speaking only to you. Says it's in connection with the Jenny Cahill murder enquiry.'

Flood sat bolt upright. 'Put him through.'

'DCI Flood?'

'Yes.'

'I understand you're the Senior Investigating Officer on the Jenny Cahill murder.' Flood detected a slight Scottish accent.

'Yes. Who are you?'

'I've got some information for you. Meet me this afternoon. Three o'clock. Nunhead Cemetery, East Dulwich. There's a bench opposite the war memorial to the Canadians and New Zealanders. You need to be on your own.'

Before Flood could reply, the line went dead. He noted down the instructions and sat back in his chair, staring at the phone. Eventually, he picked it up and asked Laura to come to his office.

'I've just received a call from someone who says he's got information on Jenny Cahill. He wants to meet me on my own this afternoon. I've no idea who this guy is. I want you as back up.'

Laura's face lit up. 'This could be the breakthrough we need.'

'Maybe. We'll go wired up. I want you to keep out of sight. We don't need him spooked. Arrange for two surveillance specialists to follow him after the meet. I want to know where he lives.'

'We'll need authorisation from the Assistant Commissioner. I'll set it up now.'

Flood raised his eyes. 'More bloody arse-covering!'

*

The freezing spell that had lasted four days had given way to overcast skies with intermittent, heavy rain showers. As Flood drove to East Dulwich, he turned to Laura. 'I hate this bloody weather. I'm sure I've got that syndrome. What is it? Sun deprivation or something.'

Laura smiled. 'It's called SAD syndrome. Seasonal Affective Disorder. Is that why you're always so grumpy when it's dull?'

'Does it show that much?'

She smiled. 'Er... yes, it does. I recognise the symptoms. Remember, I had a Swedish mother. She lived up north. They get very few hours of sunshine. She had the same problem. That's why she moved to London where she met my father. And here I am.'

Flood smiled. 'I'm glad you are.'

He drove to Lindon Grove, half a mile from the cemetery and parked. 'Laura, make your way to the war memorial. Find somewhere close enough to observe us. Meet me back here afterwards.'

'OK. Good luck.' She gave him a thumbs-up and an encouraging smile through the window after she'd got out of the car.

Two surveillance officers in an unmarked pool car had followed Flood and parked fifty yards behind him. One got out and followed Laura at a respectable distance. The driver remained in the car. Flood waited ten minutes, giving time for Laura to get into position.

The rain stopped as Flood walked through the wrought-iron gates at the entrance to the cemetery. Unsurprisingly for a damp Sunday afternoon in late February, no visitors were paying their respects.

Flood followed the instructions, pausing only to peer up at the Victorian chapel now a ruin after an arson attack in the 1970s. He found the memorial after a ten-minute walk along a heavily-wooded path.

A tall, thin, reedy figure dressed in a black waterproof coat sat on a bench opposite the memorial. A giant oak tree had provided cover from the worst of the rain.

The man's dark hair, tightly swept back and tied in a man-bun, emphasised the gaunt features of his dark-skinned face. He wore a gold stud earring in his right ear and stood as Flood approached.

'DCI Andy Flood, I presume?' Flood couldn't reconcile his slight Scottish accent with the man's ethnicity.

'Yes. And you are?'

'Robbie Barlow.' His brown eyes searched Flood's face, sizing him up.

Flood remembered the name from the Intelligence Report. One of The Goshawks gang. He searched his memory for what he'd read about Barlow and made a mental note to check it out when he got back to the station.

'You said you had some information about Jenny Cahill's murder. Well?'

'Let's sit here.' Barlow gestured at the bench. 'This is all off the record, right? If anyone knows I'm gabbing to you, I'm dead.'

'Tell me what you know.'

'You're not wired up, are you? There's no one with you?'

'No.'

Barlow put his head on one side. 'How do I know that?'

Flood bluffed. 'Check it out if you want.'

Barlow lit a cigarette, took a long drag and turned away from Flood, blowing the smoke out through his nostrils.

He turned back to Flood. 'I believe you. How are you getting on with the case?'

'I haven't come here to discuss it with you. I'm here because you said you have some information. Now, either tell me what it is or I'll leave.'

Barlow grinned. 'I dunna think you'll leave. I've a good idea who killed Jenny Cahill.'

'A good idea?'

Barlow took another long drag on his cigarette, appearing

to gain great comfort from the nicotine hit. 'I've done business with the gang responsible. The Goshawks. I'm sure the Met are aware of them. They're one of the biggest gangs in London. They wanted revenge for Jenny Cahill's acquittal. The gang's leader, Tommy Lidgate, ordered it.'

'How do you know?'

'I'm taking a huge risk in telling you this.' Barlow peered over his shoulder before continuing. 'I overheard a conversation.'

'What conversation?'

Barlow glanced over his shoulder again. 'People talk all the time. I can tell you a lot.'

'Why would you do that?'

Barlow flicked off the ash of his cigarette and took another drag. 'There's a hell of a difference between running drugs and wiping out coppers on the streets. When you do that, the cops up their game. It becomes personal.' Barlow dropped his cigarette onto the path and ground the stub into the tarmac with his boot.

Flood said, 'You say you've a good idea who killed Jenny Cahill. A *good idea* does nothing for me. I need hard evidence and reliable testimony. How soon can you get it?'

'Leave it wi' me. I'll work on it. Get you more info. Maybe take a few days.'

'You know where I am. How can I contact you?'

'I dunna think that's a good idea. I'll give you a shout when I've got stuff.'

'OK.' Flood stood and began walking back towards the cemetery entrance. Barlow remained seated on the bench and lit another cigarette.

*

Flood sat in his car and checked that the tape machine had recorded the conversation. Ten minutes later, Laura tapped the passenger window. He leant across and opened the door for her.

As she settled in the seat, she said, breathlessly, 'Sorry I couldn't get close enough to see you but I heard everything. Went well, eh? Barlow sounds like he wants to help. We've got nothing else.' She clipped on her seatbelt.

'I got the feeling he was sounding you out, making sure he could trust you before giving you any more information.'

'Could be. Something bothered me, though. His motive. Typically, informants want one of two things: a sizable bung or a *definite* guarantee of leniency for crimes they've committed. He never asked for either.'

Laura nodded. 'True.'

'And something else. According to the profiles provided by Intelligence, Barlow's a member of a ruthless gang, Laura. They'd do anything, including torture and murder, to protect their drug trade. He didn't strike me as someone who'd worry too much about a copper being killed.'

'No, he didn't. What's our next move?'

'I'm hoping the surveillance throws up something.'

'What about Martin Cahill? If Barlow's telling the truth, he's off the hook isn't he?'

'*If* he's telling the truth.'

*

Flood and Laura returned to the police station just after 6.00 pm. Before heading home, Flood retrieved the file on Robbie Barlow. He placed it in his briefcase to read again later. If he left now, he'd be in time to see his girls before they went to bed.

After supper, Pippa and Gemma showed him what they'd prepared to commemorate the anniversary of their mother's death. They'd chosen a photograph from the family album and pasted it onto the front of a folded-over, white card. Inside, they'd written in bold colours, messages to their mum: '*We'll always love you, Mummy,*' '*We'll never forget you*' and '*Hope you're happy in Heaven.*'

'That's lovely, girls. I'm sure Mummy would appreciate your cards.' Flood swallowed hard. He realised the importance of this ritual, thought it an important part of their recovery from the shock of losing their mother in such tragic circumstances. In three days' time, it would be four years since she'd died from injuries resulting from the hit-and-run.

On every anniversary, Flood, his mother and the girls visited his sister, Julie, who lived in Winchester, close to Southampton, Flood's home before his promotion to the Met. Julie and Georgina had become good friends.

After the girls and his mother had gone to bed, Flood went into his office and read the file on Robbie Barlow again. He wrote down bullet points in his pocketbook. That way, he always had something on him he could refer to.

- *Born on 1st June 1968 in Edinburgh. Afro-Caribbean descent.*
- *Family had emigrated from Martinique in the French West Indies in 1967.*
- *Attended schools in the city, left with O levels in English and French.*
- *Known to Scottish police for a series of minor drug-related offences.*
- *1988, served a six-month sentence for possession and supply of Class B drugs. His prison profile recorded him to be a model prisoner.*
- *1993, moved to London. Joined several gangs involved in drug running.*
- *1999, joined The Goshawks gang. Suspected of being involved in running Class A drugs from France into the UK. Not enough evidence to satisfy the CPS as at December 2000.*

*

The next morning, Flood checked with his team working through the miles of CCTV footage covering Cahill and Katie's routes from their homes to Epping Forest. He also checked with the rest of the team ploughing through Cahill's emails and mobile phone records. None of them had thrown up new information.

Shortly after 2.00 pm, Flood received the call he expected from DI Fuller. 'Hi, Andy. I've got the preliminary results of our investigation into Katie Brunswick's death. I've asked the pathologist to send you the results of the post-mortem directly. It should be available later today. Can I pop over now and go through the prelims with you?'

'Excellent. I'm here all afternoon.'

Fuller arrived within the hour. Flood invited Laura to join them in his office. 'What have you got for us, Harry?' Flood's voice crackled with anticipation. Fuller opened his file, put on his glasses and scanned the documents.

'The pathologist estimates the time of death at between one thirty and three thirty am on the morning of Wednesday, 21st February.'

'That's about twelve to fourteen hours after Martin Cahill said he last saw her,' Laura interjected.

Flood nodded. 'Go on, Harry.'

'The pathologist reckons Katie's body had been in situ for two-and-a-half days. We'll have to wait for the full toxicology results which will take about four weeks. However, he discovered lethal levels of alcohol and acetaminophen in Katie's body. In her car, we found three empty boxes of p*aracetamol*, the source of the drug.'

'Is that what killed her?' Flood enquired.

'Looks like it. Pathologist says the most likely cause of death is liver failure due to a drugs overdose. He's not ruling out death due to hypothermia and exposure. The high level of alcohol would have accelerated the effect.'

'Any evidence of sexual activity or defence wounds?' Flood asked.

'No. On the contrary. The pathologist found no scraping or bruising of the body. No signs of a struggle and she hadn't been gagged. Forensics found fibres on her clothes. They're checking that out. They'll have a report soon. You can get your suspect's clothes tested. See if the fibres match.'

'And the car?'

'We found two sets of fingerprints inside. One belonged to

Katie. No doubt you'll check the other set against your suspect.' Laura made a note.

'Flood asked, 'What about the handcuffs?'

'Just one set of fresh prints. Katie's.'

Fuller continued: 'We're still continuing a search of the area. There'll be a coroner's inquest, of course. God knows how long that will take.'

'Thanks, Harry. I owe you. If you get any more information, let me know.'

Flood stood and shook Fuller's hand. When he'd left, Laura said, 'I've an idea. We know Katie bombarded Cahill with texts. She threatened to commit suicide on more than one occasion. Maybe Cahill's story is true. He said he met up with Katie in her car to discuss their future.'

'So?'

'When he left her, she decided to kill herself knowing his fingerprints would be in her car and fibres from his clothes would be attached to hers. Remember, she asked him for a final hug? Then she snapped on his handcuffs around the branch of the fallen tree. All designed to put Cahill in the frame.'

Flood leaned back in his chair and clasped his hands behind his head, contemplating Laura's comments.

She broke the silence. 'Whatever's the truth, what a horrible way to die. I reckon Cahill's rejection pushed her over the edge.'

DC Tyler tapped at Flood's door, opened it and put his head through the gap. 'Sorry to interrupt, Boss. I thought you'd like to know that we've just received the post-mortem results on Jenny Cahill. She was pregnant.' Flood and Laura exchanged a glance.

As Tyler closed the door, Flood said, 'Now that *is* interesting. If forensics put Cahill at the Epping Forest crime scene at the same time that Jenny was shot, he's in the clear. But what if Cahill had found out about Jenny's pregnancy and her affair with Russell? If he assumed Russell is the father, what would he do?'

Laura screwed up her face. 'Oh, God! This is so

frustrating!'

Flood continued: 'We need a paternity DNA test. They can do that in less than twenty-four hours. Compare it with Cahill's and Russell's DNA. They'll be on the Met's medical files.'

'Do you think we should get Cahill back in?'

'Let's do it after we get the DNA results. If Russell's the father and Cahill knew, that's a hell of a powerful motive.'

CHAPTER NINE

Tuesday 27th February 2001

Laura, looking pleased, strode into Flood's office late in the afternoon.

'I pulled in a few favours from forensics. They've excelled themselves. I've got the paternity DNA results.'

After they'd discussed them in detail, Flood said, 'Let's get Russell and Cahill in for separate interviews. See what they both have to say.'

*

As Flood and Laura entered the interview room, Russell stood and whispered, 'This is about Jenny Cahill, isn't it?' His eyes darted nervously between Flood and Laura. Flood motioned Russell to sit.

He looked the exact opposite of Martin Cahill: fair-haired, diminutive and out of shape. Flood would never have guessed he was a firearms officer. Or that he'd appeal to Jenny Cahill.

As Flood and Laura sat opposite Russell, Flood replied, 'Yes it is. What can you tell us about your relationship with her?'

'I've been seeing her for the past few months. It was getting serious. She wasn't happy in her marriage. She told me that she wanted to leave her husband for me. Then I heard she'd been shot. I can't believe it. It's really shaken me up.' His eyes welled up.

'Was it a sexual relationship?'

Russell nodded. 'Yes. It was.'

'When was the last time you saw her?'

'The Friday before last. We met in a pub near my place in Camberwell.'

'Which pub?'

'The Queen's Head in the High Street.'

'Can you tell us where you were on the morning of Tuesday 20th February?'

A look of incredulity crossed Russell's face. 'You're not seriously thinking I did it, are you? I loved her. I had no reason to harm her.'

'We're talking to everyone who had recent contact with Jenny. It's routine police work as you know.'

'I was on duty at the firearms unit all day. My boss can vouch for me.'

Laura made a note and said, 'We'll check that out.'

Flood continued: 'Do you know Jenny's husband, Martin Cahill?'

Russell scowled. 'Yes, I do. Arrogant bastard. Thinks he's God's gift to women. Jenny told me she knew he was having an affair. Said what was good for him was good for her. Then it got serious between us. She told me she loved me.'

'Did Jenny tell you that she was pregnant?'

'Yes. She told me a few days before we met on that Friday evening. I asked her if she thought I was the father. She said yes. I was chuffed. We spent the entire evening discussing what we should do.'

'Do you know if she told her husband?'

'She said that she'd tell him over that weekend and that she wanted to leave him and move in with me. I was going to call her on the Monday, see how it went. Next thing I hear, she's been killed.' He began sobbing uncontrollably into his hands. Flood glanced at Laura and ended the interview.

*

An hour later in the same interview room, Flood and Laura faced Cahill and his solicitor. Cahill's first words were, 'I can't believe you've arrested me! I've told you everything I know.'

Flood placed his file on the table. 'We'll be judge of that.'

Laura placed fresh tapes into the machine and turned it on. She reminded Cahill that he'd been cautioned.

Flood opened his file and flicked to a page inside. 'Martin,

66

we've received the initial findings of the post-mortem on your wife. Makes interesting reading. Would it surprise you to learn that she was pregnant?'

'Pregnant?'

'Yes. Twenty-eight days. Did she tell you about it?'

Cahill looked affronted. 'No. No, she didn't.'

'Isn't that unusual if, as you've told us, you had a good relationship?'

Cahill spluttered, 'I had no idea. I don't know why she didn't tell me. I'd have been over the moon.'

Flood flicked over another page of his file and glanced down at it. 'When we got the results of the post-mortem, we took a paternity DNA sample and compared it to yours. It doesn't match.'

'That's bollocks!' Cahill sat back in his chair and shook his head. 'I'm telling you that's bollocks!'

'We checked the DNA with Carl Russell's. It proved a match. The Forensic team tell us that the odds of misidentification are several million to one.'

'That can't be true! There's obviously been a mistake.'

'I'm afraid not. Do you still maintain that Jenny never told you about being pregnant?'

Cahill leant forward and emphasised his words. 'No. She didn't.'

Flood glanced across at Laura and motioned to her to turn off the tape recorder. He said, 'OK. Give us a few moments.'

Flood and Laura stepped out of the interview room into the corridor. Before Flood could speak, Laura said, 'I think he did see Katie at Epping Forest at roughly the same time someone shot Jenny. Even if Jenny did tell him about being pregnant with Carl Russell's baby, which gives him his motive, he couldn't be in two places at once. Do you still think he didn't use an accomplice to kill Jenny?'

Flood shook his head. 'There's no evidence to support that. We've checked his emails, computer and mobile. Nothing points us in that direction.'

'Should we release him again on police bail?'

'I don't see how we can retain him. We can't prove he

knew about Russell. He may be the world's biggest prat but what he's said is entirely plausible. OK, let's go back in.'

Without bothering to sit down, Flood said to Cahill, 'You're free to go. We'd like you to remain available for interview if we obtain further evidence.' Scholes couldn't resist a smirk of satisfaction.

Cahill jabbed a finger towards Flood. 'I hope you realise what you've put me through. I said from the start I wasn't involved in Jenny's murder. I hope you're putting as much effort into finding her killer.'

'I assure you we are. We'll keep you in the picture.'

Cahill's eyes took on a puppy-dog look as he whined, 'I know I've been a stupid prick. I don't blame Jenny for having an affair. I really loved her, you know.'

Flood shrugged. He and Laura left the interview room. Before they returned to their offices, he said to her, 'You know I'm off duty tonight and all day tomorrow, don't you? It's the anniversary of Georgina's death. I always take the girls and my mother down to see my sister in Winchester. We visit the place where her ashes are scattered and celebrate her life.'

'I hope it goes well. Are the school OK with that?'

'Yes. The teachers think it's an important day for them. I'd better be going. Call me if anything crops up that can't wait twenty-four hours.'

*

Next morning, Wednesday 28th February, a date forever etched in Flood's memory, he drove down the M3 as weak sunlight reflected off the car's bonnet. His mother sat in the front passenger seat. Pippa and Gemma sat in the back.

They arrived at Flood's sister's house in Winchester at 11 am. The girls rushed out of the car as soon as the front door opened, shouting, 'Hi, Auntie Julie!' as she appeared in the doorway.

Julie, two years older than Flood, shared many of her brother's physical characteristics: sallow skin, tall, slim and intense brown eyes.

Flood remembered with affection, that they'd shared a happy childhood. Julie took her responsibility as the elder sister very seriously, always looking out for him. Still did in a way. He was delighted when Julie and Georgina got on so well together, acting more like sisters. They often spoke on the phone for hours. Especially when Julie went through her divorce. Julie had been the one to suggest that their mother live with Flood after Georgina had been murdered.

After the girls had shown Auntie Julie the cards they'd made, they all climbed to the top of St Catherine's Hill, a local beauty spot. It had been Georgina's favourite view of Winchester.

They looked down as the sun highlighted the glistening River Itchen meandering through the water meadows below. In the distance, the 11th-century cathedral dominated the view of the city.

Several dog walkers, their coats buttoned up against the chilly breeze, passed them, much to the girls' delight. They'd begged their father to get them a puppy. Flood had resisted. At least on this subject, Flood's mother and he agreed. She'd said, 'There's already enough to contend with in this family. I know what'll happen after the novelty has worn off. Muggins here will be the one taking it for walks.'

When they reached the top of the hill, all slightly breathless, Flood unhitched his rucksack. He took out a bottle of champagne, two bottles of lemonade and five glasses.

After opening the bottles, he popped the champagne and poured out the drinks. As they raised their glasses, he said, 'To Mummy and Georgina. We'll never forget you.' They took a sip and stood in silence for several minutes, each with their own thoughts.

They climbed down the hill via a steep path and lunched at the local Pizzeria. Afterwards, Stella took the girls to see some of their friends who they'd not seen since Flood's family moved from Southampton to London two years earlier. Julie and her brother walked the short distance to Julie's house and sat in her elegant sitting room.

Julie poured the tea. 'How are you? Is everything alright

with Mum and the kids?'

'I think so. Why do you ask?'

'No reason, really. Just something Mum said.'

'Such as?'

'She called me last week. She went on about you never being home and not spending much time with the girls. Told me that even when you are home, you lock yourself away in your study, trying to find out who killed Georgina.'

'So she asked you to have a word, did she?'

'I can see her point, Andy. I don't think you realise how unhappy she is. She came to your rescue four years ago but I think she's had enough. She's got a life as well, you know.'

'I know but what can I do? Once I get Georgina's killer locked up, everything will be all right.'

'So you're going to carry on as you are?'

'Yes. I have to.'

'Well, it's up to you. I told Mum I'd talk to you and I have. Anyway, how's the investigation going?'

'So, so.' He rocked his head from side to side.

Julie mimicked Flood's movement. 'What does "so, so" mean? Are you any nearer than you were a year ago?'

'No. I'm not, if you must know.'

'Can I say something?'

'What?'

'I know you've been through a lot in the last few years but do you remember how you were before it all happened? You always had a smile on your face and were fun to be with.' Julie beamed at the memory.

'That was then. This is now.'

Julie slowly stirred her tea. 'Do you remember when you used to do impressions at Christmas? Mum and Dad loved them. So did I. Mum loved your Prince Charles. My favourite was your Tommy Cooper. Had me in stitches. I bet you haven't done that for a while.'

'I've not exactly been in the mood, have I?'

'Mum's right about one thing. This obsession with Georgina's murder is getting you down. And it's affecting your relationship with the girls.'

'Back to that now, are we?'

'No. This is *me* talking, not Mum.'

'Julie. You don't understand. Georgina would *want* me to keep plugging away. If I had more time it would help but I don't suppose the villains in London will agree to a cease-fire will they?'

'No. I don't think so.'

Julie topped up Flood's tea. 'I'm only passing on how you're coming across. You never used to be like this. If you want to see more of the girls and keep Mum onside, you'll need to do something.'

'Sounds like you and Mum are ganging up on me.'

'All I'm saying is that you need to change.'

He knew she was right but couldn't bring himself to admit it. Flood raised his voice. '*All I'm saying* is that I need to solve the case.'

Flood picked up his cup of tea and stared out of the window before sitting down on the sofa. Julie joined him, reached over and patted his knee. 'How is work otherwise?'

'Plenty to keep me busy.' He told her about the Cahill case and mentioned his 'bagman', a certain DS Laura Miles, in glowing terms. 'She's great at her job. A real asset on my team.'

'Is she? Do you know, when you mentioned her name, your eyes lit up.'

'Did they?' Flood smiled with embarrassment. 'I've told her about Georgina. Laura understands what I'm doing. I like her... I like her a lot.'

Julie smiled, leant forward and said, 'I can sense that. Tell me more? How old? Married? Kids?'

'Don't be nosey. All I'll tell you is that she's about your age, divorced, with a married daughter who has a four-year-old girl. That enough detail for you?'

Julie's smile grew wider. 'That'll do ... for now.'

Flood stood and said, 'I think I'll call Laura before Mum and the kids get back. Get an update.' Julie collected the cups and saucers and took them into the kitchen.

'Hi, Laura. Any news?'

'Yes. I'd say so. I didn't want to worry you today of all days but I thought you'd call. Straight after Barlow left you, he went to an address in Noel Street, Islington and stayed the night. He returned last night and stayed over again. We believed it to be his home until we checked it out. According to the Land Registry, it belongs to Barry Lidgate. Remember him? The judge sentenced him to serve a minimum of twenty years three years ago for attempted murder. He's Tommy Lidgate's son.'

Flood pursed his lips and whistled.

'Anybody else living there?'

'Barry's wife, Jessica Lidgate. The surveillance team saw her entering the house, wheeling a buggy complete with a young child.' As Flood's brain raced, assimilating the possible implications, the front door opened.

'Sorry, Laura. Got to go. Good work. Keep up the surveillance. I'll see you in the morning.' He slipped his mobile into his pocket just before the girls bounced into the room followed by his mother.

*

They arrived home at 8.30 pm. After the girls had gone to bed, Stella, who'd been quiet on the journey back to London, confronted Flood. 'I don't want you to work in your study tonight. It's time for us to have a serious chat.'

'We've had that, haven't we? I know you spoke to Julie. What do you want me to do, Mum? Give up my job? Give up trying to find Georgina's killer? I can't. That's it. You'll have to accept it.'

'You know, sometimes I think you're more interested in solving the case than you are about getting justice for Georgina.'

'Mum, you're talking rubbish!'

'I don't think so. If you're not prepared to change, why should I continue looking after the girls? I love them to death but *you* need to take more responsibility for them. You owe them that much at least.'

'OK. I'll think about it.'

'No, I'm sorry, Andy. That's too vague. If you haven't made a decision by the end of March, I'm moving back to Winchester to be with my friends. I want to enjoy what's left of my life. I'll be nearer Julie too. I'm not saying I won't see the girls. I'd love to have them for the odd weekend. You'll *have* to spend more time with them.'

Flood stared up at the ceiling, considering his response. After a short silence Stella put her hands on her hips and said, 'Well?'

'Not a lot I can say, is there?'

'So, it's agreed? At the end of next month, we'll review the situation and I'll decide whether to move out or not.'

Flood softened his tone. 'Mum, I really appreciate what you've done. I couldn't have carried on with my job if you hadn't helped out. I don't know what I'd do with the girls if you weren't around. OK, I agree. Let's make a decision at the end of March.' That would give him one month to solve the case, he reasoned.

Stella hugged her son. 'Good. I'm sure it's for the best.'

Flood sloped off to his study.

*

Next morning, Barlow called Flood at the station. It had been three days since their first meeting. 'There's something I need to tell you. We need to meet.'

'OK. Same place?'

'No. Be at Speakers' Corner, Hyde Park at two thirty this afternoon.' The phone clicked off.

With growing excitement, Flood set up the same arrangement with Laura, including being wired up.

They caught the tube to Green Park and walked the rest of the way past Marble Arch to Speakers' Corner, splitting up within two hundred yards of the meeting place.

Barlow wore the same overcoat with the collar turned up against the icy March wind. He stood, shoulders hunched, stamping his feet alternately to alleviate the chill. When he saw Flood approach, he pulled his cigarette from his mouth and stubbed it out on the ground. His eyes lacked any sparkle and the puffy bags under them suggested lack of sleep.

Barlow nodded an acknowledgement to Flood and said, 'Let's walk.'

They set off towards the open spaces of Hyde Park. After walking fifty yards in silence, Barlow turned to Flood.

'I wasn't completely honest with you the last time we met.' Flood thought Barlow's Scottish accent sounded edgy.

Flood stopped walking. He stared at Barlow. 'You mean you lied to me?'

Barlow stopped too. He returned the stare. 'No. I didn't lie. There's something I didn't tell you the last time we met.'

'And?'

'I'm a Met Police undercover cop.'

CHAPTER TEN

Thursday 1st March 2001

Barlow produced a warrant card from the inside pocket of his coat and offered it to Flood.

'I knew you'd want to see proof. Of course, I don't normally carry this with me. It's usually tucked away somewhere safe.'

Flood took the card from him. He inspected the front of it closely, turned it over and back again. Satisfied it was genuine, he thrust the card back towards Barlow.

'Why wasn't I told about you? The Met know The Goshawks gang is one of my lines of enquiry.'

'They don't exactly advertise the fact, do they? For all I know, there are other undercover officers involved. The Met don't want any more people than necessary to know I'm a deep swimmer.'

'How long have you been undercover?'

'Seven years. Two on this job. My current brief is to get enough testimony and tape or video recordings to convict Tommy Lidgate. He's recently stepped up the level of violence since the East European drug gangs moved into his patch. There are so many gangland shootings; it's like the bloody Wild West these days.'

'Why didn't you tell me this before?'

'Because I wanted to know whether I could trust you. I need you to get me out of this mess. Quickly. I think my cover's about to be blown.'

'Why?'

'Last week, one of the gang challenged me. We were drinking in a pub. When I went to the men's room, he pulled a gun and pointed it at my head, saying, "You're Old Bill aintcha?" My stomach churned. I knew this villain had killed before. I put my head close to his. I yelled, "Dunna fuck with me. That's not funny." He backed off.'

Flood waited for two joggers to pass by before saying, 'Why haven't you told your handler this? He'll pull you out if he thinks you're at risk.'

'I don't trust him. I've passed stacks of information back but only a few small-fry have been convicted. For all I know, my reports have been shredded. I have to be careful.'

'Can't you talk to a more senior officer?'

'I could but, to be honest, I don't trust anyone anymore. I'm concerned that the more I feed back evidence against Tommy Lidgate, the more I'm at risk of him finding out. Then I'm dead.'

'You still haven't told me why you're taking a chance talking to me.'

Barlow started walking again. Flood followed.

'I want out of the Met. This is a fucking awful job. Look at me?' Barlow stopped. Flood stared into his bloodshot, expressionless eyes.

'I haven't slept in ages. I'm terrified about being found out. I hate living a double life. I'm sick of being a trained liar. Some days I don't know who I'm supposed to be.'

'Aren't you supposed to have regular psychological reviews?'

'You're joking! The Met are only interested in getting the job done. They say, "If you're struggling, don't worry, come and see us." There's no way I could open up, tell them how fucked up I am. There'd be a black mark agin me, I'd never be able to work for the Met again, unless it's a desk job.'

'Maybe that would suit you.'

Barlow glared at Flood. 'You think so?'

'No. Probably not. What makes you think I can help you?'

Barlow stopped walking. He tipped out a cigarette from a pack and lit up. He took an exaggerated pull on it and blew out the smoke through his nose.

'You should know that I'm living with Tommy Lidgate's daughter-in-law. Have been for eighteen months. We've got a wee bairn together. He's called Mark. Her husband's Barry Lidgate, Tommy's son. Three years ago, he got twenty years for attempted murder.'

Flood grimaced. 'Oh, that's not good. Does your handler know about this?'

'My handler knows *everything*. He dunna approve, thinks I've been *grossly unprofessional*. He's a stickler for doing things properly. Sleeping with criminals' wives is a complete no-no in his eyes. He says I've crossed the line.'

'You have.' They started walking again.

Barlow continued: 'When my handler found out about me and Jessica, do you know what he said? "There are two rules to obey when you're working undercover: Don't fall in love and wear a condom. You've broken them both." Fucking wanker.'

'I'd say that was good advice.'

Barlow stared at Flood before taking another drag of his cigarette. 'The Met have given me a month to make up my mind. Either they'll get me out on my own, which means leaving Jessica and the bairn. Or, I can resign and stay with her and the gang. I'm screwed either way.'

'Why not get out? You say you're pissed off with the Met and staying in is too dangerous.'

Barlow glared at Flood. 'I don't want to lose Jessica or my boy.'

'Does she know you're an undercover officer?'

'Yes. She found out a couple of months ago.'

'How?'

'I don't know. She wouldn't tell me. She swore that Tommy Lidgate doesn't know. She was furious with me for deceiving her. Had a massive row. Went on for weeks.'

'I'm not surprised.'

'I told her I wanted to spend the rest of my life with her. Then she said she wanted us to stay together for little Mark's sake. Told me she wanted to get away from the gang culture. She didn't want the bairn turning out to be a villain.'

'What does she think about Tommy Lidgate?'

'They don't get on. Something to do with her elder son Vinnie, being part of the gang. If Lidgate finds out Jessica knows I'm the filth and hadn't told him, he'll kill both of us, believe me.'

'Your decision's easy. Get out.'

Barlow stopped and faced Flood. 'You just don't get it, do you? Six months ago, I sat with Jessica at the hospital, holding her hand through ten hours of labour. Then I held the wee lad in my arms. I'll never forget that moment. He's my son. You think I should give him up?'

'I don't think you have a choice.'

'That's where you come in. I've checked your record with the Hampshire Police and the Met. I also know what happened to your wife.'

Flood snapped, 'What do you know?'

'I know that she was killed in a hit and run after you'd put away the leader of The Edge gang.' Mention of them brought angry bile to Flood's throat.

'What do you know about them?'

'Only that I'm sure there's a connection with The Goshawks.'

'I questioned all the leading members of The Edge gang. I've checked out their alibis. They all stack up. I never discovered a connection.'

'Well, there is.'

'What is it?'

'That would be telling, wouldn't it?' Barlow grinned, much to Flood's annoyance.

They started walking again. Flood responded, 'What do you want from me?'

'I want you to get me, Jessica and the laddie away from it all. I want you to get us fresh identities so we can start a new life. We'll need passports and driving licences. You know your way around. I want to be invisible to Lidgate, his gang *and* the Met.'

'Why should I do that?'

'Because if you agree, I'll work flat out to prove who was responsible for killing your wife. I'm your best chance of getting a result.'

Flood senses flipped from excitement to resentment at being blackmailed. 'As a serving police officer, if you discover information regarding my wife's murder, you have a duty to report it.'

'But, you'll never know what I'd found out unless I tell you. I know none of this is perfect but you must agree, if it works out, we both get what we want.'

'Except Tommy Lidgate will still be free.'

More joggers passed by, this time a group of ten. Barlow waited until they were out of earshot. 'That's true. The Met will have to find another undercover officer. There may be others already involved. I think it's only a matter of time before we get him.'

'And if I don't help you?'

'You'll be no nearer to finding out who killed your wife. We'll take our chances, do a runner. Hope Lidgate and his cronies don't find us. It's not my preferred option.'

'Why can't you go back to your original identity? The one before the Met created your legend.'

'I could, but the Met know the link. It's too risky. I don't know whose side some of my fellow officers are on. I want a completely fresh start.'

Flood shook his head. 'Sorry, I can't do it. You're asking me to break the law.'

'It's your choice.' Barlow took a final drag on his cigarette before flicking the still-lit stub into the bushes.

He turned back to face Flood. 'There is one thing you can do for me that's legal.'

'What's that?'

'If something happens to me, the Met won't give a shit about Jessica and Mark. I want you to promise that you'll look after them, find somewhere safe for them to live.'

'Why should I do that?'

'Because you know what will happen to Jessica. Same as happened to your wife.'

Barlow's comment hit Flood hard. How could he refuse?

The sound of a piercing police siren roaring up Park Lane caused Barlow to pause before continuing. 'I haven't got much time. I'm going on a drugs run to Marseilles tomorrow. I won't be back for four days. Give me your home number. I'll call you. You can let me know your decision then.'

*

Flood, his mind racing, strode back towards Green Park tube station, considering everything Barlow had said. He met up with Laura who sat at a table at a coffee shop near the entrance.

Laura, her face full of concern, said, 'I couldn't believe what I heard. I didn't see that coming. He'd obviously sized you up at the first meeting.'

Flood didn't reply. He couldn't get Barlow's proposal out of his mind.

Her look of concern turned to one of horror. 'You're not seriously considering his proposal, are you?'

'It's tempting. This could be my only chance to find the truth, Laura.'

She shook her head. 'Sounds more like a career-ending move to me. For starters you'll have to wipe clean the audio tape you're wearing, the contents of which, *I've* heard. What am I supposed to say if I'm questioned about that?'

'I don't know. All I said was, it's tempting.'

Laura turned away from Flood, avoiding his gaze. Seconds later, she faced him. 'I know you're my boss but, sorry, I can't possibly support what you're thinking of doing. It's madness.'

She got up from the table, leaving her coffee and strode out of the cafe. Flood followed. They remained silent, each with their own thoughts as they stood on the tube train full of rush-hour commuters back to Southwark Police Station. As they walked the last fifty yards, Flood ventured, 'So, how does that leave us?'

Laura shook her head in disgust, still not looking at Flood. 'It leaves us nowhere. I can't believe you haven't considered my role in this... this charade. I've got a career to think about too, you know.'

As they reached the entrance to the police station, she hissed, 'That's the trouble with you. You only ever think about yourself. I know it's tough on you, losing Georgina the way you did, but I think your mother's right. For God's sake, let it go. If you want to run the risk of losing *your* job, that's fine. But don't expect me to.'

She stormed into the station. With Laura's words ringing in his ears, Flood returned to his office, pulled down the blinds, a sign to his team that he required privacy.

He knew exactly what to do about obtaining identity documents. He'd once investigated a case involving counterfeiters in Brixton who'd provided passports and the new-style driving licences for members of a criminal gang. Flood solved the case with help from a 'fixer' working for the counterfeiters who'd turned informer. He considered his next move.

CHAPTER ELEVEN

Friday 2nd March 2001

First thing the following morning, Flood rapped on the door to Fox's office. He burst in after Fox nodded his acknowledgement.

'Why the hell wasn't I told we had an undercover officer working with The Goshawks? You know that is one of my lines of enquiry.'

Fox glanced up from his papers. 'I'm not at liberty to disclose that information, as you well know.'

'I can't believe you didn't tell me.'

'Andy, you know that it's vital that undercover cops are protected. We can't have every Tom, Dick and Harry knowing where they're working.'

Flood spluttered, 'It's not good enough. I know you didn't *have* to tell me but I'm not a rookie. We should be working together. The Met's got this one wrong.'

'Have you spoken to the undercover officer?'

'No,' Flood lied, despite being aware that Laura might give the game away. And he still hadn't decided what to do about Barlow's proposal.

'Good. Your specific job is to find out the person responsible for Jenny Cahill's murder. Leave the cloak-and-dagger stuff to the undercover officers. What progress have you made?'

Flood glared back at Fox. 'Very little. We've bailed Martin Cahill. It's looking most likely that Tommy Lidgate's gang arranged the hit, except we can't prove it. His underlings are shit-scared of giving anything away that leads back to him.'

'OK. Keep plugging away. By the way, the Borough Commander called me last night in a right strop. He's summoned me to his office later this morning to discuss a serious matter concerning you. He asked me to make sure you're around later in the day.'

'What's it about?'

'He wouldn't say.'

Flood shrugged. 'OK, I'll be around.'

*

Before holding a review meeting with his team, Flood asked Laura to come to his office. She sat opposite him, a disapproving expression replacing her usual smile.

'I thought I'd better warn you that I told Foxy I knew about the undercover working with the gang. He asked me whether I'd spoken to him. I said I hadn't.'

Laura let out a gasp before saying through gritted teeth, 'I knew this would happen. One lie leads to another. If I'm asked directly whether you've met Barlow, what do I say? You've put me in an impossible position.'

'You'll have to tell the truth. I'm not asking you to lie for me, Laura.'

'Then you'll be stuffed. Foxy will have your balls on a stick.'

'So be it. Obviously we can't mention Barlow's involvement to the team.'

'*Obviously.*'

Flood stood and picked up his file. 'Let's go to the briefing.' It yielded nothing new. Flood revealed only that a source had informed him that there might be a link between The Goshawks and The Edge gangs. He asked one of the DCs to specifically check it out with Intelligence. Flood hoped this might throw up something which would enable an official reinvestigation of the cold case making him less reliant on Barlow.

Later that afternoon, Fox buzzed him. 'Andy, can you come up to the BC's office right away.'

As Flood climbed the stairs to the top floor, a surge of uneasiness shot through his mind.

Fox formally introduced Commander Yates who sat at the head of a small conference table. Flood had met him a few times but never spoken at length. Fox motioned Flood to sit at the opposite end of the table.

Yates wore a flawlessly ironed, crisp, white shirt complete with epaulettes displaying his rank. A black tie, immaculately knotted, complemented the shirt. His perfectly cut and shaped greying hair went with his manicured nails.

Fox straightened a file on his desk, looking nervous. 'It has come to Commander Yates' attention that a serious allegation from a forensics manager has been made against you regarding the John Hartley trial last September. We discussed it in detail this morning. We'd like to put that allegation to you, get your reaction before deciding on the next course of action. Commander Yates will advise you of the allegation.'

Yates, who hadn't taken his eyes off Flood while Fox spoke, sat upright in his chair. He opened the file in front of him, looked down at his notes then directly at Flood.

'I'm sure you'll remember the John Hartley case. You were the Senior Investigating Officer.'

Flood would never forget it. John Hartley, a manipulative psychopath had paid a low-life criminal, Leroy Johnson, to set fire to a house while Hartley's ex-girlfriend, Lynne, and her two children slept. After Lynne had ended their relationship, she'd married a successful businessman, James Hamilton, and had a baby with him. Lynne and both children perished.

'You'll remember a jury convicted John Hartley for murdering Leroy Johnson. The prosecution alleged that Hartley's motive was that Johnson threatened to go the police and implicate him unless Hartley paid over a substantial sum of cash.

'The case turned on detailed forensic evidence putting Hartley at the crime scene. His jacket, trousers and trainers contained traces of Johnson's blood and DNA. Forensics found fibres from Hartley's jacket attached to Johnson's clothes.

'At the trial, Hartley consistently claimed to being set up. He alleged that someone had stolen his clothes after he'd been drugged and used them when they murdered Johnson. Then they returned them to his flat and stuffed them in a cupboard.

'As part of his defence, Hartley claimed that Hamilton's

motive for wanting to be rid of Johnson is that, despite overwhelming evidence, Johnson had got off on a technicality.'

Flood realised, with trepidation, where this was leading. Yates paused, stared at Flood and continued: 'I've learnt since that the forensic team at the Met Police lab in Lambeth ran tests to establish the validity of Hartley's defence. His saliva, urine and blood tests showed nothing untoward. However, they found a significant trace of Rohypnol, the date rape drug, in a sample of Hartley's hair. Their report stated that drug traces remain in the hair for anything up to three months, unlike bodily fluids, which show no traces after forty-eight hours.'

Yates stopped to pour water from a jug into his glass. He took a sip through his thin lips. The Commander wasn't enjoying this meeting any more than he was, thought Flood who found it difficult to breathe. He wanted to undo his tie and loosen his collar but decided against it, believing it would make him look uneasy.

Yates continued: 'The manager in charge of forensics told me that the *only* explanation is that somebody, most likely James Hamilton or an accomplice, must have injected Hartley with a solution containing Rohypnol knocking him out for over five hours. If this evidence had been presented in court, Hartley would not have been found guilty.

'The allegation is that you conspired, with a laboratory technician in the forensic service, a Michael Spenny, to ensure the deliberate contamination of the Rohypnol sample to make it inadmissible in court. We questioned Spenny, who, when faced with the evidence admitted he did it. He signed a statement saying that you asked him to. He said he owed you a favour.' Flood felt both pairs of eyes boring into him.

Commander Yates continued: 'Spenny's admitted to deliberately using a contaminated evidence bag, strictly against the rules. He told the CPS at the time that he'd made a genuine mistake. They had no choice but to advise the Met that they couldn't use it as evidence in court.'

Yates closed his file with a flourish. 'Would you like to

comment on this allegation?'

A trickle of sweat seeped down Flood's neck onto his shirt collar. 'It sounds like you're relying on one person's testimony.'

Fox jumped in. 'That's what I said to the Commander. The fact is, the allegation's been made and we have to follow it up. The forensics manager couldn't understand why Spenny used a contaminated bag. The department has sophisticated systems in place to prevent it. It could make the difference between someone being found guilty or not guilty. Spenny is willing to testify under oath, that you put him up to it.'

Flood took a large intake of breath. He put on his most authoritative voice; the one he reserved for giving evidence in court. 'Let's get one thing clear. Everybody in that courtroom, including the judge, knew Leroy Johnson started the fire deliberately on Hartley's orders. We discovered Johnson's DNA at the crime scene. The prosecution's expert witness stated that the odds on his DNA being wrongly identified were seventeen million to one.'

Flood fought hard to maintain his composure. 'Johnson's defence successfully relied on the fact that his DNA had been unlawfully retained from an earlier crime. The judge had no option but to dismiss the charges. And under the double jeopardy law, he couldn't be tried again. In other words, he got away with it. And so, too, did Hartley. If I hadn't intervened, it would have been a gross miscarriage of justice. Our job is to prevent that, isn't it?'

Commander Yates' face turned into a scowl. 'So you admit the allegation?'

Flood barked, 'Do either of you have the slightest idea what it's like to lose your family to a murderous psychopath and a lowlife cretin and the bastards remain free, just like my wife's murderer?' Flood glowered at each of them in turn. Fox broke the silence.

'I sympathise with what happened to your wife, but I think you've let your personal circumstances get in the way of doing your job. I'm disappointed in you. You're a great detective. I can't believe you'd put your career at risk.' Fox shook his head. Commander Yates stared at Flood, his lips tightening even thinner. Red blotches showed on his face.

'Your actions were not what we expect from a senior police officer. You've put the Force and me in an impossible situation. If this gets out, the media would crucify us... again. We're in danger of losing the confidence of the public. And that's not all.'

Commander Yates thrust his head closer to Flood. 'If anyone discovers what you and your accomplice did, Hartley's lawyers would demand a retrial. He'd receive a full pardon and sue the Met for zillions. You'd be tried for perverting the course of justice. There would be an enquiry. Professional Standards would crawl all over us for months.' He sat back in his chair and blew out his cheeks. 'It doesn't bear thinking about.' His intense glare bordered on hatred.

Flood hit back, 'I've always seen my job as getting justice, making the criminals, especially cold-blooded murderers, pay for their crimes. If I hadn't acted, a psychopathic killer and his dim-witted stooge would have got away with murdering a defenceless mother and her two children, one a baby. Are you happy with that?'

Yates sat forward again. 'What I'm *not* happy about are officers in my Force acting as vigilantes. Can you imagine Hartley, the judiciary and the media saying, *"Oh, that's all right, then. The Met can make up their own mind about what constitutes justice."* I don't think that's likely, do you?'

Another silence pervaded Fox's office as Flood and Yates conducted their personal staring match. Fox looked down at his desk and fiddled with some papers. Eventually, Yates continued: 'I've thought of a number of options on how we can handle this... this situation. Only five people know all the facts: your accomplice, the three of us and the forensics manager. Fortunately, he's a good friend of mine. That's why he tipped me off and no one else. All he's interested in is ensuring the Met cleans itself up, rooting out *corrupt* officers.'

Flood flinched momentarily before shouting back, 'Are you saying I'm corrupt? I hate bent coppers as much as you do. Don't put me in the same category as them.'

Yates carried on as if Flood hadn't spoken. 'Your accomplice has resigned with immediate effect. As far as you're concerned, there is only one option which ticks all the boxes. It sticks in my craw to have to cover up your actions but I've no choice. You, too, will have to resign from the Met.'

Flood's mind flashed back over his twenty-five years' service. He felt a stabbing pain in his heart. It's what he imagined people experienced in near-death situations.

'Resign? What do you mean, resign? You can't do that to me. This is my life.'

'There are conditions. Your resignation will be on health grounds. The official reason is that you're too stressed to continue in your role and that you are close to a nervous breakdown.'

'Stressed? Me, stressed?' Flood snorted.

'You'll get your pension but there are strings attached. You're to have no contact with Spenny. And, *absolutely* no disclosure to anyone else, within the Force or not. You'll be replaced as the SIO on the Jenny Cahill investigation by DI Harvey. You'll spend the rest of the afternoon briefing him. That's already been set up.'

'There must be another way of handling this,' Flood implored. 'This is all I've ever wanted to do. And I've done it bloody well.'

Fox raised his voice. 'You don't have a choice. You went a step too far.'

Yates added, 'Our decision is final. If we don't cover this up, you'll go to jail. I don't have to remind you judges come down hard on anyone, particularly police officers, found guilty of perverting the course of justice. Especially cases involving murder. You're looking at a minimum fifteen to twenty years. I don't think you'd enjoy serving time as an ex-copper. What I've suggested is as much for you as it is for the Met.'

Flood considered it ironic that the Met intended covering up his crime. Wasn't that a form of corruption? He didn't think it would do him any favours to voice his view.

Yates asked, 'Do you have any questions?' Flood shook his

head, still in shock.

'In that case I'll leave you with Detective Superintendent Fox to sort out the paperwork. Clear your desk and surrender your warrant card, computer passwords and encryption codes after you've handed over the Jenny Cahill investigation. Don't return to the station. We'll put out a statement about your resignation first thing on Monday.' He gave Flood one last contemptuous glare, picked up his file and left the room.

Fox spent the next hour going through the details of Flood's resignation. When they'd finished, Fox said, 'I'm sorry your career has ended this way. We'll miss you, Andy. I feel like a headmaster expelling my Head Boy.'

CHAPTER TWELVE

Friday 2nd March 2001

With a heavy heart and his brain on autopilot, Flood cleared out his office. He stuffed his personal items, including photos of his daughters and Georgina, into his briefcase. He nodded at a few officers still working late, as if nothing had happened. He had no recollection of the drive home except for deciding not to tell his mother or his girls what happened. Not yet anyway. After parking his car, he emptied the contents of his briefcase into the boot.

The girls had gone to bed. Stella, was watching a cookery programme on TV. She turned the TV off with the remote, stood, pecked his cheek and gave him a brief hug.

'Had a good day?'

'Er, no, not exactly.'

'You look shattered. Supper? I kept back a plate of lasagne in case you got back early.'

Flood placed his briefcase on the floor, removed his jacket and slumped into an armchair. Although his appetite had evaporated, he said, 'That would be good.'

He made every effort to appear normal as he picked at the pasta dish. His mother chatted continuously about the girls' day at school. Flood found difficulty in concentrating.

'Have you thought anymore about what I said to you a week ago? You know, about the girls?'

'Not now, Mum. I told you. I've had a really bad day. I don't want to discuss it tonight. Tell you what, I've got this weekend and the next few days off. Let's talk about it then, OK?'

'You know I'm serious, don't you?'

When he'd finished eating, Stella took his plate, loaded it in the dishwasher, turned it on and retired to bed with a book. Flood picked up the half-full bottle of Merlot and his glass from the table and headed for his study.

He sat for an hour staring at the whiteboard, glugging back the wine, trying to make sense of what had happened. It had all been so sudden. Twenty-five years exemplary service shot to bits in a few hours. How would he explain his resignation to his family? How would they react if he told them the truth? Would they think less of him?

He especially dreaded a conversation with Laura. When he finally went to bed, the wine bottle emptied, he couldn't sleep. The same questions spun around his mind like clothes in a tumble dryer.

*

Flood got up the next morning, a Saturday, feeling wretched and empty. He put on a pair of jeans, a multi-coloured check casual shirt and favourite navy sweater. At least he didn't have to wear a jacket and tie every day from now on.

He considered calling his accomplice in the forensics lab, Mike Spenny, although he didn't know him well. When Flood thought about it, their relationship simply consisted of a favour given and a favour returned.

He'd saved Spenny's job after he'd made a crucial mistake, involving the handling of vital evidence in an unrelated case. Flood didn't report it but still got the conviction through alternative evidence. He concluded he'd gain nothing by getting in touch.

He decided to devote the weekend to the girls, taking them to see *Billy Elliot,* the story of an eleven-year-old boy from the North-East who became a renowned ballet dancer. Both girls loved dancing. Flood found it desperately hard to concentrate in the cinema, his mind continuing to spin. He gained solace from glancing at the girls' faces from time to time. Billy's exploits, against all the odds, enthralled them.

He spent the next wet and windy day baking bread and cakes with the girls under Nana's supervision. He ended up getting himself covered in flour, much to his family's amusement. After a light lunch, they settled down in front of the TV. Stella sat with them, a contented smile on her face.

At teatime, she carried in the results of the morning baking session. As they feasted on the fresh pastries, she said, 'This is how a family should be.'

For most of the next afternoon, Flood's mobile hardly stopped ringing. The Met had released the official statement referring to his retirement on health grounds earlier that morning. Many of his team wanted to know more about his condition. He batted most of them away, emphasising that he'd succumbed to the stressful nature of his job and he'd finally had enough of police work.

Some wanted to arrange a farewell party. Others said how much they'd miss his dedication and brilliance at solving difficult cases. Flood expressed his gratitude, having no idea he commanded such a high level of respect.

His friend, DI Harry Fuller, left a message. 'I can't believe you've resigned. Mind you, I don't blame you for getting out. I can't wait to join you. Give me a call when you've got time.'

As he downed his third cup of coffee, Laura called. Flood struggled to nail his emotions on hearing her voice. 'What's this about resigning? You never said anything to me.'

'I've had enough, Laura.'

'Nothing to do with you meeting up with the UCO?'

'No. The Met don't know I've spoken to him.'

'What was it, then? I know you were pissed off with the Met but only the other day you'd said that being a copper was all you ever wanted. The rumour mill's working overtime. All sorts of stuff.'

'Such as?'

'The most common one is that you had a major falling out with Foxy. That you lost it, told him where to stick his job. Is that true?'

'No. Apparently, I'm on the edge of a nervous breakdown. Too stressed to carry on.'

'Really? So stressed you'd want to give it all up?'

'There's a lot I need to tell you, Laura. Can we meet?'

'Why don't you come to my place? I'll rustle up some dinner. Say about seven thirty?'

'I'll be there.' She gave him directions. As Flood ended the call, he mulled over how much he should tell her.

*

On the way to Laura's flat, Flood stopped off a local supermarket. He spent time choosing a good bottle of vintage Burgundy, which he knew Laura loved, and an exotic bunch of flowers. Laura greeted him at the front door with a half-hearted smile and an awkward embrace.

'What's this? A peace offering?'

'Yes. I'm sorry we fell out, Laura.'

She smiled. 'Peace offering accepted.' She took them from him. 'Come in. Hang your coat over there.' She nodded towards the hooks beside the front door.

As Flood followed her to the kitchen, he couldn't help noticing her tight-fitting, patterned dress emphasising her trim figure. He'd only ever seen her wearing clothes suitable for a detective sergeant. The subtle lighting and the aroma of a chicken roasting in the oven cast a spell over Flood, marginally improving his mood.

She filled a vase with water and arranged the flowers. 'These are lovely. Just my colours. Drink?'

'Glass of red would be great. Shall I open the Burgundy?'

'Sure. Pour me one. I'll carve the chicken. When it's on the table, I want to hear *all* your news. Make yourself comfortable in the dining room.'

Flood's detective eye noticed a montage of photographs taking up most of one wall. Many showed two young girls, a few years apart in age, at different times in their lives. Others showed a baby girl.

'This looks good,' Flood said, as Laura brought two plates of food from the kitchen and placed them on the table. 'Nice place, too. I love the way you've furnished the flat. Georgina loved *ikea* too.'

'Thank you. When Rich and I divorced, we sold the family house. I bought this. You don't get much for your money in Westminster but I love it here. He's pissing his share against a wall somewhere.'

'Are those your daughters?' Flood nodded in the direction of the wall.

'Yes. And my granddaughter, too.'

'You've only ever mentioned one daughter.'

'Have I? I had two. So…' Laura said, shaking out a cloth napkin before placing it on her lap, 'Why the resignation? Why so sudden?'

Flood decided that she deserved to know the truth if he wanted to continue a relationship with her. Despite their falling out over Barlow's proposition, he felt closer to her than anyone outside his family. Except he didn't know what her reaction might be to his latest news. Flood topped up their glasses.

'I know you didn't approve of me considering doing a deal with Barlow, Laura.'

'No. I didn't. I thought it was reckless.'

'This is something else. I'm going to tell you everything. It has to remain absolutely confidential. Are you happy with that?'

She frowned. 'Yes, I'm happy. And intrigued.'

Flood took a deep breath. As he exhaled, he said, 'OK.' Between mouthfuls of chicken, he told her what he'd done to ensure John Hartley's conviction. Laura had to remind him several times that his food was getting cold.

He noticed Laura's expression growing increasingly pensive. When Flood told her he'd persuaded his accomplice to tamper with the crucial evidence, she put down her knife and fork and placed both hands over her mouth. Flood wondered if he'd made the right decision in telling her the truth.

'What got to me was that everyone in that courtroom knew that Hartley and Johnson were guilty. They got off on a stupid technicality. I felt I had to act to ensure they got their just desserts.'

Laura nodded. He continued: 'I won't disguise the fact that what happened to my wife influenced me. I know I made a mistake but I did it for the best possible reasons. I believe justice was served.' Flood locked eyes with Laura to emphasise the point.

'Didn't you think of the consequences if the Met found out?'

'All I thought about was what James Hamilton went through after his wife, baby daughter and stepson had perished in the arson attack.' Flood looked imploringly at Laura.

She reached across, picked up Flood's cutlery and empty plate, put them on top of hers and carried them to the kitchen. She said, over her shoulder, 'I need time to think about this.'

Flood sipped his wine and sat back in his chair. Although relieved he'd unburdened himself, he grew fearful that Laura didn't approve. She returned with two bowls of apple crumble and placed them on the table, saying, 'I assume the Met found out.'

'Yes. The Borough Commander and Foxy had me in on Friday. They forced me to resign on the basis that I'm too stressed to continue. They don't want anyone to know what I did. Only six people know the truth now, including you.' Flood tried to read Laura's crestfallen expression.

He tested the water. 'Do you think I'm corrupt, Laura?'

She shook her head. 'No, I don't think you're corrupt. You didn't gain anything for yourself. I can see why you did it. You identified with Hamilton. He'd lost his family and you'd lost your wife all because their killers sought revenge.'

Laura continued: 'I thought about you considering dealing with Barlow. Actually, it's all I've thought about this weekend. I put myself in your shoes. It must be so frustrating not to get to the truth.' She reached for her napkin lying on the table and placed it back on her lap.

'I can see why you think Barlow's your best chance of getting a result.'

'I'm sorry if I put you in an awkward spot. I shouldn't have put you at risk.'

'It doesn't mean to say that I wasn't cross with you at the time. You didn't think about me at all. That's what hurt.'

'You're right. I'm sorry, Laura.'

She fiddled with her spoon, moving a piece of apple around the bowl. 'What are you going to say to Barlow when he calls you?'

'I'm going to tell him I'm up for it. I've got nothing to lose now.'

'That still means you'll be breaking the law if you provide him with fake IDs.'

'It's a risk I'm prepared to take. Barlow's well-connected within the gang. I'm sure he'll deliver.'

Laura stood up from the table. 'Go and sit on the sofa. I'll get us drinks. Tea, coffee, something stronger?'

'Coffee's fine. Do you have any cognac?'

'I do. It's my favourite medicine. Cures everything.'

Laura returned from the kitchen carrying a tray containing two cups of coffee, brandy glasses and a half-full bottle of 'medicine'. She poured two large measures, placed the tray on the coffee table and sat next to Flood.

She sipped her coffee and placed the cup back in the saucer. 'There's one advantage of your resignation. At least you'll have more time to spend with your mother and your girls.'

'Yes... yes, you're right.' Flood reached for the cognac and inhaled the aroma. He took a sip, sat back in the sofa and closed his eyes in appreciation. 'Oh, that's good.'

Over the weekend, Flood had thought of another advantage to his fall from grace. He'd become aware of the odd remarks, some subtle, some not so subtle, made by fellow officers regarding his burgeoning relationship with Laura. Now it didn't matter, assuming she wanted to continue.

Flood reached for his glass again. 'Sorry, Laura. I don't want to monopolise your evening. How are things with your ex? Still on the scene?'

'Oh, he's such a pain.'

'Why? What's he done now?'

'He's been bothering our daughter Liz. The one with the four-year-old. Since the divorce, he's been turning up there, pissed out of his brains. Insisting on seeing his granddaughter. Liz is beside herself.'

She picked up her brandy glass and took a sip. 'She doesn't want him near her daughter when he's in that state. If it gets any worse, we'll have to get a restraining order. He's a complete arsehole when he's drunk.'

'Has he always been like this?'

She shook her head. 'No. No. He wasn't. Quite the opposite. He was kind, gentle and treated me well.'

Laura peered thoughtfully down into her glass which she cradled in her hands. She took a deep breath. 'Something dreadful happened to my other daughter Joanne, seven years ago.' Her eyes glanced up to the photographs on the wall then back to Flood.

'It changed everything. She studied philosophy at the University of London. It was great for me because she lived with us. She had everything going for her.' Laura smiled at her memory.

'And...'

'I still find it difficult to talk about.' She stared at the floor and back to Flood.

'You told me more than once that it helps to talk about these things.'

Laura gave a weak smile. 'Yes, I did, didn't I? OK. She went out with some friends from Uni one night to celebrate a birthday. Because it was out of town and she'd be late home, she said that she'd get the night bus to Waterloo. I agreed to pick her up from the bus stop, take her the three-quarters-of-a-mile or so home to our house in Kennington. Sod's law worked its magic.'

'Always does.'

'A nasty assault case came in that night. I was called into the station to help. Rich was away on business so I told Joanne to call me on her mobile as soon as she got close to the bus stop so that I could pop out to collect her.'

'What happened?'

'She called me. I left the station immediately but the bloody traffic was awful. There'd been an accident close to Waterloo Station. I called Joanne to say I was going to be late. She said not to worry, she'd walk home. I told her to get a taxi. She said she would but she didn't. She came across a gang of idiot pissheads, off their heads with God knows what. They picked on her. Asked her for money. She refused. They started touching and fondling her.' Laura reached for a tissue tucked up the sleeve of her dress and dabbed her eyes.

'One of them pushed her. She fell badly, cracking her skull on the kerb. They left her there and ran off. She died from a brain haemorrhage in St Thomas's Hospital twenty-four hours later.'

'Oh, Laura.' Flood leant over and put his arms around her shoulder and squeezed. 'That's awful. It's a parent's worst nightmare. Did they get the bastards?'

'Yes. I don't know how I got through the court case. Rich and I went every day. I couldn't take my eyes off the three of them. They showed no remorse. I could have killed them. They each got ten years for manslaughter. They'll be out anytime soon if they've behaved themselves in prison.'

Flood shook his head. 'That's our bloody system for you.'

She fixed her eyes on Flood's. 'Nowhere near enough, is it? At times, I didn't know whether I could carry on with life. Why bother? I thought. I felt so guilty.'

'You shouldn't blame yourself, Laura. It wasn't your fault. How did Rich take it?'

'Not well. He blamed me. Said I should have organised a taxi from the party to home. Maybe I should have. He started drinking. He won't accept that Joanne's gone. Won't even discuss it. It's so stupid. We both needed someone to lean on. Someone to help us come to terms with our loss. Instead, we went into our shells. Our marriage started breaking down right there.'

'Did you consider counselling?'

'I did. But Rich wouldn't even talk about it. He didn't believe anyone outside the family could help us.'

'I assume the station knew?'

'Of course. Once the court case ended, I told them I didn't want to talk about it. It's not that I wanted to forget that it happened. I think about her every day. I don't want to be defined by it or be remembered for it. I didn't want it to feed my guilt or for people to feel sorry for me.'

'I'm sure everyone felt sorry for you, Laura. It's only natural. It's an awful thing to have happened. If anything like that happened to my girls, I'd end up a basket case.'

Laura sniffed, blew her nose with the tissue and laughed in embarrassment. 'Sounds like confession night, doesn't it?' She stood, slightly uneasily and shuffled towards a shelf holding CDs.

She scrabbled amongst them. 'I think it's time we changed the mood.' She selected a Johnny Mathis CD, popped it into the player, topped up their cognacs again and plopped down next to Flood on the sofa. She rested her head on his shoulder, saying, 'This is better.' They both closed their eyes, letting the music wash over them like a soothing tepid shower.

Flood felt the warmth of Laura's body seeping into him. He'd forgotten the power of such intimacy. Then he remembered his meeting with Barlow the next day.

As the plaintive strains of *The Last Time I Felt Like This, I Was Falling In Love* finished, Flood stretched his lanky body and stood. 'I'd better be getting back. Big day tomorrow.'

Laura stood, too, straightening the front of her dress with both hands. 'Good luck with Barlow.'

'Thanks. You must know by now how much you mean to me, Laura.'

He reached for her and hugged her tightly. His hands moved up and down the curve of her hips. His lips crashed into hers. They stayed joined together for what seemed an eternity.

As they separated, Laura said, 'Do you want to stay tonight?'

'No… I can't, Laura. I need to be on top of my game when I meet Barlow tomorrow. I've already drunk more than I should have.'

He grabbed her close to him again, this time kissing her neck repeatedly as their bodies dovetailed together like pieces of a jigsaw.

*

Flood hailed a cab on the still-busy Westminster Bridge. On the way back home, his body radiating with Laura's last kiss, he tried to work out why he'd turned down her offer, wondered if she felt upset with him for not staying. He couldn't put his finger on why he didn't stay. Was it too soon after Georgina? He reasoned that when he'd avenged her death, he'd feel differently. He fought the urge to ask the taxi driver to do a U-turn. He'd never ever thought about a serious relationship with another woman. Until now.

CHAPTER THIRTEEN

Tuesday 6th March 2001

Flood drove Pippa and Gemma to school for the second day running. 'We like this, Daddy,' Pippa said, as she bounded out of the car.

'I do, too. Very much. Be good today.'

The girls both chorused, 'We will,' as they giggled on their way to the entrance.

As Flood drove back home, the warm feeling he'd felt having the girls in the car faded. The potential possibilities of his meeting with Barlow that evening took over. Shortly after arriving, his landline rang.

'It's Martin Cahill.'

'How did you get my home number?'

'It wasn't easy. Let's say I've got friends in the Force.'

'What do you want?' Flood snapped.

'I've heard about your retirement. Stress, wasn't it?'

'That's what they say, yes.'

'I thought you'd be the last person to get stressed. You seemed to enjoy your job.'

'Why have you called me?'

'I know the plonker who's taken over the case from you. DI Harvey. From what I've heard, he's not in your league. I don't have much faith in him. My contacts tell me you're one of the best detectives in the Met. I want *you* to find out who killed my wife Jenny.'

'That's odd. As I recall, most of our chats revolved around your affair with Katie Brunswick. Now you're expressing concern about your wife's murder.'

Cahill sounded contrite. 'The Met still think I had something to do with Jenny's death. I want you to help prove my innocence.'

'That's all very interesting but I'm a retired police officer. What do you want from me?'

'After the judge acquitted Jenny, I knew the gang would take revenge.' Cahill's voice wavered. 'I should have insisted on us going into the Witness Protection Programme. I feel guilty about that.' Flood couldn't decide whether Cahill belonged on a stage or whether he genuinely felt responsible.

'As the former SIO, you have detailed knowledge about Jenny's case. I'd like you to carry on investigating privately. Prove I wasn't involved.'

'The Met are on the case. There's nothing I can do while that's going on.'

'I'm prepared to pay you.'

'Save your money.'

'Think about it. Call me when you've made up your mind. Here's my number.'

*

Barlow called Flood later that morning. 'I'm back. We arranged to meet, remember? Be outside Churchill's Cabinet Rooms in Whitehall. Six thirty pm.' Flood hated being dictated to about where and when he should meet. He usually called the shots.

By the time he arrived at the meeting point, the bright, sunny day had turned to darkness and the temperature had plummeted again. Barlow wore his long, black coat buttoned up to the collar, as usual.

As Flood got closer, he smelt stale tobacco on Barlow's breath as he nodded and said, 'Let's walk.' He turned into Whitehall setting off towards Trafalgar Square. Flood fell in beside him.

'Thought any more about my proposal?' Barlow sounded like a life insurance salesman, thought Flood.

'Yes. I have. If you get me the information I want, I can get you new IDs. It's risky and it takes time. At least a week.'

'So you think you can still help me despite the fact you've resigned from the Met?'

Flood stopped abruptly and turned to him. 'It's obviously public knowledge. This means that the only way I can get

102

what you want is by using my criminal contacts. You could do the same.'

'I can't do it. If Lidgate finds out I'm planning to leave the gang, it would confirm his suspicions. He'd kill me.' Barlow reached for a cigarette packet in his pocket. Flood noticed his hands trembling as he pulled one out.

Flood asked, 'How are you going to get my information?'

After Barlow lit up, he said, 'We're collecting another consignment of cocaine soon. The stuff's arriving in the south of France by container ship. We'll pick it up and bring it back to the UK.'

They started walking again. Barlow continued: 'I'm going with two members of the gang. I think they're the ones responsible for murdering your wife and Jenny Cahill.

'I'll be wired up while we're travelling in our Transit van. I'll bring up your wife's case. And Jenny Cahill's. Talk about the link between The Edge and Goshawks gangs. They'll speak a lot of bollocks in between but they love bragging about jobs they've done. It's bloody risky but you'll be able to hear everything they say.'

'Won't your handler want to know what's going on?'

'I don't tell him everything. I've told you before. I don't trust him. I'd rather trust you to get me out of all this.'

'Who's your handler?'

'Jeff Swanson. A DI based in Islington.'

Flood made a mental note to check him out. 'When are you back?'

'We leave tomorrow night. Back in about three days. I'll give you a shout when I return. Swap notes then.'

'Before you leave, I'll need two passport-size photos of you, your girlfriend and the baby. How old is your girlfriend?'

'She's thirty-eight, five years younger than me.'

'I'll need cash. Fakes change hands for a grand each these days.'

Barlow smiled. 'OK. I'll see you outside WH Smiths on Waterloo Station tomorrow night, same time. I'll hand over the cash and photos then.'

Flood nodded as Barlow added, 'I'll be leaving

immediately afterwards.'

'How do you get the drugs into the country?'

'We've got a system.' Barlow grinned. 'Probably best if you don't know the details. See you tomorrow.'

*

Flood spent the following dull, grey morning walking through Greenwich Cemetery at Shooters Hill, close to his home. After an hour-and-a-half, he'd got what he wanted. He came across a couple, Steve and Carol Harris, who'd died on the same day, Flood presumed in a car crash. Their ages were within a year or two of Barlow and his girlfriend. He'd use these names for the passports and driving licences.

Later that day he met up with Barlow at Waterloo Station who handed over an envelope containing £3000 in used notes and the photos, saying, 'I hope these are suitable.' Flood opened the envelope and inspected the contents.

Jessica's photo revealed an angular, narrow face with dark chocolate-brown eyes. A glossy lipstick covered her sensuous lips. Her black hair cascaded down the side of her face, highlighting her prominent cheekbones. Flood though she looked sexy rather than pretty.

The baby lay on a white sheet, highlighting his dark skin. Cushions and pillows propped him up. Flood said, 'They'll do fine,' and then replaced the cash and the photos in the envelope before putting them in his inside pocket.

Barlow's face creased into a smile. 'Good. When I get back, we'll meet up. Let's say Monday night at the bandstand in Regent's Park, about seven thirty. We can swap everything. Then we'll both have what we want.'

*

Flood called Laura and arranged to visit her later that evening. Over drinks, he brought her up to date on his meeting with Barlow.

'So, you're actually going to get Barlow and his new family

fake IDs?' Laura questioned.

Flood put down his glass. 'I need to, Laura. This is the closest I've ever been to knowing who killed Georgina.'

'I totally understand why you want to do this but it's bloody risky. If the Met find out, you'll go to prison. Ex-copper or not. Then what?'

'I know. To me, it's worth the risk.'

'What about your kids? Is it worth depriving them of a father if you get caught?'

'I don't think I'll ever be a proper father to them until I get this sorted. I want them to know that I did everything in my power to find out who murdered their mother.'

Laura topped up Flood's glass. 'I can see your mind's made up.' They stared at each other, not sure what to say.

Flood broke the silence. 'Do you know a DI called Swanson, Jeff Swanson? He's Barlow's handler. Works out of the Islington station.'

'No, I don't. Would you like me to check him out?'

'Would you? If you can get me his details and a mug shot, I'll watch him for a while.'

Early next morning, Laura emailed Flood with Swanson's address, an apartment in Highbury Grove, nor far from Arsenal's football ground. She attached a head and shoulders photo.

She'd written:

Nothing much to report. Been with the Force for twenty years. Done most of his time in North London stations. Known to be competent but not a high flyer.
Good luck.
Love, Laura.

*

Later that day, Flood visited his counterfeiter informer, a Nigerian calling himself 'David'. He possessed film-star good looks and always wore a khaki linen suit with an open-necked floral shirt. He worked out of a room at the back of a cafe on Brixton High Street specialising in Caribbean food. When

Flood asked to see David, the Jamaican owner looked Flood up and down.

'Who wants to see 'im?'

'Tell him Andy Flood's here.'

The Jamaican disappeared to the back room and returned a minute later. 'He's in there,' nodding back in the direction he'd come from.

David welcomed Flood like an old friend. 'Good to see you. I assume this is business not pleasure?' His smile revealed pristine, perfectly aligned white teeth.

'Yes. I need passports and driving licences pronto. How soon can you get them if I give you the photos, names and cash now?'

'About three days. Used to be quicker. There's so much demand these days.'

'Three days is good.' Flood foraged in his inside jacket pocket and handed over the envelope.

David counted out the notes as efficiently as any bank teller. 'That's fine. I'll call you when they're ready for collection.'

*

That evening, after Pippa and Gemma had gone to bed, Flood decided to drive over to Swanson's home. He told his mother he was working on a surveillance job and wouldn't be home until late.

'I thought you'd finished with going out all hours of the night.'

'It's something that has to be done.'

Her voice softened. 'Please be careful, son.'

He arrived at Highbury Grove just after 9.00 pm and parked across the road with a good view of Swanson's first-floor flat. The lights remained on until 12.30 am. Flood waited a further half-hour before deciding to return home.

While he sat in his car, he fantasised about Barlow's mission; talking to his 'friends' in the confines of a Transit van. He hoped Barlow's time was proving more fruitful than his.

Flood repeated his surveillance the following night, sustained by swigging tea from a thermos flask he always carried on such jobs. His body tensed as the lights to the flat went off and the front door opened just after 9.30 pm. He drained the remains of his tea and screwed the cap back on the flask.

After slamming the front door, Swanson's squat frame hurried down the steps to ground level. Flood slumped down out of sight in his driver's seat as Swanson pointed and clicked his remote key to a blue Peugeot parked four cars in front of him. Swanson got in and drove off.

Flood followed, driving for a mile up the Seven Sisters Road towards Manor House Tube Station in heavy traffic. Swanson turned left into a side street and stopped behind an Audi. Flood noticed someone sitting in the driver's seat as he drove past.

He parked a hundred yards in front of both cars, got out and crept back towards the Audi using the buildings as cover. He got close enough to see Swanson sitting in the passenger seat talking to the driver. Flood made a mental note of the car's number plate. Half-an-hour later, Swanson returned to his car. Flood followed him back to his flat and then drove home.

He called Laura early the next morning and told her what he'd witnessed. He gave her the registration number. 'Can you find out the registered owner?'

'Sure. Don't get too excited. It's probably one of Swanson's informants. I'll call you back later.'

She did. 'The car's registered to a Billy White. I passed the details on to Intel. He's got form, mainly to do with drugs. But get this: they believe he's linked to The Goshawks gang.'

Flood let out an audible whistle. 'Why on earth would Swanson want to talk to him?'

'Could be that White's either working undercover or he's an informer.'

'Or Swanson's on Lidgate's payroll? Barlow told me he didn't trust him.'

'It's a possibility, I suppose. But that means Swanson

would have already told Lidgate about Barlow being undercover.'

'Shit! Barlow's right to be worried about him if that's the case.'

'Is it worth talking to Swanson? Say we know about Barlow, Billy White and Lidgate, get a reaction?'

'There's no point, Laura. He'll tell us nothing. He'll protect his man. It may even put Barlow's life in danger if we declare our hand. How's the rest of the investigation going?'

Laura groaned. 'We're getting nowhere. This case is like trapping fog.'

*

Flood spent Sunday with his girls, taking them to the supermarket to do the week's shopping. He rewarded them by a visit to the ice rink. He joined them, having to concentrate all his efforts on remaining upright. Whenever he fell, the girls skated to his rescue. They laughed together as they pulled him to his feet. When he finally managed a complete circuit, the girls embarrassed him with a cheer. As Flood drove them home, he realised he hadn't once thought about his meeting with Barlow.

*

Flood arranged to meet Laura at a pavement cafe on the South Bank the following morning. Laura had arrived first. Flood hugged her tightly and kissed her on the lips.

For the first time in ages, the sun put in an appearance and glistened off the murky Thames. They felt the warmth on their backs as they sat outside, raising Flood's spirits.

'Any developments?' he asked.

Laura opened a sugar sachet, poured half the contents into her cup and began stirring.

'Not really. Harvey's not up to speed yet. Some of the guys wish you hadn't retired. They want you back.'

Flood huffed. He put his cup back on the table. 'Don't rub

it in. When I think of all the hours I put in, all the villains I banged up. I can't get over being kicked out of the Force.'

Laura shook her head. 'It's the Met's loss.'

'Not sure that's how they see it. There is a positive, though. I'm spending more time with my girls. I'm enjoying it.'

'I'm glad.' Laura stroked Flood's hand resting on the table. After a short silence, she continued: 'Did you get Barlow's IDs?'

'I'm collecting them this afternoon. I'll see Barlow afterwards. Hope he can get the evidence I need.'

'I hope so, too.' Laura finished her coffee and stood. 'I'd better be getting back. Harvey will wonder where I am.'

Flood finished his coffee. 'I'll walk with you.'

Laura linked her arm inside his as they strolled along the embankment towards Southwark. Within a hundred yards of the station, Laura stopped walking and turned to him.

'I'll be thinking of you. Good luck.' She drew him close to her and hugged him. He watched her walk away, aching to run after her and kiss her again. Everything appeared to be falling into place.

CHAPTER FOURTEEN

Monday 12ᵗʰ March 2001

David proved as reliable as ever. Back at his office at the rear of the Brixton café, Flood inspected the immaculate documents. He hadn't told him he no longer worked for the Met. He reasoned that there were some things you kept to yourself and that David would have assumed that he had some credit in the bank.

Flood arrived at Regent's Park grandstand half-an-hour early for his meeting with Barlow. He engrossed himself in a newspaper as much as he could, finding it hard to concentrate as thoughts of what he might discover in the next hour dominated his mind. He checked his mobile frequently, making sure he had a signal.

Fifteen minutes passed. Then twenty, twenty-five, thirty minutes. One hour. Nothing. No phone call or text either. After waiting another half-hour, he called Laura.

'Bloody Barlow's a no show.'

'Oh, no! I'm sorry. What do you think has happened?'

'Either Barlow's panicked, done a runner, with or without his new family or, if Swanson's straight, he's got him out, put him in a safe house somewhere. If he's bent and learnt about Barlow's plans, he's probably tipped off Tommy Lidgate.'

'What's your money on?'

Flood hesitated. 'Before I answer that, I'll visit Jessica, see if she's still there. You have her address, don't you?'

'Give me a sec… yes, here it is.'

As Flood jotted it down, he said, 'I need to know more about Swanson. Might be worth a longer spell of surveillance.'

'Of course, there is another explanation.'

'Which is?'

'Could be Customs held Barlow up. He may still be in one of the ports.'

'Can you check that out? See who they've recently

detained. That's our best hope.'

'Are you going to Jessica's now?'

'Yes. I'll let you know how I get on.'

'Do you want me to come?'

'No. You make your checks. I'd better be going.'

'Be careful. Remember, Jessica is Tommy Lidgate's daughter-in-law. We don't know how she feels about him.'

*

Flood drove to Islington, full of gastro pubs and fancy restaurants these days. He parked outside a smart block of four large Regency houses surrounded by black-painted railings.

He checked the house number Laura had given him. He was at the right place. Through the curtains he spotted lights on in the hall and living room. He rang the bell. The door opened as far as a sturdy chain would allow.

'Yes?' A woman's face peered through the gap. Flood recognised Jessica from the passport photo he carried inside his jacket pocket.

Ditching his usual police tone, he smiled broadly, trying to sound friendly. 'You must be Jessica. Sorry to worry you. I had a meeting arranged with Rob Barlow tonight. I understand he lives here. I'm a friend of his. He asked me to pick him up. Is he in?'

'He never told me that. He tells me everything. Nah, he's not in. Don't know when he'll be home. Who are you anyway?' Jessica flicked her long, black hair away from her eyes with a perfectly manicured hand.

'I'm Andy Flood.' He noticed her eyes, heavily ringed with eye-liner and mascara, widen in recognition of his name.

'He's got my number but here's my card.' He handed it to her. He'd had them printed with his contact details and the words 'Private Investigator' written on them. Without his Met Police warrant card he felt helpless.

'Can I wait for him here?'

She unlocked the chain and opened the door wide enough to pop her head forward. As she looked up and down the road full of parked cars, she said, 'OK. Come in quick. Don't think it's a good idea for me to be seen talking to an ex-copper.'

He followed her into the living room. She appeared more petite than the photo depicted; almost anorexic. The contemporary furniture and decorative glass wall coverings in bold colours came straight from the *Ideal Home* magazine. A child's buggy was parked in the hallway.

Jessica turned off the barely audible TV. 'Sit down. My little boy's asleep upstairs. It took me ages to get him off tonight. I think he's missing his dad.'

'Have you heard from him?'

'Nah. He's on one of his trips. He don't usually call me unless it's urgent. Should be back tonight, though.'

'Did he tell you about me and our plan?'

Jessica fiddled with her hair, something she did regularly. Flood recognised it as a sure sign of nervousness. 'Yeah, he did.'

'Are you happy with it?'

'Not much bloody choice, is there? It's circumstances.'

'What circumstances?'

'When I first met Robbie, I fell for him. Big time. Good looking and smart. I'd never felt that way before about no one. Our little boy Mark is the result.' She flicked her head upwards to his room. 'Everything seemed fine. Then I found out six weeks ago about Robbie being a bloody undercover cop. We had the biggest row ever. Men can be bastards, can't they?'

Flood imagined that she'd had some experience in the matter. 'I can't deny that. Only some men, though.'

She snorted. 'He was acting a bit strange. Hiding stuff from me. I got the quiet treatment, that sort of thing. I thought he was having it off with someone. I asked a close friend of mine to follow him. She's nothing to do with the gang. Anyway, she tracked him to a flat in Marylebone. Robbie visited it twice a week. I don't know how my friend found out but it's a bloody safe house used by the filth. I didn't know which was worse; a love-rat or a fucking copper in our midst.' Her dark eyes blazed at Flood.

'I went ballistic. I told him to fuck off. I said, "I don't even know your proper name or nothing about the real you." Everything he told me was a lie. Everything.'

'How did he react?'

'He begged me to forgive him. He cried a lot. Told me he loved me. Said he wanted to spend the rest of his life with me and Mark. He promised he'd find a way to get out of the Met. Run away, start a new life together.'

'You believed him?'

'I didn't know what to believe. We spoke about it all the time for weeks. I didn't like being conned and humiliated. I felt he'd used me. I asked him whether he'd slept with me, hoping I'd cough up some juicy bits about the gang or whether he really loved me?'

'And?'

She sighed. 'He kept saying over and over that he loved me, that he wanted the best for our little boy. Both of us agreed: we didn't want him growing up in a gang. I suppose you know about the Lidgate family?'

'I know your husband's banged up and that your father-in-law's a well-known criminal. That's why Robbie infiltrated the gang.'

Jessica nodded. 'He begged me not to snitch on him. The cops have no idea how much working undercover affects these guys. Robbie's a mess. He said he'd grown sick of leading a double life. He didn't know who he was half the time.'

'The Met could have got him out.'

'Nah. Robbie wasn't having any of that. Since we had Mark, the Met couldn't give a shit about us as a family. Robbie told me all they want is Tommy Lidgate. They won't do nothing until they get him.' She fiddled with her hair again at the mention of his name. 'I hate that man!'

'Any particular reason?'

'I just hate him!' She glared at Flood, her dark brown eyes fixed on his. 'I love Robbie. I decided to keep my gob shut.' She drew a hand across her lips like closing a zip. 'If Tommy Lidgate finds out that I knew Robbie was the filth and didn't tell him, he'd kill me.' Jessica hugged herself in an effort to stop her skinny body shuddering.

She composed herself. 'Once Robbie knew how I felt, he told me about you. Said you could get us out of all this crap. Can you?'

'I've done everything Robbie's asked. We made an arrangement. If he keeps his side of the deal, then, yes, I think you'll have a chance to start a new life.'

Jessica relaxed back in her chair. She fiddled with her hair again. 'Do you think Robbie's alright?'

'I hope so. One thing worries me. Could the friend who discovered the safe house have mentioned it to Tommy Lidgate or anybody else in the gang?'

'She's a good friend. Trouble is, you can't trust nobody these days.'

Flood looked at his watch, stood and said, 'Doesn't look like Robbie's going to get here tonight. Ask him to call me as soon as he gets back.'

'I will.' She walked with him to the front door. Flood heard her slide the chain in place behind him.

Driving home, Flood recalled every detail of the conversation with Jessica. He felt sorry for her. She could be at considerable risk. Her future happiness depended on Barlow turning up and giving him the information that he required. His quest to discover Georgina's killer rested on the same premise.

*

Shortly after taking Pippa and Gemma to school the next morning, Flood received two calls on his mobile in quick succession. Laura called first. 'I've checked the ports. There's no record of anyone matching Barlow's description being detained. Sorry. How did you get on with Jessica?'

He explained what happened, ending with, 'I don't think he'd leave her high and dry. They've got something special going on together. We're down to the other possibilities. The Met got Barlow out or Tommy Lidgate's taken action.'

'Is there anything else I can do, Andy?'

'I don't think so. I can't do much until Barlow gets in touch. Got time for a quick lunch?'

'Sure. Shall we try that new Italian in Bermondsey High Street? See you there at one.'

The second call came through immediately Flood had rung off. 'You haven't called me.'

'Why should I call you, Cahill?'

'You said you'd keep in touch. That you'd think about my offer.'

'I said no such thing. I don't have to talk to you if I don't want to.'

'That's a pity. I want to get the Met off my back. Get the bastard who killed my wife.'

'I suggest you call DI Harvey. I'm a civilian now, as you well know.'

'Come off it! You won't let it go. You hate unsolved cases. I'll call again in a day or two.'

*

Lunch with Laura provided Flood with a much-needed break from his concern at Barlow's disappearance. He asked, 'Any news on the Jenny Cahill murder investigation?'

'Nothing. Harvey hasn't got a clue, frankly. He's out of his depth. The morale in the team is shot.'

As she finished the sentence, her mobile rang. Plucking it out of her bag, she glanced at the caller's name. She looked at Flood. 'Sorry. It's Gerry from the station.'

He watched Laura's expression turn from concern to horror as he heard her say, 'There's no doubt about the identity?'

She gazed at Flood who'd stopped eating. He concentrated on her every word.

'OK. I'll be there in half-an-hour.'

Laura replaced the mobile back in her handbag. 'You're not going to like this. Barlow's dead. We discovered his body this morning in a disused swimming pool pump room in Shoreditch. Looks like he's been tortured.'

Flood groaned, threw his head back, looked up at the

ceiling and shut his eyes. He cursed under his breath. If he'd not been in a public place, he'd have thrown or kicked something.

Laura reached across the table. She placed a sympathetic hand on his. 'I'm sorry. I don't know what to say. I know how much you depended on Barlow.'

Flood hissed, 'Tommy Lidgate's got to be responsible.' He rested his elbows on the table and placed his head in his hands. Laura stood, patted his back and leant down to kiss him on the cheek.

'I'd better be going. There's a briefing at three o'clock. I'll call you when I've got more details.'

Flood sat motionless for five minutes, staring at the partially-eaten meals. He repeated under his breath, nodding in time with each word, 'Shit! Shit! Shit!'

CHAPTER FIFTEEN

Tuesday 13ᵗʰ March 2001

Later that afternoon, Laura called Flood. 'All hell's broken loose here!' Her voice sounded strained. 'Plenty of overtime being offered. All leave is cancelled. Top brass are panicking.'

'I can't believe what happened. That's it, for me. Barlow was my last shot.'

'I know. It's a bugger. One of the guys from Covert Operations came to see us. Foxy must have told them you'd found out about Barlow's existence. They told us to play down the undercover policing bit. They knew about his affair with Jessica and them having a kid together. Told us to keep it under wraps. I think they're terrified about the media getting hold of the story.'

'All the bloke's guilty of is falling in love. Did they talk to you?'

'Yes. Fortunately, they didn't ask me any direct questions. I didn't have to lie to them.'

'Sorry, Laura. You're in a difficult spot. I don't want you to lose your job. You have to do what's best for you.'

'I will. I thought you'd like to know that they interviewed Jessica this afternoon.'

'Poor woman. She'll be in a hell of a state. Be interesting to know what she told them.'

'I've got to go. See you soon.'

Flood decided to call on Jessica. He worried about her safety. She might also know something about the tapes.

*

He arrived at her house at 6.15 pm. A large blonde woman wearing a baggy jogging outfit answered the door. She opened it only as far as the chain allowed and squinted at Flood through the gap in the door.

'You're not the fuzz again, are you?'

'No. I'm not the police. I'm a friend of Robbie Barlow and Jessica. My name's Andy Flood.'

'I don't care if you're Brad Pitt. We're seeing no one.'

As she started closing the door, Flood heard Jessica shout from the sitting room. 'It's alright, Val. Let him in.'

'You're honoured,' said Val, as she unhooked the chain and opened the door wide. Flood followed her into the hall, past the buggy and into the living room. Jessica sat on a sofa with her baby son in her arms, gently rocking him to sleep. Her red-rimmed eyes looked puffed. She wasn't wearing make-up and her unkempt, dark hair hung limply by the side of her face.

'Take a pew. Don't mind Val. She's my sister. Come over to keep an eye on us. I suppose you heard about Robbie?'

'Yes, I did. That's why I'm here. I'm worried about you.'

'Thanks.'

'Can we have a chat?'

'Yeah, I'd like to.' Jessica offered up the baby to Val. 'Can you look after Mark for a bit?'

Val, looking suspiciously at Flood, leant over and carefully took the baby from her.

'C'mon sleepy head. Aunty'll take you upstairs.' Flood's eyes followed Val's progress to the door, making sure she'd left the room.

'Jessica, I'm so sorry. I know how much Robbie meant to you.' She reached for a tissue in the box on the table and dabbed her eyes.

'I can't believe he's gone. He was a good man. When I first met Robbie, I was a druggie. Had been for a long time. Complete waste of space. He straightened me out. That and having the baby. Been clean ever since.' She wiped away another tear with the tissue. 'Why have you come to see me? We don't need your help now. We're not going nowhere.'

'I know. I'm sorry to have to talk about this, but it's important. You said Robbie had explained our arrangement?'

'Yeah, he did. He told me he was getting some information for you. Said that if it all worked out, we could get away from the Met… and the fucking gang.'

'Did you mention any of this when the police interviewed you this afternoon?'

'You're joking, ain'tcha? I never had much time for them anyway. Even Robbie told me not to trust them. Only trust you.' He breathed a sigh of relief.

Jessica opened her mouth to say something. Nothing came out. Flood waited patiently. Still no words. She started sobbing and dabbing her eyes again.

'Maybe it's too early to have a chat. Shall I come back later?'

'No. Don't go. I'd rather talk to you than the filth. Fucking obvious who done this, isn't it?'

'Tommy Lidgate?'

She nodded. 'He's a controlling, dictatorial shit.' She'd found her voice now. Flood encouraged her.

'Last time we met, you told me that you hated him. You never told me why. After all, he is your father-in-law.'

She spat out her reply. 'I regret every minute of every day I got involved with this family. Barry, my husband, started off as a petty criminal working for his father. I didn't mind at first. I was young. We was loaded. Spent dosh like it were going outta fashion.'

'What happened?'

'Barry got more and more involved in the nasty stuff, dealing with other gangs muscling in on the business. He wanted to impress his father. Show him how tough he could be. But that's not why I hate him.'

'Why?'

'Because he's fucked up my eldest son. With his father in and out of jail, Tommy groomed him to be a gangster. Vinnie's twenty-one now. From the age of fourteen, he and Tommy became thick as thieves. Lidgate taught him to use guns, torture people, anything to help protect the gang's business and territory. Vinnie did time in that Young Offenders place in Feltham. Worst thing that could have happened. Place is more like a fucking college for criminals.' She stared at the floor before looking up at Flood. '*That's* why I hate Tommy Lidgate.'

'I can't say I blame you.'

'Now you see why I went along with Robbie's plan to get us out of all this crap. I didn't want little Mark to grow up to be like Barry, Tommy or Vinnie. That idea's screwed now.'

She sobbed so hard, Flood stood, walked over to the sofa, sat on the arm and cuddled her shoulder. 'Have the Met offered you any protection?'

Jessica composed herself, twisting the damp tissue in her hand. 'No. Robbie told me they wouldn't want to know. All because of us having a baby.'

'You told me you were worried what Tommy Lidgate would do to you if he found out that you knew about Robbie and hadn't told him. Have you passed that on to the police?'

'No. Robbie told me that if anything happened to him, tell the police nothing.'

'Jessica, I think you're in danger if you remain here. Why don't you stay at my house in Southampton? It's empty. I'm between rentals. If you don't mind the decorators, you can stay there for a while. Take your baby… and Val if you want.'

Jessica looked relieved. 'Are you sure? I think I *would* like to get outta this place for a bit. I'll have a chat with Val.' She walked to the door and climbed the stairs. Five minutes later, she reappeared. 'Val thinks it's a good idea.'

'We should go now. Pack a case; bring whatever you need for the boy. Where does your sister live?'

'About five minutes away.'

'Good. Once you're ready, I'll take you.'

'OK.'

Flood waited downstairs while they packed, brooding over Barlow's demise. He didn't think it would come to this. He still had the fake passports and driving licences in his inside coat pocket. He'd kept his part of the deal. Flood wondered whether Barlow had kept his. If he had, what had he done with the tapes?

*

Flood had forgotten how much paraphernalia babies need. The

buggy took up most of the boot. Val sat in a rear passenger seat with a case on her lap. Jessica fixed the baby carrier next to her and placed a sleepy Mark in it. After she clicked the seatbelt in place, she sat in the front with yet another case resting on her knees.

They spent the first half-hour of the journey mostly in silence, each caught up with their own thoughts. Jessica occasionally snivelled. Her sister stroked her shoulder several times.

Flood broke the silence. He turned to Jessica. 'I know this is probably the wrong time to talk to you but did Robbie mention anything to you about audio tapes?'

Jessica fiddled with her hair. 'Yeah, he did. Told me that if anything happened to him to tell you that he'd hidden them in the van they used to go to France. Sorry. I'm all over the place. I should have told you. I'm trying to think what else he said.'

She frowned. Then she said, 'Oh, I remember. He said he'd put them in the van's First Aid kit.'

'Where is the van usually kept?'

'In a lockup on Shaftsbury Trading Estate in Finsbury. I think it's Unit 14, 'bout a mile from where we live. Robbie told me that he left a spare set of keys to the lockup and the van in the soap drawer of the washing machine at home. I've been in such a state. I should have told you about all this before we left the house.'

She sniffed, holding back more tears. 'God, I miss Robbie.'

*

They arrived at Flood's former home just after 9.30 pm. He wanted to head back to Jessica's house immediately to check out the van. Instead, he left the sisters to settle in the house while he popped round to the local Tesco Express to pick up provisions.

By the time he returned, Jessica had tucked up Mark in bed. Val had gone to bed too. Flood made a pot of tea for Jessica and said, 'I'd better be getting back. Can I borrow your house keys?'

She fumbled in her handbag and gave them to Flood saying, 'Yeah. Val's got a spare set.'

'Give me your mobile number. Mine's on the business card I gave you. Call me if you need anything.'

*

As Flood drove back to London up the M3 in light traffic, he called Laura, told her what he'd done and filled her in with the details of his conversation with Jessica.

'Playing Fairy Godfather are we?' she teased. 'Actually, I think it's a good idea.'

'Barlow asked me to look out for Jessica and his son.'

'And you are.'

'Any decent evidence discovered at the Barlow crime scene?'

'Forensics are analysing it as we speak, especially DNA. Should have the initial results soon. Where are you now?'

'I'm on my way to Jessica's house to get the keys to the lockup and the van. I'm hoping the tapes are there. I have to know if Barlow got the information.'

Laura paused before replying. 'You shouldn't do this alone, Andy. Everything we know about Tommy Lidgate is bad news. Why don't you let the Met handle it from here?'

'We can't trust them, Laura. Swanson may be legit but why did I see him talking to Billy White, one of Lidgate's gang? Maybe Barlow's paranoia wasn't misplaced.'

'OK. What time will you be at Jessica's?'

Flood looked at the clock on his dashboard. 'Around twelve thirty.'

'I'll see you there.'

*

Flood sat in his car parked outside Jessica's house waiting for Laura. Heavy rain hammered onto the roof. Within five minutes, she arrived and parked in the only other free space, fifty yards away. He got out of the car and rushed to meet her, holding his coat over both of their heads as they made their way through the puddles to the front door. 'Thanks for coming, Laura. You don't have to do this, you know. You could get into all kinds of trouble if the Met find out you're here.'

'I think you've more chance of getting a result than the Met. We're going round in bloody circles at the station.'

Flood turned the key in the lock. He went inside, flicked on the light switch in the hall then strode to the living room. Laura followed.

Flood looked around the room. 'Shit! Looks like a tsunami has swept through the place.'

Laura followed Flood's gaze. 'Bloody hell!'

Furniture had been tipped over, ripped and torn. Open drawers hung from their moorings, their contents spilling out onto the floor. Kitchen cupboards were half-empty. Cups, saucers and plates lay partly smashed on the floor. They checked the other rooms. The tsunami had swept through them, too.

Laura turned to Flood. 'Someone's looking for something. Thank God Jessica and her baby weren't here. Good idea of yours to get them away.'

Flood headed to the utility room next to the kitchen with Laura on his heels. A gleaming white washing machine stood against a wall. Flood approached it and opened the soap drawer. As he did so, he thought about crossing his fingers.

Two sets of keys glinted back at him. Flood couldn't help letting out a triumphant, 'Yes!' as he cradled them in his hand.

Flood nodded. 'Let's go to the lockup. See if the van's there.'

He raced to the front door. Laura switched off the lights and joined Flood. They both dashed through the rain to their cars and sped off.

CHAPTER SIXTEEN

Wednesday 14th March 2001

Flood always thought one of the best parts of his job, when he had one, was feeling the exhilaration of being on a mission. Much better than the form-filling and political correctness that he'd endured in his latter days at the Met.

Although the rain had slackened off, the spray from the cars in front splashed against his windscreen, refracting the headlights of the oncoming cars. Flood was forced to slow down, much to his frustration.

He parked directly outside Unit 14. Laura's car drew up behind him minutes later. The limited street lighting gave off just enough light for Flood to read the sign above the doors: *Williams and Co. Ltd. Paint Supplies. Import/Export Specialists.* The 1970's building was in darkness.

Flood opened the pedestrian door with the key. He fumbled up and down the right-hand side of the wall with his fingers, finally finding the light switch. An adrenaline rush hit him as he noticed a white Transit van facing the rear wall of the building.

With the pungent smell of paint and thinners assaulting his nostrils, Flood rushed towards the rear doors of the Transit. He felt inside his pocket for the keys as Laura looked around the building. Flood unlocked one of the doors and pulled it open. The lights came on automatically. Stepping up into the empty van, he scanned the interior, looking for the first aid kit. He noticed a green box with a red cross prominently stencilled to the lid fixed behind the driver's seat.

He unhooked it and carried it out of the van. He felt his breathing accelerate as he opened the box. He tipped it upside down on the painted concrete floor. Plasters, dressings, cleansing wipes, and all the usual paraphernalia fell out and rolled in different directions. Flood fumbled amongst the contents with his hands, finally concluding that the tapes weren't there.

'Bugger!' Flood hurled the empty box back into the van and looked around the lockup, considering whether another hiding place existed.

Laura looked up. 'What's the matter?'

'There's nothing here. What have you found?'

He noticed Laura examining a pool of liquid on the floor, well back from the entrance. He walked over to her as she knelt, prodded her finger into the sticky mess and inspected it.

'Blood stains,' she said.

'Barlow?'

'Could be.'

'You'll need to get it checked, Laura.'

Flood peered around the lockup again. 'Didn't you say the Met found Barlow's tortured body in a disused swimming pool not far from here? I reckon this is where they tortured him. Then they took him to the pool. Poor bastard.'

'Look at this?' Laura pointed out more patches of blood lying underneath two stanchions attached to a wall.

Flood shook his head. 'This doesn't look good, does it? Now we don't know whether Barlow had the tapes and they discovered them or they killed him just for being a copper.'

He kicked one of the tyres of the Transit. 'Shit! My plan's fucked now.'

'I'll have to call this one in, Andy. It's a full-blown crime scene.'

'How are you going to explain how you found this place?'

'I'll tell them I got an anonymous tip-off. That someone heard something going on inside the unit and called me.'

Laura reached inside her handbag and retrieved her mobile. She punched in the numbers and spoke to an inspector on the team, urging him to send a backup unit to the lockup. She returned her mobile to her bag. 'Let's hope whoever dealt with Barlow left enough evidence to get a trace back to Tommy Lidgate.'

'That doesn't help me get closer to knowing Georgina's killer though, does it?'

Laura touched Flood's arm. 'You're going to have to think

of another angle. You'd better go. I'll stay here until the backup unit arrives.'

'OK. I'll call you tomorrow. Thanks, Laura.'

Heavy rain started to pour again as Flood got into his car. Before driving off, he pounded the steering wheel with his fists, muttering, 'Back to fucking square one.'

*

The following afternoon, Flood drove his girls home from school. As he entered his front door, his mobile burst into action. Fox's curt, clipped vowels cut straight to the point.

'I need to talk to you. Be at my office within the hour. I don't care what you've got on, drop it. This is urgent.'

Flood returned his mobile to his pocket. He'd never heard Foxy sound so furious. He drove to the police station immediately and made his way to Fox's office on the first floor. He nodded to colleagues who acknowledged him. That's as far as he wanted to go.

As he got closer, he noticed Laura sitting opposite Fox's desk, looking down at her nails, deep in thought. Before Flood had a chance to speak to her, Fox appeared behind him with a file under his arm. With a grim look on his face, he gestured at Flood to sit in the seat next to Laura. Fox slumped down in his chair and threw the file down on his desk. He looked about to go ballistic. He leaned forward and looked at both of them in turn.

'I can't believe you two could be so stupid.'

Flood frowned. 'What do you mean? What's this about?'

'In the early hours of this morning, Miss Marple here,' he nodded at Laura, 'reported that she'd been tipped off about a possible crime scene at a lockup on the Shaftsbury Trading Estate. We sent a backup unit and, sure enough, there is evidence of a crime. One of the first things one of my officers did was to check for eye witnesses. We got lucky. A particularly observant worker was working a night shift at a unit opposite. We've taken a detailed statement from him. Makes interesting reading. I guess you both know what I'm going to say next.' Flood and Laura exchanged a glance.

'The eyewitness told us that in the early hours of yesterday morning, he noticed a white Transit van arrive with three passengers. He saw them drive the van into the unit. An hour later, one of the men left and returned, driving a black BMW Estate car. He parked it outside the entrance.

'He entered the building and ten minutes later, the same three men emerged and got into the car. One of them had to be supported. Because of the poor lighting, the eyewitness could only give us a sketchy description of the men.'

The mention of a BMW Estate car rocked Flood. Such a model was used in the hit and run killing of Georgina. He questioned whether it was a coincidence.

Fox continued: 'The men locked up and drove away. The eyewitness thought it all a bit odd but didn't bother to call us. However, at around one fifteen this morning, he noticed two cars arrive, one driven by a male and the other by a female. This time, he jotted down the reg numbers. Surprise, surprise, the cars are registered to you two.'

Fox stopped to glare at them before continuing. 'He saw them enter the lockup. Says they stayed for between twenty and thirty minutes. He saw the male drive off. Minutes later, the place was surrounded by police.'

Flood inwardly cursed. He'd checked for CCTV and found none. He thought that the lights from some of the other units were left on for security reasons. He opened his mouth to speak. Fox held up his hands, palms facing Flood.

'I haven't finished yet. I've got a list as long as your arm of the rules you've broken, especially you, DS Miles. For starters, I can't believe you'd run the risk of contaminating forensic evidence at a crime scene. You know how important that is.'

Flood managed to interrupt. 'It's my fault. I asked DS Miles to provide backup for me. I had good reason to believe that the lockup may reveal evidence which would help solve the murder of Jenny Cahill. My source gave me the location and the keys to the lockup. I wasn't sure what we'd find.'

Fox, his face reddening, addressed Laura. 'Why didn't you

call this in as soon as Inspector Clouseau here, asked you to back him up? Why tell us someone *tipped you off?*'

Laura muttered, 'I wanted to protect Andy. He's worked so hard on this case. I thought he'd be in more trouble if the Met knew he was still involved in the investigation.'

Fox glowered at Flood. 'I made it abundantly clear to you that your investigating days with the Met are finished.' He opened the file on his desk and flipped through the wad of papers until he reached one particular sheet. He scanned it and said, 'From what Intel has said, I suspect your source is Jessica Lidgate, the UCO's girlfriend. I'll get her in. I'll interrogate her myself. She obviously knows what's going on.'

'I don't think that if the bloody Commissioner himself interrogated her, she'd give him anything. She doesn't trust the police. With good reason.'

'What do you mean?'

'For a start, Barlow told Jessica that he thought his handler was bent.' Flood added that he'd witnessed DI Swanson's clandestine meeting with Billy White.

'UCOs are always paranoid about their handlers. It's part of their makeup.'

'I can only tell you what I saw. You should keep an eye on Swanson.'

Fox glared at Flood. 'Don't dictate to me how to run this operation.'

'You'll get nothing out of Jessica Lidgate. But she trusts me. That's why she told me about the lockup and the Transit van.'

Fox sat back in his chair and twiddled a pen between his fingers.

Flood pushed home his advantage. 'Why don't you admit it? The Met are getting nowhere on charging Tommy Lidgate. I believe he's ultimately responsible for the killing of Jenny Cahill and Robbie Barlow. Not to mention a host of other gang-related murders over the past few years. I'm the only one who can help you, now that Barlow's out of the game.'

'Haven't you've forgotten something? You're no longer part of the Met.'

'All I'm saying, is that with the Met's resources and my contacts we can get Lidgate.'

Fox folded his arms and raised his eyebrows. 'Oh, yeah?'

Flood played his ace card. 'I spoke to Robbie Barlow before his last drug-running trip.'

'You did what?' Fox gripped the sides of his desk and sat forward.

'I met up with him. Had a long chat. He told me he was close to getting a result but feared what would happen to Jessica and his baby if his cover was blown. He didn't trust his handler. That's why he contacted me. Said he believed that the Met had abandoned him once they knew about his relationship with Jessica and fathering a child.'

Fox responded, 'He knew the rules. His relationship was a no-no. He should have got out of it.'

Flood nodded. 'I agree he went too far, but Barlow trusted me. Wanted me to look after his family if anything happened to him. In return, he'd find out more about the gunning down of Jenny Cahill and my wife's murder. He said he believed that there's a link between The Goshawks and The Edge gangs. I'm convinced The Edge were responsible for Georgina's murder. You know the circumstances.' He tried not to sound cynical. He didn't think he'd pulled it off.

'You know better than anyone how these investigations work. We always have to assess our priorities.'

Flood sat forward, looked Fox in the eyes. 'She was my wife. A copper's wife. With two little kids. How do you think I felt when the police gave up on the case?' Laura placed a hand on his thigh in an effort to calm him down. Both men silently stared at each other.

After a few moments, Fox said, 'How was Barlow getting the information?'

Flood explained Barlow's plan to record incriminating conversations with the gang members and pass them back to Flood. 'When he didn't turn up, I visited Jessica. When she learned about Barlow's murder, naturally, it upset her, big time. She's certain Tommy Lidgate's responsible. She wants me to get enough evidence to prove it.'

'That's our job, not yours.'

'How many times must I tell you? She doesn't trust the Met. Before this last trip, Barlow told her that if anything happened to him, he'd leave the tapes in a first aid kit in the back of the van they used to bring in the drugs from Marseilles. She told me where the spare keys to the Transit and the lockup were located. That's how much she trusted me.'

'I assume you didn't find the tapes?'

'No. Right now, I don't even know whether they exist or not. Or, if they do, whether Lidgate and his cronies discovered them.'

'And where are Jessica and the baby now?'

'I was concerned for her safety. If Lidgate discovered that she knew about Barlow being an undercover police officer and hadn't told him, her life would be at risk. She's staying in my house in Southampton for now.' Fox raised his eyes in surprise.

Flood continued: 'I wouldn't like that fact broadcast. We don't know if Barlow's handler is straight. I think you owe it to Jessica to provide protection for her.'

'The Met won't agree to that. Barlow got himself into the relationship. He should have thought of that before he got involved.' He turned to Laura. 'And you, DS Miles. I should suspend you, ask Professional Standards to get involved. You'll possibly go back in uniform, be put on admin duties.

'You acted in an utterly unprofessional manner. I think your judgement's been clouded by your relationship with Flood, here. I hope you realise that.' Laura stared at the floor in embarrassment. Another silence followed. Fox rested his elbows on the desk and clasped his hands together.

'I've made a decision.' He turned to Flood. 'You'll hand over to the new SIO, DI Harvey, all the information you have to date regarding your relationship with Barlow and his girlfriend. You'll work as an informant to DS Miles. This is highly irregular. I'm taking a huge risk here. My only objective of this approach is to get Tommy Lidgate banged up.'

He turned to Laura once more. 'I want you to pass on to DI Harvey every last piece of information this informant gives you from now on.' Fox nodded in Flood's direction. 'I'll allow you to provide resources and intelligence to *ex*-DCI Flood after you've passed it by me first. Do you both understand?' Laura and Flood nodded.

'You've got forty-eight hours. After that, if we've made no progress, I'm going to throw, not just the book at both of you, but the whole bloody library.'

Laura glanced at Flood, then at Fox. 'Thank you, sir. I appreciate your trust in us.'

Fox replied, 'Before you go, there's one more thing you ought to know. I've received the pathologist's preliminary report on Barlow. It's not pretty reading. Three fingers on each hand had been severed. Most likely at the lockup. Then they slit his throat at the disused swimming pool, typical gangland style. Just for good measure, the letter 'G' had been carved on his back. We're dealing with dangerous people. I don't want either of you to take more unnecessary risks.'

CHAPTER SEVENTEEN

Wednesday 14th March 2001

As they left Fox's office, Flood turned to Laura. 'We need to talk. Let's go to that cafe on Borough High Street.' She nodded. Flood sensed several pairs of eyes following them as they walked through the main office to the stairs.

Once they'd settled with their coffees, he said, 'I'm sorry, Laura. I shouldn't have asked you to come to the lockup with me. I've put you in a bad situation.'

'Don't worry. I'm a big girl. I chose to go. I'm just pleased that Foxy's given us a chance to sort out this mess.'

'He didn't have much choice. We don't have a lot of time, though.'

'What's our next move?'

'Let's start with the eyewitness descriptions of the two guys at the lockup. I know they're not great, but can you compare them to the photos in DC Collins' Intelligence Report? Remember? The one he produced at the start of the enquiry into Jenny Cahill's murder. If the descriptions and photos match, we'll have names and addresses. The Met can pay them a visit; question them about the BMW, Barlow and the missing tapes.'

'Assuming they exist.'

Flood groaned. 'Oh, don't say that.'

'I'd better be going. I'll give you a call when I've got something.' He walked her back to the police station, hugged her and kissed her cheek.

*

Flood arrived home hoping to see his girls before they went to bed. As he parked on his driveway, it surprised him to see the house in darkness and the curtains downstairs drawn. Usually, the girls left every light on in the house at this time of the evening. His threat to deduct the cost of the electricity bill from their weekly pocket money usually proved ineffective.

He turned the key in the lock, pushed the door open and switched on the hall light.

'Anyone home?' His question was met with silence. He walked into the kitchen, turning on the light as he went.

'What the fuck...?' He almost tripped over the contents of drawers and cupboards which covered the floor. It was the same in the living room. He headed to his study. The door, usually locked, had been forcibly jemmied open, as had the desk drawers and filing cabinets. Papers and folders covered the carpet.

With mounting anxiety, he took the stairs two at a time and went into the girls' rooms to find them empty. He ran back downstairs and dashed to the garage. His mother's car was parked inside. Flood couldn't decide whether that was a good thing or not.

As he returned to the hallway, he heard strange noises coming from the cupboard under the stairs. Lifting the latch, he opened the door. His mother lay on her side, her mouth covered with duct tape, her hands and feet bound together. She made a burbling, unintelligible sound. He kneeled down beside her and helped her out of the cupboard.

'Oh, my God! Who did this? Where are the girls?'

The look of terror in his mother's tear-filled eyes shocked Flood. He carefully undid the tape sealing her mouth. She gasped, 'Oh, Andy! They've taken them!'

He freed her hands and legs and helped her to her feet. She collapsed into his arms and gripped him tightly. Flood felt her body trembling. He led her to the kitchen table and sat her on a chair. He stroked her hair as he fought to contain his anger. 'Who are *they*? Can you tell me what happened?'

She gabbled her words out between gulps of air in an unsuccessful attempt to suppress her tears. Flood passed her a tissue from a box on the kitchen table.

'I couldn't stop them. Two young men came to the door, said they were police officers. I didn't think to ask to see their warrants. They said they... they wanted to come in and talk to me about something personal. I thought they had some bad news about you. Once they got inside, they attacked me, tied me up and bundled me under the stairs.' She started sobbing again.

He held his mother's hands in his and stroked them with his thumbs. 'It's alright, Mum. Take your time.'

She recovered sufficiently to say, 'After a while, I heard them go up the stairs to the girls' rooms. They screamed then it went quiet. I heard them coming down the stairs and the front door slam. What are we going to do, Andy?'

Flood felt as if his head was about to burst. He forced himself to remain calm for his mother's sake.

'I'll sort this out, Mum. Don't worry.'

'This is all to do with your job, isn't it?'

'I think so.'

She found the strength to shout, 'I knew it! For God's sake, Andy, give it up!'

Flood yelled back, 'I had no idea *this* would happen. It's one of the most despicable things anyone could do. Did they say what they wanted?'

'No. They didn't. Oh God! They won't harm them, will they?'

'I don't think so. How long ago did it happen?'

'I lost track of time. The girls went up to their rooms after tea so I think I must have been in the cupboard for over an hour.' She shuddered.

'I know you're in shock, Mum, but can you tell me what they looked like?'

An expression of disgust crossed her face. 'Both in their early twenties, I'd say. One was particularly aggressive. Mean eyes. Thin, too. His head was too big for his body. He had sticky-out ears. Should have had them pinned.'

'And the other one?'

'Fat. Scruffy. He had dark skin with long, black hair. The other one had fair hair.'

She paused, searching her memory. 'Oh, I've just remembered something. Another man, older, well-built, in his thirties, I'd say, called at the door about an hour earlier. He asked to speak to you. I told him you weren't here, that you'd probably be back much later. Do you think he's part of it? Checking up to make sure you weren't home?'

'Could be.' Flood stood and gazed around the kitchen. He noticed a large hand-written note stuck with one of the numerous fridge magnets the girls had collected. He was certain it wasn't there when he'd left that morning.

His mother watched him as he walked over to the fridge and pulled off the note. 'What does it say, Andy?'

A chill ran through Flood's body as he read out the bold scribbled words. *You'll be getting a call from us soon.*

'Who is *us?*'

'I've got an idea, but I can't do anything until I know what they want. How could anybody do this?' Flood slumped on a chair opposite his mother as he re-read the note.

The landline rang. He jumped up and yanked it out of the holder and said, 'Andy Flood.'

A mature, cultured voice spoke slowly and deliberately. 'We've got your girls. You'll get them back when you hand over the tapes you've received. We'd advise you not to involve the police. If you do, we'll know about it and send bits of your little girls back to you in the mail. We'll call again tomorrow morning. Give you further instructions.'

Flood yelled down the phone, 'Who is this?'

The line went dead. The call lasted less than twenty seconds. Flood dialled 1471 to be told the number had been withheld.

His mother stared up at him. 'Was that them?'

Flood nodded.

'Well? What do they want?'

'They think I have information incriminating their gang. They want it in exchange for the girls.' He repeatedly pumped his fists hard down on the kitchen table alternately. 'I don't have anything!'

'Andy! This is awful!' She started sobbing again, so deeply, that Flood noticed her shoulders bob up and down. Flood hated seeing her like this. He channelled his anger by switching into detective mode and focussed on practical issues realising that he'd have to leave the house at some time to deal with this crisis. But he couldn't leave his mother alone in the house in her state.

Flood called his sister, Julie, to explain what had happened. His voice choked as he described finding their mother under the stairs.

'Can you come and collect Mum, take her back to your place for a while? She's obviously in shock. She needs a lot of TLC. I have to be here to deal with this.'

'Poor Mum! I can't believe someone's taken the girls! Why would they do that?'

'I don't know, Julie. I need to get this sorted.'

'Of course. I'm on my way.'

Typical Julie, Flood thought. Always reliable in a crisis. He told his mother what he'd planned.

'Shouldn't I stay here with you in case the girls come back home?' she said.

'You need someone to look after you, Mum. You'll be better off at Julie's. Why don't you pack some clothes? She'll be here in a couple of hours.'

As his mother went upstairs, still sobbing, Flood thought about his options repeatedly, reluctantly concluding that he could do nothing until he heard from the kidnappers in the morning. He felt like screaming at the top of his voice and punching a wall.

Flood carried his mother's case downstairs. As they sat waiting for Julie to arrive, he sensed her disappointment with him between her sobs. She didn't need words to convey her feelings that his obsession had led to his girls being kidnapped.

He thought back to two nights earlier. After the girls had gone to bed, he'd told her about the circumstances of his resignation.

When he'd finished, she'd said, 'I'm proud of you, son. You got justice for that poor family. That's what you always wanted.'

Several questions bugged Flood. He assumed that the gang had sussed out Barlow, found the tape recorder attached to him but not the tapes. So what had happened to them? If Barlow had hidden them in the Transit van, surely they'd have found them? And why did Lidgate think he had them?

When Julie arrived, she made a fuss of her mother and checked that she had everything she needed. Flood hugged her before she got into Julie's car. She said, 'You will get them back home safely, won't you?'

'Yes. I promise, Mum.'

Shortly after they'd left, Flood's landline rang again. He rushed to it, hoping to hear something positive about his daughters.

'It's Martin Cahill. You never rang me back. You promised to keep in touch.'

'I'm sorry. There's a lot on my mind at the moment.'

Flood was about to return the phone to its cradle when he heard Cahill say, 'I know where your girls are.'

'What? What do you mean, *you know where my girls are?* I hope you're not fucking with me?'

'I wouldn't do that. I witnessed the whole thing.'

'Witnessed what?'

'I've got time on my hands after being suspended following my arrest. Your guys are still making checks regarding Jenny's murder, which is bloody ridiculous by the way. Anyway, I decided to visit you earlier to have a chat since you didn't call me back.'

'Never mind the chat. What did you witness?'

'Your mother told me you weren't in but that you'd be home later. I decided to park up the road and wait for your return. As it got dark, a black BMW Estate pulled up outside your house. Two guys went in and returned twenty minutes later with two young girls. I assume they're your daughters.'

Flood, concentrating on Cahill's every word, said, 'Go on.'

'They manhandled them into the rear of the estate car. They didn't put up much of a fight. I think they may have been drugged or something. I noted down the registration number and checked it out with one of my colleagues back at the station. They're using cloned plates. The original belongs to a retired dentist in Norwich.' Cahill continued: 'I took a punt. I followed them.'

137

'Where to?'

'Fifteen to twenty minutes from where you live.'

'Why didn't you call me earlier?'

'Because your mother told me that you wouldn't be home until later and I only had your home number. Also, I wanted to make sure they didn't take them anywhere else. That's why I've been watching the place for the last three hours. I'm still here. I think they're settled for the night.'

'Where are you?'

'In Dulwich Village. I'm sitting in my Volvo parked close to a nineteenth-century hunting lodge. Here's the post code.'

Flood wrote it down. 'I'm on my way.'

Before leaving, he called Laura and told her about the kidnapping and ransacking of his house. She gasped. 'What a nightmare! Your poor mother! And the girls!'

'I got a phone call. I'm certain it was Lidgate. He's convinced I've got the tapes. Wants to swap them for the girls. God, I hope they're alright, Laura.'

Flood felt himself close to tears. He pulled himself together and asked, 'Did you get anywhere with comparing the eyewitness descriptions with Collins' file?'

'Yes. I was about to call you. There's a strong resemblance. One of the guys looks like Vinnie Lidgate, Jessica's son, Tommy Lidgate's grandson. The other could be another member of the gang, Jack McBride. Foxy's already put out an alert to get these guys in for questioning based on their suspicious actions at a crime scene.'

Flood bellowed down the phone, 'That's exactly what I didn't want to happen, Laura. *I* need to deal with it. This is not good.'

'Why not?'

'Lidgate made it very clear that he'll harm my kids if I get the Met involved.'

'But we agreed we'd work with Foxy, didn't we?'

'Yes, but my girls' lives weren't in danger then.'

'What makes Lidgate think that you've got the tapes?'

'I don't know.'

'So you're not going to tell Foxy that Lidgate's been in

touch?'

'I daren't, Laura. It's too risky to involve the Met. Don't forget the handler, Swanson. He may be in on it. I'd never forgive myself if anything happened to Pippa and Gemma.'

'God, what a situation!'

'There's something else. Martin Cahill called.' Flood explained what Cahill had witnessed. 'I'm going to meet him there as soon as I put the phone down.'

'That's a stroke of luck. At least you'll know where the girls are.'

'But then what? Thing is, I can't give Lidgate something I don't have. Without the tapes, I'm fucked.' He kicked out at an armchair so hard that it toppled over and crashed to the floor.

CHAPTER EIGHTEEN

Thursday 15th March 2001

A full moon lit up a crystal-clear sky, emphasising the chilliness in the air as Flood rushed out to his car and headed down the A2 as fast as he dare.

Fifteen minutes later, he pulled up behind Cahill's Volvo parked close to a pair of solid wooden gates tucked away at the end of a dimly-lit road. A ten-foot high fence surrounded the lodge. Flood got out of his car, rushed to Cahill's and jumped in the passenger seat next to him.

Cahill nodded at Flood and then towards the lodge. 'The BMW passed through those gates. No one's gone in or out since.'

Flood noticed the high level of security: a keypad next to the entrance, two alarm boxes and a discrete camera fixed underneath the eaves, a pulsing light giving it away. Lights shone through the gaps in the drawn curtains of some of the bedrooms.

Flood reigned in thoughts of commandeering Cahill's car and smashing it through the gates, breaking and entering the lodge and rescuing his girls by force. Instead, he asked, 'Do you know who owns this pad?'

'I've had someone check the Land Registry. It's in the name of a company registered in Monaco. I also checked out the electoral roll. There's no one registered. I'd say it's worth about three million quid.'

'Did the gang hurt them when they bundled them into the back of the BMW?'

'They were a bit rough with them. I told you, the kids looked out of it. It all happened in a flash.'

Flood spat out, 'If they've harmed them, I swear I'll make those bastards pay.'

'Why did they take your girls?'

Flood felt he owed Cahill an answer. He explained his deal

with Barlow and Lidgate's phone call.

Cahill let out a low whistle. 'What do you think happened to the tapes the undercover promised you?'

'I wish I knew. I've got nothing to offer these scum.'

'Is any of this related to Jenny's murder?'

'It looks like the same gang are involved. The Goshawks. Tommy Lidgate's gang.'

'Bloody hell!'

Flood looked towards the lodge once again. 'Why would he bring my girls here?'

'It's the perfect place. Respectable, upmarket, secure. Who'd think anything untoward would happen here? Brings a new meaning to the term, working from home.' Cahill smiled at his own one-liner.

'How the hell do I get inside and get my daughters back?'

'Don't ask me. You're the detective.'

'I need to convince Lidgate that I have the information he wants. At least that'll get me inside and talking.'

Cahill asked, 'How sure are you that he's responsible for killing my Jenny?'

Flood baulked at the expression, *my Jenny*. He decided against reminding Cahill about his tempestuous affair with Katie Brunswick.

'The UCO said he'd get proof. He'd be wired up. Record evidence.'

Cahill nodded. 'What do you want to do?'

'I can't do much now. I need to be home when Lidgate calls tomorrow. I'll put a plan together. Are you still up for helping me?'

'We've got something in common, you and me. I want to know who killed Jenny just as badly as you want to know who killed *your* wife. I want to clear my name. Yes, I'm up for it.'

'OK. Stay here; keep an eye on this place. Make sure we know where my girls are at any time.'

*

When Flood arrived home, he didn't bother getting undressed.

He lay on his bed and tried to get some sleep. It proved impossible. His brain looped round continuously, visualising what his girls might be going through as he sought a solution to the question: how to free them *and* get justice for the murders of Georgina, Jenny Cahill and now Barlow? Two problems dominated his thoughts: he couldn't involve the Met and he didn't have the tapes.

The ringtone on Flood's landline startled him. He checked his watch. 9.00 am. Lidgate's voice boomed. 'I thought I'd give you a reminder of what your girls' voices sound like.' Flood sat bolt upright, suddenly fully awake.

Before he could respond, he heard shuffling, then, 'Daddy!'

'Pippa. Are you alright? How's Gemma?'

'We're both OK, Daddy.'

Flood heard her sniff back a tear. 'But we want to come home.' Her voice caught in her throat. 'We don't like it here. Please come and get us, Daddy.'

Lidgate spoke again. 'I hope you've got my tapes.'

'Never mind that, you bastard. If you harm my girls, I'm telling you, I'll come after you. I won't care what happens to me.'

Lidgate's cold, unemotional, cultivated voice countered, 'If I don't get the tapes, your girls will suffer. You've got until six this evening. I'll call you then to make arrangements for the swap. Remember, don't get the Met involved.' The line clicked off.

Flood called Cahill. 'What's happening?'

'Nothing. I've been here all night. I'll stay put; keep watch for as long as long as it takes. I've got a pal who'll cover for me if I need a break. Don't worry. We'll have the lodge covered every minute of the day.'

Flood washed, changed his clothes and sat brooding over a cup of coffee in his ransacked, silent house. Normally at this time of the morning, it bustled with activity: his mother getting the girls' breakfasts, making up their sandwich boxes and chivvying them up so they wouldn't be late for school.

Pippa's plaintive plea, *Please come and get us,* rang repeatedly around Flood's head. He tried not to think too deeply about the abduction. Every time he did, an anchor seemed to drag him down to the depths of depression and helplessness.

An hour later, Flood's front doorbell rang. 'Parcel for you. You need to sign for it.' A surly Royal Mail postman wearing shorts despite the coolness of the day thrust a bulky jiffy bag towards Flood. He placed the package under his arm and scribbled his name. The postie mumbled, 'Thanks,' and disappeared through the front gate into the foggy morning.

As Flood closed the door, he peered at the front of the parcel and noticed a label reading, *La Poste Colissimo*, France's post office tracking service with a Marseilles postmark. He felt his heart pumping against his ribs as he rushed to the kitchen. Taking a knife from a drawer, he slit open the package with trembling hands and tipped out the contents onto the kitchen table.

Three audio cassettes labelled, *Play First, Tape One*, and *Tape Two*, half-a-dozen photos, two police pocket notebooks, a letter and a key spilled across the surface. Flood picked up the photos showing two young men sitting at a bar unaware they were being photographed. He turned them over. The names, Vinnie Lidgate and Jack McBride had been scrawled on the reverse. They matched his mother's description of her attackers.

Flood flicked through the pocketbooks. He recognised them as the sort undercover officers used to prepare their weekly report for their handlers. They revealed the most recent extent of The Goshawks gang's criminal activities.

Placing the contents back into the package, he carried it to his office. The door hung loosely next to the splintered frame. He retrieved his cassette player from underneath a pile of papers and plugged it into the socket, placed the cassette marked *Play First* on the deck and pressed 'start'. With mounting excitement, Flood heard Robbie Barlow's slight Scottish accent, sounding resigned and downcast.

'Here it is. The information you wanted. But first, I want you to know that I've told Jessica all about you. I told her you'd be in touch if I didn't survive this trip. She knows about

our plan to get us away, start a new life together. I also told her to tell you that if anything happened to me, you'd find the information you need in the First Aid Kit in the Ford Transit van. I since decided not to do that. It's too risky. I'm sure I've been rumbled. It's only a matter of time until they deal with me, find the tapes and destroy them.

'When we got to Marseilles, I decided to send everything to you by registered post. You'll find everything you need in this package: proof of the identity of your wife's killer and Jenny Cahill's assassin.'

Flood stopped the tape and stared at it, feeling the four years of anguish of not knowing who killed his wife drain from his body. He pressed 'start' again, anxious to hear more.

'I've included my most recent pocketbooks. I lodged all the others I'd completed since I've been undercover in a safe deposit box at The Capital Safe Deposit Company in Hatton Garden. I've enclosed the key and a pin number. You'll need to talk to the manager Brian Sharpe. I've included a letter of authority for you to get access. I've called him, told him what I've done.

'I prepared weekly reports for my handler, DI Swanson, from these pocketbooks. I don't think they've been acted upon. You know why I think that is. You should tip off the Met. It's been an absolute bloody waste of my time. They have no idea of the risks I take every single day.

'You'll remember that I told you I thought there was a connection between The Edge and The Goshawks gangs. It's confirmed on Tape One by Vinnie Lidgate. It goes back a long time. I don't know how the Intelligence team missed it.

'You'll find details in my pocketbooks of how the gang get the drugs from Mexico via Marseilles and into the UK. They've set themselves up as international paint importers. I deliver to three so-called paint companies in London. They dilute the drugs with cutting agents. That's where the big money is. It's a neat arrangement. You'll find stuff here proving that the whole thing is masterminded by Lidgate.

'My training should ensure that the tapes can be used as evidence. I've not led the conversations in any way; these stars

are only too happy to brag about their exploits. It's their way of promoting their credentials as so-called hard men, especially in the eyes of Tommy Lidgate. He's their Svengali.

'I have a confession... you'll hate me for this but I knew that Vinnie Lidgate had driven the car directly at your wife. He acted on his grandfather's orders. You'll hear more details on the other tapes. I'm sorry I couldn't tell you. I needed collateral to get you to obtain the fake IDs for us.'

Flood wanted to stop the tape again to think about what he'd just heard but felt compelled to continue to listen.

'Jessica doesn't know about this. I didn't know how she'd react. Although she'd disowned Vinnie years ago, he is her son. I feared she'd take agin me if I shopped him.

'I desperately wanted my relationship with her to succeed. She's been part of a criminal family all her life. When she discovered I worked undercover, she found it difficult to accept. I'm the enemy. Despite that, she told me she still loved me and wanted us to start a new life together. Looks unlikely now.

'I've kept my side of the bargain. I trust you to ensure Jessica and my boy are given a chance to have a good life outside the underworld and protected from them. I love them so much. Now you know. Please make sure these murderous bastards don't get away with what they've done.'

Flood sat back in his chair and exhaled deeply. He shook his head and muttered over and over, 'I can't believe this!' realising that he'd be facing his wife's murderers in less than eight hours' time.

He reached inside the package again and played the cassette marked *Tape One*. It consisted entirely of conversations between Barlow, Vinnie and McBride, mostly banter and everyday chitchat. Barlow cleverly engineered a conversation about how the three of them had joined The Goshawks.

Barlow: 'What about you Vinnie? I suppose you've always been a Goshawk, what with your father and grandfather bossing up the gang.'

Vinnie: 'Nah. Not always. When I got outta that Young Offender's shithole in Feltham four years ago, Papa insisted I

*should do some jobs outside London for a bit. The first one he
gave me was for a pal of his, a geezer who'd started The Edge
gang yonks ago. Papa met him in Spain where he lived most of
the year. After the geezer got banged up, he got word to Papa
to ask him a favour. Papa said it would be a good job for me.
Said I had to prove myself if I wanted to join The Goshawks.
Bit like a test.'*

McBride: *'Couldn't wait, couldya?'*

Vinnie: *'Too right.'*

Barlow: *'What was the job?'*

Vinnie: *'Papa told me that this particular filth had put
away his mate and forced the gang to break up. His mate
wanted to show the fucker a lesson. I had to find out where his
wife lived, somewhere in Southampton, case the joint for a
while; learn their habits.'*

McBride: *'Proper little detective, eh?'*

Vinnie: *'Yeah, suppose I was. She left her house, regular as
clockwork, about half-eight every morning on her bike. I
followed her in the car a few times so I knew which way she
went. Once I got that sussed, Papa wanted me to hit her hard
with the Beemer they let me drive, knock her off her bike.
Show the filth we weren't happy with what he done. He'd have
to live with that for the rest of his life.'*

McBride: *'Did a good job, too, didn't yah? Killed her
dead.'*

Vinnie: *'Yeah. She was only a copper's wife but I proved
myself. Papa let me join The Goshawks.'*

Flood pressed the stop button on the recorder, his hands
trembling. If Vinnie had been within throttling distance, he'd
be dead. His brain struggled to understand how anybody could
intentionally aim a car at a defenceless mother of two small
children while she cycled to work.

He stood, walked to the window and stared out. Tears
welled up inside him, finally surfacing and dribbling down his
cheeks. He couldn't reconcile the senselessness of Vinnie's
cowardly actions and believing them to be a badge of honour.

Thinking about the link between The Edge and The
Goshawks gangs, he remembered that there was no mention

of it in the Intelligence Reports. Did Intel screw up or was it covered up?

Desperate to hear more, he wiped away his tears and sat back at his desk. He pushed the start button again and heard the three of them chatting about the football results, the girls they'd shagged or would like to shag, the drug-fuelled parties they'd gone to and who was doing what to whom in the TV soaps.

Flood skipped the tape forward and backward several times until he heard reference to somebody being 'taken out'.

Barlow: 'I heard you're good with guns, Vinnie?'

Vinnie: 'Yeah. Papa taught me how to shoot. Gave me my first gun when I turned fourteen. I love guns. Gotta have one these days. Used it a few times. You can go a long way with a gun.'

McBride: 'What about the last time you used it? You know, the one where your Papa wanted that copper taken out for getting away with killing Terry Connor.'

Barlow: 'I heard about that. I didn't realise you were involved.'

Vinnie: 'Yeah. She deserved it. Papa said it was her word against 'Arry Lewis who sat in the car with Terry at the time. Fucking judge should get it too. Me and my driver here, Michael Schumacher, sorted her out.' Flood heard Vinnie cackle.

McBride: 'I got fuck all credit for getting you there and away pronto.'

Vinnie: 'Any stupid bugger can drive a fuckin' car.'

Tape Two provided detailed proof and confirmation of other serious crimes The Goshawks had committed under Lidgate's leadership. Mainly drugs importation and the intimidation of witnesses. Vinnie and McBride described the beatings, torturing and murdering of competitors with relish.

It was clear to Flood why Lidgate wanted these tapes and pocketbooks back. They'd provide enough evidence to lock him up forever. He thought that not even a corrupt undercover handler could prevent it.

He made a cup of tea and considered his options,

scribbling them down. When he'd finished, he called Laura and updated her on his meeting with Cahill, their trip to the lodge and the call from Lidgate reminding him of the deadline.

'Laura, it's awful. All I can hear in my mind is Pippa's voice begging to come home. I'd do anything to be with them. Anything.'

When he told her about the package turning up, Laura let out an audible gasp. 'That's good news, isn't it? What are you going to do?'

'My first thought was to do what they want; swap the package for my girls. But that still leaves these murderous bastards walking the streets.'

'What about the Met? Why don't you hand over the package to them?'

'And leave Pippa and Gemma at the mercy of Lidgate and his crew? No way. Foxy'll want to play by the book, conduct endless threat reviews that'll take forever. Then he'll hand over to negotiators with loud hailers, asking Lidgate to please release them and come quietly. Do you honestly see that happening?'

'I have to agree with you. I don't.'

'There's also the possibility of a leak. Barlow's handler could tip off Lidgate. He's made it very clear what he'll do if I get the Met involved. There has to be a better way.'

A short silence followed. Laura said, 'Do you want me to pop over, talk through some ideas?'

'It could cost you your job Laura. It's best if you don't get involved.'

'I can't see how you can get your girls back *and* sort out Lidgate and his crew without the Met's involvement. On the other hand, they must be going through hell.' After a short silence, she said, 'I really want to help you get them back home.'

'Thanks, Laura. I can't tell you what that means to me. I'll get Cahill involved, too. I don't like him much but he's capable, desperate to help and wants justice for Jenny. I'll play you extracts from the tapes and show you the photos and pocketbooks. We couldn't wish for better evidence. It's a treasure trove.'

CHAPTER NINETEEN

Thursday 16ᵗʰ March 2001

Knowing that his next contact with Lidgate wouldn't be until six o'clock, Flood asked Cahill to come to his house. Cahill agreed, saying that his pal would cover the lodge. As soon as he and Laura arrived, Flood wasted no time in showing them the photos and pocket books before playing Barlow's tapes.

When they heard Barlow say, *you'll find everything you need in this package, proof of the identity of your wife's killer and Jenny Cahill's assassin*, Laura raised her eyebrows and exchanged a glance with Flood.

Cahill couldn't take his eyes off the tape recorder, transfixed by the spooling of the tape. When Barlow admitted he knew Vinnie was responsible for killing Flood's wife, Laura reached over and touched Flood's arm sympathetically. As the tape ended, she gasped and said, 'I see what you mean about a treasure trove. This is dynamite.'

'Wait till you hear the rest,' Flood said, as he placed the cassette marked, 'Tape One' in the recorder and fast-forwarded it to where Vinnie bragged to Barlow and McBride about killing Georgina and Jenny.

Cahill burst out, 'Thank God! That means I'm off the hook.'

Flood stopped the tape and said, 'There's loads more stuff here. Lidgate's henchmen must have told him what they'd discussed with Barlow. No wonder he wants these tapes.'

Cahill said with a tremulous voice, 'This is my fault. I persuaded Jenny not to go into the Witness Protection Programme. None of this would have happened if I hadn't.' He slammed his fist onto the table. 'We've got to get them!'

Laura, a puzzled look on her face, said to Flood, 'I don't understand. Why is Lidgate so sure that you've got the tapes?'

'He can't be certain. All he knows is that the tapes are missing from Barlow's recorder. He'd have checked whether they'd been sent to his handler Swanson. Lidgate could have assumed Barlow sent them to Jessica. Remember, they turned over her place. After Swanson and Jessica, I guess I'm the most likely recipient. Especially if he'd discovered that I'd met her.'

Flood fiddled with one of Barlow's pocketbooks absent-mindedly. 'It's possible that Swanson's told Lidgate about Barlow. Lidgate's not stupid. He probably reasoned that the gang were bound to be targeted. By getting Swanson onside, he could control the information being passed back. It's only when the tapes go missing and I get involved that Lidgate acts.'

Laura said, 'Foxy told us that according to the initial post-mortem results, Barlow's body showed signs of torture. Is it possible that they forced him to say he'd sent the package to you?'

'I don't buy that. Barlow didn't strike me as the kind of copper who'd give up any information, whatever the circumstances. Remember, he'd been working inside the gang for a couple of years. He desperately wanted to get a result.'

Laura nodded. 'I still think you should get the Met involved. Lidgate doesn't know that we know where your daughters are. And we've got arrest warrants for Vinnie and McBride in connection with Barlow's disappearance.'

'Sorry, Laura. That's the last thing I want to do. Lidgate's already threatened to harm the girls if the Met are involved.'

'Yes, but you'll be taking a huge risk if you don't involve them. Especially if Lidgate finds out that you lied to him.'

'I'm banking on the fact that he can't know *for sure* that I've got the stuff. I think it's worth bluffing him, say I don't know what he's talking about. Tell him I'm no longer a cop. That all I want is the girls returned, unharmed. That I'm not interested in his criminal past.'

Cahill whistled. 'That's one hell of a long shot. Are you saying you're happy for these bastards to remain at large?'

Flood turned on him, shouting, 'No, of course I'm bloody not.' He lowered his voice. 'All I'm saying is that we can bring the Met in *after* my girls are safely home. I've got an idea. Are you both happy to help?'

Cahill replied first. 'I feel so guilty about Jenny. I decided to break off my relationship with Katie so that I could spend the rest of my life with her.' He stabbed his finger at the tapes and pocketbooks strewn across the table. 'Those scumbags took Jenny away from me. I never thanked you for trying to save her life. I want to return the favour. I'm in.'

Flood nodded. He turned to Laura. 'What do you think?'

'We told Foxy we'd work with him to get a result. I'm in a bloody difficult position here.'

'I'll understand if you want out.'

'I'm in too deep already, Andy. We've got to get your girls back. They must be terrified.' She looked up towards the ceiling and held her gaze for ten seconds before turning to face Flood. 'OK. I'll do whatever you want me to do.'

Flood breathed a sigh of relief. 'Thanks, Laura.' He pulled a foolscap paper pad and a pen from his briefcase resting against the side of the table. He'd already scribbled some notes.

'Martin, I think it's important we know that the girls are being kept at the lodge. I know you haven't had much sleep but can you go back there, report to Laura or me any movement?'

'No problem. I'm used to it.'

'Good. When Lidgate calls, I'll say that unless I personally see that the girls are unharmed, there's no deal. That should get me into the lodge. You'll be able to track me, too.' Cahill nodded.

Flood continued: 'I'll take these tapes and pocketbooks to the Capital Safe Deposit Company in Hatton Garden now. I'll use them as bait to flush out Lidgate. I'll also have a look at the stuff Barlow's already deposited. Laura, can you stake out the premises during their office hours?'

'Sure.'

'Be good if you can take over one of the offices opposite. You can maintain your surveillance from there.'

'Do you want me to take the tapes back to the station, get the techies to copy them?'

'I don't think that's a good idea. We can't trust anyone in the Met in case it gets back to Lidgate. We'd also have to prove in court that they were unaltered, not been tampered with.'

Flood looked at his watch. 'Anyway, we don't have a great deal of time.'

'When did you say Lidgate's calling you?' Laura asked.

'Six.'

'How can we stay in touch?'

'I don't think we can. There's no point in me going in wired up or taking my mobile. I don't want to spook Lidgate. My first objective is to get into the lodge. See that the girls are OK. After that, I'll have to play it by ear.'

Pippa's plaintive voice pleading to come home flashed through his mind for the hundredth time that day. 'Any questions?' he asked. Cahill and Laura exchanged glances and both shook their heads.

Flood went over the plans in more detail before saying, 'Let's crack on. If you have any other ideas before six, call me. I can't tell you both how grateful I am for your help.'

*

When they'd left, Flood called the safe deposit company and made an appointment to see the manager. Then he packed his briefcase with the tapes and pocketbooks.

As he approached Hatton Garden, he recalled the last time he'd visited the area. Twelve years previously, he'd taken Georgina to London's jewellery centre to pick out an engagement ring after she'd accepted his proposal, thrilled at the prospect of becoming Mrs Flood.

The Capital Safe Deposit Company Ltd's office sat between two jewellery shops. CCTV cameras covered the entrance. The windows had been blacked-out with the name of the company stencilled across them. An LED keypad lay to the right of the entrance door. He pressed the button marked, 'Reception'. Immediately, a woman's cultured voice answered.

'May I help you?'

'My name's Andy Flood. I have an appointment to see the manager, Brian Sharpe.'

'Wait a moment, please.' Her self-important tone of voice grated with Flood. A minute later, Miss 'Superior' said, 'That's fine, Mr Flood. Please enter. You'll be met by security.' Flood heard a buzzer and the door clicked open.

A fit-looking, heavily-built man in his fifties got up from his chair as Flood entered an outer office. The guard wore a light-blue shirt with the firm's prominent logo above the pocket.

'I need to check you over, sir. Raise your arms, please.' Flood felt the guard's hands run over his clothes.

'Would you open your briefcase?' Flood clicked it open. The guard rummaged inside it and took out the package.

He inspected the contents closely. Satisfied, he pressed a buzzer next to another door which opened into the reception area. The guard ushered him inside saying, 'Thanks for your cooperation.' A tall, elegant, bespectacled forty-something-year-old woman, impeccably dressed in a navy-blue suit, sat behind a desk.

'Take a seat,' she said, pointing at four comfortable chairs and a table with several magazines fanned out on top. The room reminded Flood of a doctor's surgery.

A minute later, a door opened and an equally well-dressed, middle-aged smiling man entered and held out a hand. 'It's nice to meet you, Mr Flood. Let's go to my office. Follow me please.' Brian Sharpe's face seemed familiar. After they'd sat down, Sharpe asked, 'How can I help you?'

Flood reached inside his briefcase and showed him the letter from Barlow. Sharpe read it and said, 'That's fine. Can you show me some ID?' Flood had expected the question so had brought his passport which he handed over. Sharpe inspected it before placing it face down on the photocopier behind him. He placed the copy in a file on his desk and returned the passport back to Flood.

Sharpe continued: 'I received a call from Mr Barlow a few days ago telling me to expect you. He told me that he sent you the key and the pin number to his box. Do you have them?'

'Yes. I'd like to inspect the contents. I'd also like to open a separate account. I've got something I need to deposit. Can you arrange that?'

'Of course. I'll get Pamela to set it up immediately. There's a form to fill in. Should only take a few minutes. When we've done that, I'll take you down to the vaults.'

After Flood had completed the form, Sharpe buzzed Pamela who came to his office immediately. He asked her to process the application without delay. When she'd left, Sharpe said, 'Let's go.'

Flood followed him to a door leading down twenty steps to the underground vaults. At the bottom, they stood before a reinforced steel door with a large wheel attached to the front.

Sharpe deftly swung it this way and that, something he'd clearly done many times. Eventually, the door swung open. They stood in a brightly-lit room half the size of a soccer pitch. Flood gazed at thousands of numbered safe deposit boxes stacked in neat rows from floor to ceiling. No one else seemed to be there. 'How do I find the box?' Flood asked.

'There's a reference number on your key.'

Flood reached inside his pocket and pulled it out. 'It says, F 214.'

'It's a simple grid system. It's in row F then search for the number. Your key will enable you to retrieve the box. You can take it to one of the private viewing rooms at the back of the vault.' He waved in the general direction. 'Insert your pin number on the side of the box to access the contents. When you want to leave, press the buzzer at the door we came through. I'll catch up with you later.' Sharpe turned and left the vault.

Flood found the box, took it to a viewing room and opened it. Barlow's pocketbooks, going back to September 1999 when he'd first infiltrated The Goshawks gang lay inside.

He knew that when undercover cops produced a report for their handler from their pocketbook, they usually destroyed them. They didn't want them falling into the wrong hands. He realised Barlow must have doubted his handler from an early stage in the investigations. Either that or paranoia had got the better of him.

Flood studied the pocketbooks in detail. Barlow had listed the location of the factories in London where they processed the cocaine before passing on to the dealers. He'd also annotated every Marseilles trip bringing in thirty-five kilos of cocaine each time. Flood estimated the street value of each load to be between £25m to £30m.

When he'd finished, he returned the box and pressed the exit buzzer. Sharpe met him at the door. 'Your account has been approved. Here.' He handed Flood a key and a scratch card. 'Your pin number is on there.'

Flood deposited the latest tapes and pocketbooks and returned to Sharpe's office. Then he remembered where he'd met him.

'Did you ever work for the Met?'

'Yes. Why do you ask?'

'I thought so. We've met before. You were a DS working for the Met out of Marylebone. You provided intelligence to our team. Two years ago, I think. Nasty GBH case.'

'Oh, yes. I do remember. You still on the job?'

'No. I left. Doing private stuff now.'

'Don't blame you. The Met's changed. I couldn't stand it anymore, all that paperwork and pussy-footing around. I got out. This job's great. No hassle.' Flood thought Sharpe could prove useful.

*

As he made his way back home, his girls' situation dominated his thoughts. Were they being well-treated? Were they being fed? Were they tied up?

With a heavy heart, he opened his front door. He barely had time to hang up his coat when his landline rang. Flood rushed to it, hoping the call might have some relevance to the girls' kidnapping.

'How much longer do I have to stay down 'ere? It's driving me well crazy!' Jessica's London accent magnified her despair.

'What do you mean? It's a perfectly safe place for you to be at the moment.'

'Safe but boring as hell. I'm so lonely. I miss my friends. Me sister's gone back. She couldn't stand it no more. It's just me and the baby. Don't think I can put up with it much more either.' Flood heard her sob.

'Jessica, believe me, now is not the best time for you to return home. It's still too dangerous.' He thought about telling her what had happened but chose not to.

'When, then?' Jessica hissed.

Flood thought, compared to his situation, her life was idyllic. He replied, speaking slowly, spelling it out so that she knew where he stood. 'I'll tell you when. Not now. There have been some developments. I'm trying to sort them out. I'll come back to you soon.'

'Have you found out what happened to Robbie?'

'That's what I'm working on.' Flood, desperate to get her off the phone, said, 'Jessica, I promise I'll call you soon, OK?'

Defeated, Jessica said, 'OK,' and rang off.

As Flood thought, *Just what I need,* the phone rang again. 'Hi. It's me. Julie. Your sister. Remember me? Any news?'

'Sorry, Julie. You know there's a lot going on. I'm desperately trying to sort things out. How's Mum?'

'Not too good. Still struggling. She's worried sick about the girls. What with the shock of them being kidnapped and her being tied up and bundled in the cupboard, I'm amazed she's still sane.'

'I know, Julie. I feel so guilty about what happened to Mum. Tell her I love her. Tell her I'll have the girls back soon.'

Julie would not be patronised. 'I don't think you have any idea of what Mum's gone through. Why haven't you got the TV companies involved? Surely an appeal would help, wouldn't it?'

She wasn't usually so accusative. Flood knew that if anything, she idolised him. He decided not to rise to the bait.

'Yes, I think it would, but all I can say is, I don't have

control over those things now. I can only assume the Met are working to a strategy. Sorry, Julie, I have to go. I'll call you tomorrow. I'm sure I'll have better news then.'

Flood put down the receiver and checked his watch. It showed 5.30 pm. He ran through his plan of action in his head for the umpteenth time. He called Laura and Cahill to make sure they were in place and waited for Lidgate's call.

CHAPTER TWENTY

Thursday 16th March 2001

As the hand on his office clock clicked to 6.00 pm, the shrill ringing of his landline broke Flood's concentration.

'Have you got the tapes?' Lidgate's refined voice cut through him. He assumed he'd cultured his speech over many years, believing it gave him an air of respectability in gangland.

'I'm not playing your game unless I see my girls. I want to know they're safe and well.'

A short silence followed. 'I can arrange that. Be at the end of your road where it meets Broad Avenue in half-an-hour. Bring the tapes. You'll be picked up. Let me remind you that if I hear from my contacts that the Met are involved, all bets are off. You'll not see your girls again.' Before Flood could reply, the line clicked off.

He glared at the mouthpiece and yelled, 'You fucking bastard!' After he replaced the phone, he took an ultra deep breath, opened his briefcase and stuffed it with files from an unrelated investigation.

Then he called Laura. 'I've heard from Lidgate. They're picking me up, taking me to see my girls. They'll be here soon.'

'Good luck. Have you told Cahill?'

'He's my next call. I hope he's still got the lodge in his sights.'

Twenty minutes later, Flood pulled on his coat, picked up his briefcase and walked out of the front door, slamming it hard behind him. Another clear, cloudless sky resulted in the temperature plunging to a degree above freezing. Pulling up his collar, he walked to the end of the road and waited.

Within minutes, a black BMW Estate car with blacked-out windows cruised past Flood and did a U-turn. It stopped a few feet away from him. The driver's window silently opened.

The driver said, 'Get in,' indicating the rear seats with a backwards jerk of his head. Flood recognised Jack McBride from the photos Barlow had sent. He climbed inside, clutching his briefcase. Vinnie Lidgate, wearing a black baseball cap back to front, sat in the front passenger seat.

Flood's revulsion at sitting behind his wife's killers, yet powerless to act, forced his body to shake. It was compounded by the thought that this was probably the same car driven at his wife while she rode her bicycle to work on that fateful day four years ago. It took all his powers of concentration not to lunge at Vinnie, throttle him with his bare hands.

Nobody spoke as the BMW headed west. Minutes later, it turned off into a little-used, secluded road without streetlights. McBride stopped the car. Vinnie turned around to face Flood and said, 'Get outta the car.'

Vinnie emerged from the front seat and walked round to the rear passenger door. Flood got out, resisting the urge to smash a fist into Vinnie's scrawny face. 'Turn around. Put your mitts on the roof.' Vinnie ran his hands up and down Flood's torso and legs, airport security style.

'Put your hands behind your back.' Vinnie tied them together with a coarse rope. Without warning, he wrapped brown duck tape over Flood's eyes then guided him back into the rear passenger seat and pushed him in.

McBride drove for another ten minutes before stopping. Flood heard the whoosh of an electric window opening followed by the bleeping of a security code as McBride punched in the numbers.

The car moved forward again. Hearing the crunch of gravel, Flood assumed they'd returned to the lodge in Dulwich. So far, so good. He hoped Cahill had spotted them.

'Get out,' commanded Vinnie, clearly enjoying being in charge. Flood stepped out onto the gravel. Vinnie guided him to a door.

'There are steps going down. Go in front of me.' When they'd reached the bottom, Flood heard another door opening. Vinnie pushed him through it.

Flood stood still as he heard Vinnie dragging a chair across a stone floor and position it behind him. He untied his hands and tore off the tape covering Flood's eyes, forcing him to blink as they grew accustomed to the light.

McBride entered, carrying Flood's briefcase which he threw down on a table in the centre of the room.

Flood peered round the cellar. He noticed two settees, four chairs and a table, all of which had seen better days. A sink with a cupboard underneath took up one of the corners. The walls, painted battleship grey, served to make the room appear and feel inhospitable.

For the first time, Flood took a good look at Vinnie and McBride. They couldn't have appeared more different. Vinnie, slightly built with a pinched, mean face, seemed constantly agitated and fidgety.

McBride's belly stretched his T-shirt to bursting point. His jacket remained permanently open; there wasn't enough material left to fasten it. The belt on his trousers fought to contain the mass and he moved at the pace of a sloth. His down-turned mouth suggested he didn't like Vinnie running the show.

He barked at McBride. 'Get the girls.' McBride reluctantly trudged out of the cellar.

'Where are they?' Flood shouted, as he rubbed the circulation back into his wrists.

Vinnie, sitting on one of the settees, picked up a car magazine and flicked though it.

'Sit down. You'll see 'em, soon enough,' he sneered.

'If you've hurt them, you'll pay for it. I promise.' Vinnie shrugged.

A minute later, Flood heard movement outside the cellar. The door opened. McBride ushered Pippa and Gemma into the room. Flood rushed to greet them. They both ran towards him, almost knocking him over. They screamed, 'Daddy! Daddy!' and hugged him hard, squeezing the breath out of his body.

Flood inspected the girls closely. Their hair, always their crowning glory, lay lank and untidy on their heads. Their crumpled dresses hung loosely. Their complexion appeared deathly pale. Flood had seen corpses with more colour. Both girls'eyes, too, after brightening up on seeing their father, returned to being dull and lifeless. Dried tears stained both girls' cheeks.

He stroked each girl's hair. 'Have they hurt you?'

They glanced at each other, not sure what to say. Pippa spoke first.

'They said as long as we behaved ourselves and did what they said, they wouldn't hurt us. But we don't like them, Daddy. Can we go home now?'

'Soon, I promise. Have they fed you?'

'Sort of,' said Gemma.

The door opened. Tommy Lidgate strode into the cellar. Flood recognised him easily. He hadn't changed much from the photo the Met had on file; plumper and greyer maybe, and now sporting a pair of designer glasses.

Dressed in an immaculate grey suit, white shirt, red tie and highly polished brogues, he looked like a head teacher or a bank manager. He also wore a gold ring on his little finger and a matching earring, which Flood thought contradicted the image.

'Sit over there,' he said to the girls, pointing to the other settee. 'I need to talk to your father.' They stood still and stared at Flood.

'Do as he says, girls. We'll all be home soon.'

Lidgate pulled up a chair opposite Flood and sat on it back to front. 'So... you've seen your girls. Perfectly safe and well, I'd say.'

Flood yelled back, 'I told your goon here, if you've harmed them, you'll pay for it.'

Vinnie flinched at the word, *goon,* stood and moved towards Flood. Lidgate waved him back down onto the settee.

Lidgate said, 'They're a little upset, that's all. They shouted their heads off last night. It didn't matter. No one can hear anything from down here. I'll say one thing; they've got attitude. Especially that one.' He turned and pointed at Pippa.

Despite being two years younger than Gemma, she always called the shots at home. She'd inherited Flood's indomitable personality whilst Gemma possessed her mother's more gentle, tender temperament.

Lidgate continued: 'You know the deal. You give me what I want and you can take your girls home.' He leaned forward, picked up Flood's briefcase lying on the table and reached inside. 'In here, are they?'

As Lidgate rummaged through the papers, Flood said, 'I don't know what you're talking about. I've resigned from the Met. I don't give a shit about what you've done in the past. All I want is my kids safely back home.'

'So, what's this?' Lidgate held up a file of papers from the briefcase.

'It's a private investigation I'm working on. I take my briefcase everywhere. Force of habit.' Lidgate stood, threw the papers and the briefcase on the floor and pressed his face close to Flood.

He snarled, 'I *know* you've been sent some tapes. Don't fuck with me. Do you know how I know?' Flood shook his head. 'We had a chat with that dimwit undercover cop Barlow, or whatever his real name is. Know him?'

Flood shook his head again, recalling how the initial post-mortem on Barlow showed signs of torture. He noticed the girls, wide-eyed, huddling together on the settee behind Lidgate.

'One of my men,' Lidgate nodded in the general direction of Vinnie, 'saw Barlow go to the post office in Marseilles with a package. He thought it odd so he followed him and retrieved a receipt Barlow had thrown in a rubbish bin outside the building. Sometimes, he can be quite smart.' Vinnie grinned.

'It was a receipt for a recorded delivery. It had your name and address on it. Now, I don't suppose he sent you a box of French chocolates, did he?' Lidgate cocked his head to one side and continued: 'Barlow posted the package in plenty of time to reach you. Do you still deny having it?'

'I'm sorry. I don't know about any package from Marseilles or anywhere else for that matter.'

Lidgate immediately, without warning, swung round on his chair. He flashed the back of his hand across Pippa's head, the sound of the slap reverberating off the walls. He repeated the action, this time hitting Gemma's face. Both girls shrieked as their heads rocked. The ring on Lidgate's finger caused a trickle of blood to run from Gemma's nose. They both screamed so loudly, Flood's eardrums felt about to burst. They put their hands up to their faces expecting further blows.

Flood leapt to his feet and smashed a fist against Lidgate's jaw forcing him to his knees. His glasses flew off onto the floor. Vinnie rushed to protect Lidgate. He and McBride overpowered Flood, pushing him back onto his chair and held his arms behind his back.

Lidgate stood, picked up his glasses and carefully put them on. He gingerly felt his jaw with one hand and lashed out with the back of his other hand again. This time, the ring caught the fleshiest part of Flood's cheek. Blood spurted like a geyser onto his jacket, the force of the swipe sending him crashing back down onto the floor. Pippa and Gemma screamed.

Flood shrugged off Vinnie and McBride and attempted another attack on Lidgate. This time, Vinnie stood between them and shoved Flood down onto the chair once more. He walked behind him and held Flood's neck in a crook lock.

Lidgate thrust his face close to Flood's again. 'You do anything like that again and I'll kill you *and* your precious ones. Now, where are the tapes?'

Flood spoke with difficulty. 'I'll tell you when this cretin stops strangling me.'

Lidgate nodded at Vinnie. 'Let him speak.'

He shook off Vinnie's arms and took a handkerchief from his pocket and used it to stop the blood running down his cheek. Flood realised that Plan A had seriously backfired. He'd have to employ Plan B.

'OK. It's true. I did receive them. I don't have them with me. I've lodged them in a safe deposit box. It's the best place for them.'

'Where?'

'The Capital Safe Deposit Company in Hatton Garden.'

'Do you have the key?'

'Yes. It's on my key ring in my pocket.'

'Show me.' Flood reached inside his pocket and held it up.

Lidgate snatched it from Flood's grasp, squinted at it through his glasses and put it in his pocket.

'Did you make a copy of the tapes, pass them over to the filth?'

'No.'

'If I find out you have, you'll never see your girls again. Understand?'

'I wouldn't be so stupid. I'm not interested in anything else except getting my girls back home.'

Lidgate sat back in his chair. 'What time does the place open on Saturdays?'

'Nine thirty, I think.'

'Good. Here's what's going to happen. You and the kids will stay here tonight. First thing tomorrow, you'll be taken to the safe deposit company and be given back the key. You'll get the tapes and be brought back here. Then you'll get your girls back.'

Flood glared at him with contempt, wanting to express his repulsion for using his girls as bait. He decided this wasn't the time to make the point.

Lidgate continued: 'If this is a trick, remember I hold the trump card or should I say two trump cards.'

Pippa and Gemma started crying again, clinging to each other like clams. Lidgate ignored them. Instead, he fiddled with the ring on his little finger. 'Right. I think we're done for now.' He nodded at Vinnie and McBride and headed for the door. His henchmen followed. Vinnie grinned at Flood on the way.

He heard a key turn in the lock and two bolts being rammed home. Then Pippa and Gemma's audible sobs filled the room. Flood wanted to magically whisk them away.

He gently wiped the blood off Gemma's nose using his handkerchief. Then he pressed it hard against his bloody cheek. When he finished, he sat between them, put an arm around each of their shoulders and drew them close to him.

'Don't worry, princesses. We'll all be safely home tomorrow.'

CHAPTER TWENTY-ONE

Friday 16th March 2001

Flood checked his watch which showed 8.30 pm. Half-an-hour later, the lights went off. He wasn't looking forward to spending the next twelve hours incarcerated in this dark, cold, stale prison.

As the girls eventually fell into a fitful sleep, he carefully extricated himself from their clutches, took off his jacket and placed it over them before sinking into the other settee.

He lay awake in the pitch darkness and questioned how the hell he'd got his family into this situation. He reconsidered his decision not to bring in the Met. Despite everything that had happened, he still believed it to be the right one. At least they are safe... for now.

An hour later, Flood felt Pippa shaking him. 'Daddy, I need to pee!'

'Look in the cupboard in the corner. There's probably a bucket there. If not, you'll have to use the sink.'

'I can't,' she wailed. 'I don't want you to hear me.'

'You'll have to, Pippa. I can't see you. I'll cover my ears, OK?'

He heard her stumbling to the cupboard and dragging out a bucket. When she'd finished, she edged her way to his settee and sat on his lap. 'What's going to happen to us, Daddy?' she whispered.

'We'll be fine. Try and get some sleep.'

'Will we really be going home tomorrow?'

'Yes. I've promised you, haven't I.' She kissed him and returned to lie down next to Gemma.

Flood checked his watch frequently in between catnapping. The luminous hands appeared to hardly move. His mouth grew parched. He fumbled his way to the sink and turned on the tap and held his mouth open underneath it. Water never tasted this good, he thought.

Now he needed to pee. Pulling the bucket out, he, quietly as he could, emptied his bladder praying that the girls remained sleeping. He made his way back to the settee, slumped down and tried, unsuccessfully, to get some sleep.

After what seemed an interminable length of time to Flood, the lights clicked on and he heard the bolts to the cellar door being drawn. He checked his watch again. 8.00 am.

McBride's huge frame entered, carrying a tray with a plate of buttered toast and three mugs of tea. He set them down on the table and waddled out of the room without a word, locking the door with the bolts and the key.

Pippa and Gemma sat up, disoriented at first. When they saw the toast, they hungrily stuffed it into their mouths. Flood took a gulp of tea and though it scalded his lips, he luxuriated in the feeling of warmth in his stomach.

The cellar remained chilly. It smelt of stale bodies and urine. He sensed the girls' discomfort. They'd never experienced anything like this before in their short lives.

'Why don't you two wash your faces? I know it's only cold water. You'll feel better for it. I've got a comb in my pocket. You can do each other's hair, too.' Flood thought this would give them something else to focus on other than their predicament.

He watched as first, Pippa, then Gemma carefully untangled each other's locks with the occasional, 'Ouch!' and 'Careful!'

Flood took the last swig of his tea. 'When I'm gone, do as they say, OK? I'll be as quick as I can, be back in no time. Then we're away from here.'

Gemma, who seemed to have almost lost her voice, whispered, 'I hope so, Daddy.' She peeked up at him with sorrowful eyes. Flood realised she'd been badly traumatised and would need counselling when he got her home.

Half-an-hour later, Flood heard a key turning in the lock and the bolts being drawn again. McBride lumbered into the room. He nodded at Flood saying, 'Let's go.' The girls rushed to their father and threw their arms around him.

'Girls, I've got to go. Remember what I said.' He kissed

them on the top of their heads and gave them each a final hug before retrieving his jacket from the settee and pulling it on.

Pippa and Gemma cried again. Flood fought back a tear of his own as McBride ushered him through the door and locked it behind him, saying, 'You know the drill. Turn around.'

He wound duct tape around Flood's head, covering his eyes, and tied his hands behind his back before pushing him up the steps. Back on the gravel driveway, Flood gulped down the cold, sweet, fresh air. Raindrops spattered his face as McBride led him to the car and guided him into the rear passenger seat.

Flood remembered that the car had blacked-out windows and realised that if Cahill had kept up his surveillance of the lodge, he wouldn't know who sat inside. He'd have to make a decision. If he believed the girls were being transferred, he'd have to follow them. If he assumed they were still in the lodge, he'd need to stay put.

After ten minutes travelling in the silent car, McBride pulled over into a side road and got out. Flood heard him open the rear passenger door. Then he felt him untying his hands and pulling off the tape covering his eyes. Flood squinted out of the window. In the light drizzle, he recognised the park opposite the road, Tabard Gardens.

Ironically, McBride had parked less than half-a-mile from Flood's old police station in Southwark. He considered overpowering McBride and frog-marching him there but immediately discounted the idea, putting his trust in his Plan B and hoping that Laura had the safe deposit company covered.

McBride drove in heavy rush-hour traffic through the drizzle, careful not to shoot any red lights. He parked the car in a two-hour parking meter slot fifty yards away from the safe deposit company premises. Retrieving Flood's briefcase from the front passenger seat, he got out of the car, opened the rear passenger door and thrust the briefcase towards Flood.

'The keys to the safe are in here. When you get the tapes, put them inside.'

The drizzle had subsided by the time they walked to the entrance to the premises. Flood glanced around for signs of being watched. He felt McBride's breath on his neck as he kept uncomfortably close to him.

He pressed the buzzer on the security pad, gave his name and explained that he had a colleague with him. They both passed through the usual security searches before entering the reception area.

'Miss Snooty' smiled an acknowledgement at Flood and looked McBride up and down. Flood pressed out the creases in his trousers, trying not look as if he'd slept in them. 'I've come to collect something from my safe deposit box.'

'That's fine but I'm sorry, Mr Flood, your friend will have to stay here in reception. Only authorised people with an account are allowed into the vault and private viewing rooms.'

'OK, I'm happy to go through whenever you're ready.'

'Mr Sharpe won't be long. Please take a seat.' McBride looked uncomfortable and shifted his considerable weight from one foot to the other before reluctantly sitting down.

Five minutes later, Flood heard the buzz of the entrance security pad and Pamela, clearly in on the act, say, 'Please enter.' McBride stared at the reception door, looking concerned.

It burst open. Laura dashed in accompanied by two burly DCs. One of them immediately overpowered a surprised McBride and handcuffed him before he had time to react. The other DC stood in the doorway, preventing an escape. Laura nodded at Flood and approached McBride.

'Jack McBride. I'm arresting you in connection with the kidnapping of two minors, Pippa and Gemma Flood and the kidnapping and murder of Robbie Barlow. You do not have to say anything but it may harm your defence if you do not mention, when questioned, something which you later rely on in court. Anything you do say may be given in evidence.'

McBride glared at Flood. He spat out, 'You'll pay for this! I don't think you know who you're dealing with.'

The DC frisked him, finding a four-inch knife strapped to his leg, a mobile phone and the keys to the BMW in his pocket. He placed them in a bag before hustling him away to the unmarked police car parked directly outside the building.

Flood turned to Laura. 'Listen, we don't have much time. Lidgate's expecting us back at the lodge with the tapes. Where are you taking McBride?'

'Southwark nick. I have a confession to make. I had to tell Foxy your plan. I warned him about the bent handler, too. He said he'll deal with him.'

Flood bawled at her. 'Oh no, Laura! What did I say? The girls are in real danger. I bloody well hope Foxy's not going in gung-ho. If the Met do, it's all over.'

Laura fired back. 'I thought about it a lot after you'd left. I decided that it was not a great idea for you to go in alone, after all. Remember what Foxy told us about the way the gang dealt with Barlow? You and the girls could have been killed.'

'But we agreed, Laura.'

'Look, I didn't have an option. I couldn't get the surveillance you wanted without his authority.'

Flood glared at her. 'Christ, Laura!'

'Calm down. Look, Foxy's OK with this. He's agreed to the rest of your plan. He even thinks it's a good idea for you to watch me interview McBride. Two heads and all that.'

'I'm not at all happy with this.'

'It wasn't exactly an easy decision for me either. Come on, I'll give you a lift.'

As they drove to Southwark Police Station, a brooding Flood gave her every detail of Pippa and Gemma's incarceration.

'Oh, my God! That's awful! Your poor girls. Thank goodness we know where they are. Once we get McBride to cooperate we should get a result.'

'You know what, Laura? I think I should have taken the tapes with me. Swapped them for the girls. Worry about Lidgate and The Goshawks gang later.'

'That's if you think Lidgate could be trusted to keep his side of the bargain. I don't think he can.'

'No. You're right. Have you heard from Cahill?'

'He called me early this morning. He sounded tired but confirmed that he'd seen you arrive at the lodge last night. I assume he's still there.'

'I hope so. I'll call him, see where he is. Can I use your mobile?' As they stopped at a zebra crossing, Laura passed it over. Flood dialled the number, listened for a moment, then dialled it again.

'Shit! Keeps going to his message service.' After he'd dialled the number for a third time, he left a message. 'Cahill. Where are you? Please call this number ASAP.'

By the time they arrived at Southwark Police Station, the custody sergeant informed them that McBride would be processed as a matter of urgency and taken to an interview room.

'He's asked for the duty brief to be present during the interview. I've sorted one out. He's due here any minute.'

Flood asked, 'Who is it?'

'Tim Fellows.'

'Good.' He turned to Laura. 'I've worked with him before. He's a reasonable guy.'

As they walked to the viewing room, she said, 'I'll explain the urgency to Fellows before he sees McBride. I don't want them using stalling tactics.'

'Laura, we don't have much time. You may have to get McBride to call Lidgate. Say there's been a delay.'

'OK. I'll give it my best shot. I'm taking DC Saunders in with me.' Flood remembered him as a tough, no-nonsense Scouser who'd previously worked on his team.

A PC knocked on the viewing room door and peered around it. 'Duty brief's here, Sarge. You said you wanted a word.'

As Laura left, Flood sat down and stared at the video screen showing the empty interview room. He tapped the table with his fingers wondering how long this would take. Ten minutes later, Laura returned.

'Fellows' got the picture. He's seeing McBride now, explaining the charges. Once he's satisfied, he'll buzz me and we can start the interview. Foxy says he wants a word with you. He's coming up to the viewing room shortly.'

Flood shrugged. 'I thought he might.'

Twenty minutes later, the PC poked his head around the

door again. 'Duty brief's happy for you to interview the suspect now, Sarge.'

Laura nodded and left the viewing room. Flood peered at the screen and seconds later, he watched McBride enter the interview room with a glum expression on his face. He slumped down on a chair. Tim Fellows, a dark-haired, smartly dressed man in his early thirties followed McBride and sat next to him. Laura and DC Saunders sat opposite.

Superintendent Fox entered the viewing room. He acknowledged Flood with a nod and sat next to him. 'I hope everything goes according to plan here. If not, I'm considering authorising a raid on the lodge immediately.'

Flood, his mouth contorted with anger, said, 'Are you sure that's wise? My girls are in serious danger.'

'We've got a team of trained hostage negotiators standing by.'

'For Christ's sake! Lidgate's a psycho. He won't respond to that. Anyway, we don't have the time.'

'Let's see how the interview pans out, shall we?'

Flood ground his teeth together, silently seething. They watched as Laura and DC Saunders went through the preliminaries, reminding McBride that he was being interviewed under caution.

'Do you understand?'

He nodded.

'Let's deal with the kidnapping and murder of Robbie Barlow first. Do you know him?'

'No comment.'

'Have you ever travelled to and from Marseilles in the last year?'

'No comment.'

'Do you know Vinnie Lidgate?'

'No comment.'

'Do you know Thomas Lidgate?'

'No comment.'

'Have you ever visited an industrial unit on the Shaftsbury Trading Estate in Finsbury?'

'No comment.'

'Have you ever visited a disused swimming pool at Stevenson Street near Crystal Palace?'

'No comment.'

'Are you or have you ever been a member of a criminal gang known as The Goshawks?'

'No comment.'

Laura glanced down at her notes and back up again.

'Let's talk now about the kidnapping of two young girls, Pippa and Gemma Flood. A reliable eyewitness, a member of the police force, has told us that you, together with another, kidnapped them from a house in Westcombe Park. Threats have since been made to kill them. Do you deny that?'

Flood leant forward in his chair, glaring at the viewing screen.

'No Comment.'

'Have you ever visited a former lodge in College Road, Dulwich Village?'

'No comment.'

'Do you know the whereabouts of Pippa and Gemma Flood at this moment?'

'No comment.'

The interview carried on in the same vein for another ten minutes. DC Saunders remained silent as part of the strategy. He concentrated on McBride's reactions to Laura's interrogation. Flood knew this always unnerved suspects. Made them more conscious of the severity of the situation.

Flood recognised the techniques Laura used. Most of her questions were based on information she knew as fact. Now she'd present the evidence. The problem with this approach is that it took time. He wanted to shout at her: *for Christ's sake, get to the point.*

'You see, Jack, we know that you knew Robbie Barlow. We've got you on tape talking to him about all sorts of things including your role in the assassination of a firearms officer, Jenny Cahill. What do you say to that?'

McBride remained silent.

'We also know that you travel to Marseilles every other week, collecting Class A drugs and distributing them to various locations in London. You discussed your trips with Vinnie Lidgate and Robbie Barlow. It's all on the tapes. I could play them to you if you like.'

DC Saunders broke his silence for the first time, piling on the pressure.

'We have photos of you and Vinnie in Marseilles taken a few days ago. An eyewitness described three people – you, Vinnie Lidgate and Robbie Barlow – arriving in a white Transit van at a lockup on the Shaftsbury Trading Estate. Later he also describes seeing you and Vinnie bundling another person we believe to be Barlow, into the rear of a black BMW Estate car. We found his bloodstains all over the floor of the lockup. We believe you and Vinnie tortured him there. What do you say to that?'

'No Comment.' McBride had found his voice again.

Laura continued: 'Another eyewitness has identified you as the driver of the same BMW when you took him to the address in Dulwich where the girls are being kept against their wishes. Would you like to explain why you did that?'

McBride paused for a moment, as if considering what to say. Eventually, he said, 'No comment.'

Laura referred to her pocketbook lying on the table in front of her. She looked up at McBride once more. 'Our forensics team have been working flat out on the crime scenes at the lockup and the disused swimming pool where we found Barlow's body. We'll get the DNA results from both locations later today. Given the evidence we already hold, we fully expect one of the DNA results to match yours, putting you at both crime scenes.'

Saunders added, 'They'll no doubt be fingerprints, blood samples, tyre marks and loads of other stuff as well. If they point to you, then you're finished. Are you happy to take what's coming to you?'

'No comment.'

The detectives remained silent to ensure the words sank in.

Laura broke the silence. She leaned towards McBride. 'I hope you realise the serious position you find yourself in. We have enough evidence to ensure you're put away forever. The drug-running offence alone is worth twenty years. Especially given your previous convictions. You can add another fifteen at least for the kidnapping. Plus another twenty years if your DNA or fingerprints are found at the pool and at the lockup.'

McBride bowed his head. DC Saunders turned to face Laura. 'You forgot to inform our suspect about how many years he'd get for torturing Robbie Barlow.' He smirked at McBride. 'You won't have any time left to draw your old age pension at this rate.'

McBride turned to Tim Fellows sitting next to him and then turned to face the detectives. 'I want to talk to my solicitor in private.'

'That's fine. We can arrange that. Before you do, I'd like you to consider this. If you cooperate with us in getting Pippa and Gemma Flood back home safely, we may be able to lessen some of the charges. We can't promise. We'll do the best we can.'

Fellows spoke for the first time. 'What would my client's cooperation involve?'

Laura explained the plan Flood had conceived with Fox. Fellows made notes. When he finished writing, she said, 'The ball's in your court. We don't have much time. You've got twenty minutes max. If your client doesn't want to play ball, we'll charge him with everything.'

CHAPTER TWENTY-TWO

Saturday 17ᵗʰ March 2001

As soon as the interview was over, Fox turned to Flood. 'DS Miles did well. Let me know how McBride reacts.' He left and minutes later, Laura returned to the viewing room.

Flood said, 'Well done, Laura. McBride can be in no doubt about the deep shit he's in.' He checked his watch. 'We've been gone nearly three hours. I expect Lidgate to call McBride. Is his mobile being monitored?'

'Yes. Of course. I'll check it out now.' She left Flood and moments later, returned with it in her hand. 'Lidgate sent a text twenty minutes ago.' She passed the mobile to him. He read, *where the fuck are u? call me*. The text was timed at 11.55 am.

He handed the mobile back to her. 'Great. Text back, *been delayed. sorted now. on our way.*' Laura expertly thumbed the digits and pressed 'Send' with a flourish.

Ten minutes later, a PC put his head around the door again. 'The duty brief wants to continue the interview with McBride.'

Flood stood silently watching the video screen from the viewing room as they reassembled. Fellows began: 'My client's happy to cooperate with the Met on the understanding that they'll do everything they can to mitigate any charges they want to make. In particular, he says he never agreed to the kidnapping of the girls. He wants to make a statement to that effect.'

Flood, who'd been pacing the viewing room, clenched his fists and shouted, 'Yes!'

Laura said, 'Good. We'll take his statement later.' She turned to McBride. 'What's the entry code for getting into the lodge?'

McBride mumbled, 'Three, four, two, five.'

Laura scribbled it down in her pocketbook, stood and said,

'Come with us.'

Flood rushed to Fox's office and told him that McBride had agreed to cooperate. He said, 'Good. I'll authorise the plan. I'm taking a huge risk here. The only reason I'm taking it is that I still have faith in you, Andy. For God's sake, don't let me down.'

'I won't.'

'Do you have the keys to the safe deposit box?'

'Yes.'

'Hand them over. We'll need the contents as evidence.'

Flood reached inside his briefcase and passed them to Fox, saying, 'I'd better be going.'

'Be careful, Andy.'

Flood joined Laura, DC Saunders and McBride at the parking lot behind the police station. McBride's mobile pinged again just as he reached them.

Laura pulled it from her bag and looked at it before saying, 'Message from Lidgate.' She showed the text to Flood. He read; *do you have the tapes?*

'Text back, yes.' She did so and handed the mobile to Flood.

'Here. It's probably better for you to have this from now on.'

Eight uniformed Senior Firearms Officers wearing bullet-proof vests, helmets with goggles attached and carrying semi-automatic pistols and rifles, stood beside two unmarked Range Rovers. Laura ripped out the note from her pocketbook showing the entry code and passed it to the senior officer, saying, 'You'll need this.'

Flood climbed into the front passenger seat of the BMW Estate which had been driven by a DC from Hatton Garden to the police station. Laura pushed McBride into the driver's seat. Two of the SFOs sat in the rear passenger seats. The other six followed in two Range Rovers.

A speeding police car led the way with blue lights flashing and sirens blaring. Flood ordered McBride to keep up with him for the four-mile journey to the lodge. The Range Rovers followed with Laura and DC Saunders bringing up the rear in

Laura's car.

Heavy traffic and roadworks on Denmark Hill held them up. Flood pummelled the dashboard in exasperation several times. He checked his watch constantly.

A mile from the lodge, Flood turned to the officers sitting in the rear seats. 'Not far to go now. You'll find some tape and cord on the floor. Can one of you put the tape around my eyes and loosely tie my hands behind my back? I'll need to be able to undo it later.'

Half-a-mile from the lodge, the driver of the police car stopped its lights and siren and turned into a side street, his job done. Two minute later, the BMW approached the entrance to the lodge. Flood told McBride to punch in the entry code and the gates slowly opened. Flood's heartbeat thumped against his ribs at the thought of seeing his girls again. He ordered McBride to park as close to the rear entrance as possible, aware of the security cameras monitoring them.

He told McBride, 'Carry my briefcase and lead me towards the door of the cellar. Open it, push me inside and leave the door ajar. Don't even think about tipping off your cronies.'

Once they'd passed through the doorway, Flood carefully walked down the stone steps putting his hands out towards the walls to steady himself. The plan required the two SFOs to follow them down after two minutes, apprehend Vinnie and Lidgate and free the girls. The other officers would surround the property and await further instructions. For the first time since his girls' abduction, Flood felt good about the situation.

He expected to hear his girls' joyful greeting as he entered. Instead, silence. Flood freed his hands and ripped off the tape around his eyes. Looking around the room, he turned to face McBride yelling, 'Where are they?'

McBride looked puzzled. 'I've no idea.'

'What do you mean, *you've no idea?* You must know where they are. Don't lie to me!'

The two SFOs burst into the cellar, Glock pistols at the ready followed by DC Saunders and Laura. 'They're not here,' yelled Flood. He jabbed his elbow hard into McBride's gut. 'Fatboy here, says he has no idea where Lidgate's taken my girls.'

He said to DC Saunders, 'Guard him,' then turned to the two SFOs. 'Search the rest of this place.' Flood and Laura followed closely behind them as they swept stealthily through the rooms one at a time, stepping inside, commando style.

When they'd finished downstairs they repeated the process upstairs. When it became obvious the occupants had fled, Flood and Laura returned to the cellar. Flood hurled himself at McBride, grabbed his jacket lapel and forced his bulky frame against the wall.

'Where the fuck are they? If I find out you've double-crossed us, you'll spend the rest of your life in jail.' Flood spotted fear in McBride's eyes as both SFOs pointed their pistols at him.

'I... I don't know.' Flood balled his fists, longing to smash them into McBride's face. He used all the willpower he possessed to restrain himself.

'Where else do you do your dirty work, apart from here and the lockup?'

McBride recovered his composure. 'You asked me to cooperate, bring you lot here. I done what you asked.'

Flood tightened his grip on McBride's jacket and thrust his face close to his. 'Do you want to go down as someone who uses little girls to protect his freedom?' He let go of McBride in disgust.

He turned to the SFOs. 'Give this place one more sweep. See if you can find *anything* which will give us a clue to where they've been taken.'

The senior SFO glanced at Laura seeking her approval. She nodded. When they'd left the room, Laura turned to Flood. 'I think Lidgate got spooked by McBride's response. Maybe they had a code or something.' Laura reached for her mobile. 'I'll put out an all-persons alert to every police station in London.'

Flood slumped onto a chair. Laura turned to DC Saunders. 'Cuff this piece of shit and take him back to the station. Go in one of the Range Rovers. I'll get the charges prepared as soon as I get back.'

As they left, McBride yelled, 'What about my deal? I told you I never agreed with the kidnapping.'

Flood shouted back, 'The deal's off!' He looked at Laura, 'Take me back to my house. I need to pick up my mobile, check for messages. I'll check my emails too. I'm hoping Lidgate's been in touch. You realise that if he finds out about this raid, he'll probably kill the girls.'

Laura closed her eyes. 'Oh my God! What a mess.'

As she drove to Flood's home, he said, 'What the hell's happened to Cahill? Surely he'd have called you if he'd seen the girls being taken somewhere else? And he'd have seen the BMW leaving the lodge when we went to the safe deposit company.'

'I've heard nothing since he called me early this morning.'

'What's he playing at? Maybe I shouldn't have involved him. All that stuff with Katie Brunswick. I was never convinced we got to the bottom of that, you know. But I felt I owed him after he'd found out where the gang had taken my girls.'

Flood's voice faltered as he spoke, remembering that he'd promised them everything would be alright. 'Christ knows what they're going through.' He turned his head away from Laura and gazed out of the window, not wanting her to see how upset he was.

*

When they arrived at Flood's house, he opened the front door and dashed inside. Laura followed, saying, 'I need to use your loo.'

Flood stomped directly to his study and checked his emails first. Ignoring the usual spam, he noticed one sent an hour previously with an attachment marked, *Urgent: Your Girls,* in the subject box.

Opening the email with trembling fingers, he read, *'McBride texted me earlier to say he has the tapes. I've tried getting hold of him ever since. He's not answering. I'm running out of patience. I'm attaching a video you might want to see. I want the tapes delivered today. Tell McBride to bring them to Billy's place. He'll know where that is. We'll be there. Don't follow him or there will be consequences. If I don't get the tapes by 6.00 pm today, don't expect to see your girls alive again. This is your last chance.'*

Flood opened the attachment. After watching the first few frames of the video, he shouted, 'Laura. Come and see this.' She entered the room and stood peering over his shoulder.

They saw Pippa and Gemma sitting side by side with their hands tied behind their backs. Duct tape covered their mouths and their reddened cheeks were damp with tears. They fidgeted on their chairs and uttered muted, whimpering squeals. A hand gripped Pippa's hair to stop her wriggling. The other hand used scissors to cut off large chunks of her golden locks. Both girls cried incessantly.

Gemma received the same treatment. Their bodies trembled as 'Scissorhands' then ran a battery shaver crudely over their heads.

Flood gasped out loud, horrified, not believing what he was seeing. Within a minute, both girls were completely bald. He shut his eyes and shook his head, hoping the image would disappear.

Laura put both hands over her mouth. 'We've got to get these bastards,' she spat out at the screen. 'Your girls don't deserve to go through this.'

Flood stopped the video, unable to take any more. 'I've screwed up big time, Laura. I don't know where they are and the bloody tapes will be in evidence bags by now.' He stood and kicked out at the desk.

She said, 'Lidgate's smart. He knew you'd go home to check your messages. He's stopped calling McBride, doesn't want the calls traced.'

Flood rummaged in his pocket for McBride's mobile hoping there might be a recent message on it. There wasn't. The latest text from Lidgate, timed at 12.30 pm, had read, *do you have the tapes?* Flood cursed. He hadn't bothered trying to get a trace on the phone's location at the time believing that his girls were still at the lodge.

Laura said, 'I think we should get McBride's phone to the techies as soon as we can. They may be able to get a bearing on the location of Lidgate's calls. You never know, he may have used it from Billy's place, wherever that is.'

'I don't see the point, Laura. We don't have enough time.'

'Do you think Lidgate's guessed that McBride's been arrested?'

'That's what worries me. It's all over if he finds out. I don't know if I'll ever see Pippa and Gemma again.'

CHAPTER TWENTY-THREE

Saturday 17th March 2001

Flood opened a desk drawer and picked up his mobile. He'd left it there before going to the lodge. The message icon showed four voicemails. The first three were from Julie, the fourth from Jessica.

Julie's messages grew increasingly hysterical with each call.

'This is the third time I've called. For God's sake, answer! Mum's been taken to Southampton General Hospital with a suspected heart attack. I'm not surprised after all she's been through. I'm at the hospital now. She's being examined by the specialist. She's so fragile. I hope she's going to be alright.'

Flood groaned and flung his mobile back onto the desk. Laura flinched. 'What's up?' she said.

'My mother's had a heart attack!' Laura covered her mouth with her hands again.

Flood thumped his desk and shouted, 'Lidgate's caused this!'

Picking up his mobile, he played the message from Jessica. *'I'm coming back. Little Mark's not well. He needs to see a doc at the hospital in London. He's dealt with him before. I'm going up the fuckin' wall here. I can't think of nothing but Robbie. It's not fair his life ended like it did. Can't stand it here on me own...'*

Flood hit the speaker button and replayed the message so that Laura could hear it. When it finished, he flung the mobile back on the desk again and said, 'That's all I need.'

'You'll have to call her; stop her coming back.'

'I will. Better call my sister first.'

Before Flood could say anything, Julie screamed down the phone, 'Where have you been? Do you realise how serious this is?'

'Sorry, Julie. Of course, I do. How is she?'

'Still in Intensive Care. They won't tell me anything other than that she's holding on. Can you come down?'

'Julie, it's complicated. I'm trying to get the girls back. I can't come down right now. I'll come as soon as I can.' He thought about going into more detail but decided it would only upset her.

'Well, I only hope you're not too late. That's all I can say.'

A stabbing pain of guilt passed through Flood as Julie ended the call. Laura stared at him closely. Flood guessed she may be judging him badly for his decision not to go to Southampton. He returned her stare. 'What else can I do?'

'I don't think you can do anything. At least, Julie's there with your mum. You've got to see Lidgate. He's expecting you to deliver the tapes.'

Flood felt powerless and drained. He'd barely slept for the past two nights. Images of Pippa and Gemma's bald heads flashed through his mind constantly. What must they be going through? he thought.

Something compelled him to look at the video again. Laura stood behind him to watch.

As the shocking scene unfolded, Flood shook his head. 'I can't believe what I'm seeing, Laura, how could anybody do this to two little kids?'

'Because Lidgate and Vinnie are evil shits.'

They watched the camera operator focussing only on the girls' heads and the hands wielding the scissors, then the electric shaver. Flood noticed something in the background which appeared vaguely familiar. He rewound and replayed a section of the video several times, peering closely at the screen. He paused it. In the top left-hand corner, he noticed a tiny section of wallpaper. It had a creamy background with distinctive, garish red stripes.

He sat back in his chair and said, 'Laura, I've seen this wallpaper before.'

'Where?'

Flood closed his eyes and raked through his memory. After a few seconds, he turned to her and shouted, 'It's Jessica's house! They're at Jessica's house!'

'Are you sure? Why take them there?'

'Have a look for yourself. Recognise it?'

Laura squinted at the screen. 'Sorry, I can't remember. I wasn't inspecting the decor at the time.' She stepped back. 'When you think about it, Lidgate would assume it's the last place we'd expect to find them. They know it's empty. They've been there before. Could be that Jessica's son Vinnie has a key.'

Flood jumped up and grabbed his jacket. 'I'm going there now. I need to be with my girls. Are you coming?' He picked up his car keys and rushed towards the door.

Laura shouted after him. 'Are you mad? What are you going to do? Act like Superman? Sweep them up and fly them back home?'

Flood stopped and turned back to face her. 'Lidgate and Vinnie are waiting for McBride to turn up at Billy's place with the tapes. They won't realise that I know the girls are at Jessica's.'

'It's too dangerous, Andy. Let the Met handle it. They can be there in minutes. Get them out safely.'

'It's too risky, Laura. Just the smell of a copper and they'll kill Pippa and Gemma. Especially if they know we led the raid on the lodge.'

'I can see it's useless arguing with you when you're in this mood. Let me at least organise backup. I'll explain to Foxy that it needs to be discreet.'

Flood bellowed at her. 'For Christ's sake Laura, that's the last thing I want you to do. You heard what Lidgate said.'

She implored, 'But you can't do this on your own. You've already screwed up your career by being reckless. You're doing it again.'

'I haven't got time to argue with you, Laura.'

She yelled back, 'That's the trouble with you. You're so bloody stubborn! Don't you realise you could get yourself and your girls killed?'

'It's my one chance to free them,' Flood shouted back as he yanked open the front door.

'That's it.' Laura shook her head. 'I can't go through with

this. Count me out.'

As Flood stepped over the threshold, he snapped back over his shoulder, 'Do what you like!'

'What about Jessica? You need to stop her coming back.'

'She's not my problem, right now.' He slammed the front door shut, slid into the driver's seat and started the engine. The tyres squealed, leaving black skid marks on the damp tarmac as he gunned the accelerator. The car lurched forward, narrowly missing a passing van.

As he shot through several red lights, Flood thought again about his girls' bald heads. They'd spend hours every day fiddling or plaiting their long hair. Sometimes they did each other's, taking great pride in how it looked and making adjustments after inspecting the result in the mirror. Having their heads shaved was about the worst thing that could happen to them.

He thought, too, about Georgina and wondered how she'd feel if she'd seen the video and whether she'd approve of his actions. He concluded she would.

Then he focussed on his mother. Despite not being religious, he offered a silent prayer for her survival. Thank goodness Julie was there to support her.

He parked his car a hundred yards away from Jessica's house in Islington as darkness fell.

The curtains to the ground floor and bedroom windows of the Regency end-of-terrace house were drawn. He opened the front door with the key Jessica had given him earlier and hurried to the living room with the distinctive wallpaper.

Everything remained as before; flipped-over furniture and drawer contents spilling onto the floors. Except now, he noticed clumps of his daughters' blonde hair on the carpet. Taking the stairs two at a time, he peeked into each of the three bedrooms; no sign of the girls.

He dashed down the stairs and noticed a door off the hallway. He opened it and flicked on a light switch which showed steps leading down to a basement. The sight that greeted him caused him to gasp.

Pippa and Gemma, their bald heads gleaming, lay on the

painted concrete floor with duct tape wound round their hands, feet and mouths. Their red-rimmed eyes expressed the sort of fear he'd only ever seen in wildlife programmes on TV; young wildebeests cornered by a lion.

He rushed towards them and began ripping off the tapes. He said in a soft voice, 'You're going to be OK now, girls. It's over. I'm taking you both home.'

After he'd removed all the tapes, both girls clung to Flood, shaking and sobbing simultaneously. They wouldn't let him go. Flood commanded, 'C'mon, girls. Pull yourselves together. We've got to get out of this place... now.'

He struggled to disengage them. They hung on to him like marooned sailors clinging to a wreck. Flood shouted at them, more forcibly pushing them away. 'C'mon, let's go! Let's go!'

He shoved them up the basement steps into the hall then towards the front door. As he opened it, Lidgate, wearing a fedora and black coat, stood in their way. 'So, you found your girls.' He reached inside his pocket and pulled out a gun and pointed it at them.

Flood yelled at the girls, 'Run to the back door! Run as fast as you can.' Pippa, always the ballsy one, did so. Gemma, traumatised by the sight of the gun in Lidgate's hand, stood transfixed, clutching her dad. 'Go, Gemma!' Flood shouted again. She remained attached.

He watched as Pippa opened the back door and heard her scream as she was confronted by Vinnie. She dummied to go to his right and darted through the tiniest of gaps to his left. As she got over the threshold, Vinnie caught her by her dress and dragged her back inside before slamming and locking the door.

'Always the pain in the arse, aren't you?' He slapped her twice around her head to stop her screaming.

Pippa hit back, pumping her fists into his stomach, saying, 'Get off me, you creep!'

Flood tried to move towards Vinnie but Gemma wouldn't let go of him. He bellowed at Vinnie, 'Leave her alone, you bastard!'

Lidgate jabbed his gun into Flood's ribs. 'Let's all settle

down, shall we? Vinnie, take the girls down to the basement. Mr Flood and I have some business to attend to.'

CHAPTER TWENTY-FOUR

Saturday 17th March 2001

Lidgate waved the hand holding his gun in the direction of the living room. 'Move,' he barked. Once there, he pointed at one of the upturned chairs. 'Sit there.' Flood righted it and slumped down. Lidgate put his gun in the right-hand pocket of his jacket before removing his coat and fedora, which he threw onto the settee. He righted another chair and sat opposite.

Flood wanted to hurl himself at Lidgate, fancying his chances of overpowering him. He decided against it for the moment, concerned that Vinnie might harm his girls in retaliation.

Lidgate sneered at Flood. 'Don't you read your emails?'

Flood glared back, recalling the barbaric nature of the video clip. 'I suppose you're proud of yourself doing what you did to my girls. Why didn't you pick on me?'

He smirked. 'I thought it might get better results.' His expression changed. 'Let's get down to business. I need to know what happened to McBride. He said he had the tapes but he didn't show up at Billy's.'

Flood's brain raced, thinking of a plausible explanation. 'McBride's definitely got them. He said he'd deliver them to you. He told me if you were happy, you'd release my girls. I wanted to go with him, make sure you would keep your side of the deal. He said that wasn't possible.'

Lidgate sat back in his chair. 'If McBride had the tapes but didn't get my message, he'd have brought them to the lodge. When he found out we'd moved on, he'd have called me. So why didn't he?'

'I can't speak for your men. Now, I want my girls.'

'I don't think you're telling me the truth. I hope the visit to the safe deposit company wasn't a trick, because if it was, I promise you, I'll kill your girls. I never make threats I'm not prepared to carry out.'

Lidgate reached inside his jacket pocket and pulled out his gun again. 'Get up. Go to the basement.' Lidgate moved behind Flood, prodding the gun into his back. He felt his mobile vibrate in his pocket for the third time since Lidgate's return.

Flood looked around the basement which had been transformed into a workshop. An array of chisels, saws, hammers and screwdrivers covered a wall. They glinted under the light emanating from a single bulb hanging from the centre of the ceiling. An open shelf system held cans of paints, lubricants, and various boxes containing light bulbs and batteries.

A set of garden chairs lay collapsed in a corner. Against the wall opposite the door, a metal-clad bench ran the entire length of the basement. On top, lay a tool box next to a powerful vice.

Vinnie, sitting on one of the garden chairs with his gun in his hand, peered down at Pippa and Gemma who were lying face-down on the concrete floor.

Flood rushed towards them and knelt down. He turned and yelled at Lidgate, 'For Christ's sake, let them be!'

Lidgate thrust his gun into Flood's ribs. 'Get up. Vinnie, bring one of those chairs over here. Tie him up.'

Vinnie slipped his gun into the belt of his trousers. He picked up a length of rope lying on a shelf and dragged a chair towards Flood who slowly got to his feet, powerless to act. Vinnie pushed him down onto the chair and tied his hands tightly behind it. Returning his gun to his jacket pocket, Lidgate dragged another chair over towards Flood, set it up opposite him and sat down.

He spoke as if addressing a two-year-old. 'Let's get this sorted. We can resolve *everything* once we have the tapes.' He turned to Vinnie. 'Bring the mouthy one next to the bench.'

A supercilious smirk crossed Vinnie's face as he hauled Pippa to her feet by pulling at her wrists. 'Get your hands off me, you jerk,' she said, as she tried, unsuccessfully, to wriggle free from his grasp as Vinnie dragged her towards the bench.

Lidgate nodded to Vinnie who grabbed one of Pippa's

hands. Flood watched on helplessly as Vinnie used his superior strength to force her fingers deep into the jaws of the vice. With his free hand he turned the arm so that the jaws held her fingers so tightly, she couldn't escape. Her knees buckled. Gemma squeezed her eyes shut.

Flood screamed at the top of his voice. 'No! No! You can't do that. Do it to me if you must but not to her!'

Pippa tried to scratch Vinnie's face with her other hand but he moved out of reach. Her eyes darted between her hand and her father. She screamed, 'Daddy! Daddy! Do something.'

Flood roared, 'Stop! Stop!'

Lidgate said in his ultra-calm voice, 'I think we're in a position to have a chat now. I'm going to ask you once again. Where is McBride and where are the tapes?'

Flood hollered, 'I don't have them. For Christ's sake, stop!'

'I'll tell Vinnie to stop when you tell me the truth.'

Flood thought about telling Lidgate that he'd lied. That the tapes were still in the safe deposit box and that he'd get them if he stopped torturing Pippa. He realised that if Lidgate found out the Met had them, they'd all be killed. He couldn't take the risk.

'I've told you the truth. Call McBride. How many more times do I have to tell you? He's got the bloody tapes.'

'I've tried calling him. There's no response. Maybe he's in police custody. I hope not for your sake.' Lidgate leant towards Flood. 'Well?'

Flood cursed his stupidity. What had he done? He blamed himself – his reckless obsession had led to this.

Vinnie's face expressed the sadistic pleasure he derived from being the inflictor of pain. He waited for further instructions from his grandfather as Pippa and Gemma snivelled.

After thirty seconds, Lidgate nodded at Vinnie again who wrapped his fingers around the arm of the vice.

*

The sound of the front door slamming and the tired wail of a baby interrupted proceedings. Flood heard Jessica's soothing voice, although indistinct, calming down the baby.

'Fuck! What's she doing back here?' Lidgate hissed, not addressing anyone in particular.

He eyeballed Flood and the girls. 'Don't say a fucking word, any of you.'

He turned to Vinnie. 'Switch off the light.' They sat in silence in the darkness of the basement, relieved only by a smattering of light from the hall seeping underneath the ill-fitting basement door.

Flood looked at the dim tableau in horror. A bald Pippa, close to passing out, barely standing; her fingers tightly wedged in a vice; Vinnie, champing at the bit, itching to turn the vice tighter; Gemma, also bald, lying on the floor, badly traumatised; Lidgate, the interrogator, cool, in charge, sitting opposite him.

They heard Jessica climb the stairs to the bedroom from the hallway, presumably putting her son to bed. Five minutes later, they heard her come back down. Almost immediately, they heard her running up the stairs again and every door being opened and slammed as if she was searching for something or someone. She retraced her steps back downstairs.

Flood kept his eyes on the handle to the basement door. Eventually, it slowly turned down and the door opened. Jessica stood in the doorway, her silhouette framed in the light from the hall. She held a baseball club in one hand and flicked on the light switch with the other. She stared at the players in the bizarre tableau one by one with an increasing degree of alarm, her eyes doubling in size when she saw Pippa's fingers stuck in the vice.

'Christ alive! What the fuck's going on here?'

Flood barely recognised her. Usually, she wore heavy make-up, especially bright red lipstick and let her hair cascade around her face. Now, her face looked pale and wan. She'd tied her hair back scruffily against her head.

'This is nothing to do with you, Jessica,' Lidgate said. 'Why don't you go out for a while? We'll be finished here shortly.'

She yelled back, 'Are you kidding me? Let those girls go.'

Flood shouted, 'Jessica, don't put yourself and your baby in danger. I can handle this.'

Nodding towards his hands tied behind the chair, she yelled back, 'Oh, yeah. I don't think so. Bloody place has been worked over. I thought I'd been burgled. Didn't think I'd see my son torturing a kid!'

She turned on her heel, smacking the baseball club against the door with all the force she could muster. It rocked on its hinges. Vinnie made a move to follow her, whether to reason with her or harm her, Flood couldn't decide.

'Stay where you are, Vinnie. Close the door,' barked Lidgate. 'She knows what's best for her.' He turned to Flood. 'Now, where were we? You were about to tell me the whereabouts of the tapes.'

'I've told you. McBride's got them. Please let my girls go.'

'Only if you tell me the truth.'

Before Flood could reply, a tearful Jessica stood in the entrance, a .22 pistol in her hand. She pointed it at Lidgate. Her shrill, intense voice echoed in the hard surroundings.

'You bastard! You tortured Robbie. Then you killed him. You knew he meant everything to me. He was me only chance of getting away from the *shit* life with your *shit* family.'

Lidgate spoke quietly but with menace. 'Barlow was the filth. Lowest of the low. He deserved everything he got. You should have told me about him being an undercover cop. Now, put the gun down, Jessica. I'm sure we can sort this out.'

'Yeah, c'mon, Mum. This is business,' Vinnie said.

Lidgate cut him off. 'Leave this to me, Vinnie.'

Jessica wailed, 'I regret the day I married into this family. I'm sick of it all. Sick of crime. Sick of looking over me shoulder. Most of all, I'm sick of you two.' Her eyes blazed with hatred as she continued to point her gun at Lidgate. Flood watched on helplessly as her father-in-law reached inside his right-hand jacket pocket.

CHAPTER TWENTY-FIVE

Saturday 17ᵗʰ March 2001

Jessica's gun exploded twice, the sound reverberating off the basement walls, deafening Flood momentarily. He and Pippa instinctively ducked. Gemma flinched as she lay on the floor. The acrid smell of gun-smoke hung in the air. Lidgate roared with pain as the first bullet shredded his left kneecap. The second tore into his right shoulder.

He screamed, 'You fucking bitch!'

Flood yelled, 'Untie me, Jessica.'

She put her gun down on the bench and began untying the rope. As she did, Flood watched Lidgate slump down on his chair, clutching his knee with his left hand trying to stem the gushing blood. His right arm swung loosely by his side, like a ribbon in the wind. He roared at Vinnie. 'For Christ's sake, do something!'

Vinnie stood like a statue, not sure what to do. Flood looked on in horror as he finally drew a 9mm Beretta from his waistband and pointed it at Jessica. He switched his gaze from her to Lidgate and back again several times as he faced his dilemma; obey his grandfather or appear weak in his eyes. His hesitation gave Flood the opportunity he'd been waiting for.

Once freed, he leaped from his chair and slammed the full force of his body into Vinnie who crashed to the floor, still holding the gun. As Flood tried to wrestle it away from him, he shouted at Jessica, 'Get the girls out of here!'

She quickly unwound the vice. Pippa, sobbing profusely, withdrew her hand and hugged it close to her chest with her other hand. Flood, still grappling with Vinnie, shouted, 'Run upstairs out of the way, Pippa.'

She didn't need telling twice. She rushed up the steps from the basement, still crying. Jessica dragged Gemma to her feet, pushed her up the basement steps and followed her out of the door.

Vinnie, using his wiry frame to good effect, managed to slip out of Flood's grasp, still holding his gun. He dashed up the basement steps and turned in the doorway to face Flood, pointed the gun directly at him and fired. Flood heard the bullet whooshing past his head, missing by an inch at most.

Lidgate yelled out in pain again. Flood thought he'd been hit. He glanced at him and watched him trying to move his right hand to the pocket holding his gun. His busted shoulder prevented any movement.

Flood reached the top of the steps in time to see Vinnie disappearing through the back door. By the time he reached it, he saw him undo the bolt on the garden gate, dart through, and turn left onto the Regent's Canal towpath. The twenty residential narrow boats moored on the canal were mostly in darkness. Dickensian streetlights every fifty yards cast a pallid, creamy yellow glow onto the deserted path.

Flood chased Vinnie who constantly looked over his shoulder. As his lead reduced from forty yards to twenty, Vinnie stopped running. He turned to face Flood, took aim with his gun and fired. Flood heard the bullet fizz past, close to his left ear this time.

Four years of rage at the injustice of Georgina's murder welled up inside Flood. He reeled in the final yards as Vinnie flagged. Flood got close enough to hear him struggling for breath.

He timed his rugby tackle to perfection. Vinnie's knees crunched against the unforgiving tarmac. Flood stayed on top of him, ensuring a soft landing for himself.

He'd hit Vinnie so hard, the momentum resulted in them splashing into the oily darkness of the canal in a twenty-yard gap between two narrow boats. The freezing water took Flood's breath away. Vinnie thrashed his arms and legs in the murky water in an effort to shake off Flood who seriously considered pressing Vinnie's head under the water, holding it there until he drowned. He rejected the idea, preferring to see Vinnie banged up for twenty or thirty years in a prison where his crimes against two young girls would draw unwelcome attention.

Vinnie grappled with Flood like a dervish, finally getting on top of him and forcing his head under the water. Flood held his breath and with an almighty effort, pulled his head out of Vinnie's grasp. He summoned up enough strength to crook his arm around his neck. With his other arm, Flood managed a form of backstroke, lifesaving style, and swam towards the bank. When he reached it, he dragged Vinnie onto the towpath.

Pinning him to the ground face down, Flood sat astride him, grabbing one of his arms and forcing it up behind his back until Vinnie screamed in pain.

Four narrow boat residents, three men and a woman, gathered around the soaking men, their breaths adding to the misty, freezing air. They stood silently staring, shocked at what they were witnessing. Flood turned to them. 'Everything's under control now. I'm a police officer,' he lied. 'We may need statements later if you saw or heard anything. Please return to your homes.'

As he spoke, he drew his mobile from his sopping-wet trouser pocket with his free hand and punched in a number with his thumb. Getting no response, he inspected it, shook it and pressed the digits again. Nothing. He turned to the youngest of the bystanders who'd remained, a pony-tailed hippy type wearing only shorts, a T-shirt and canvas shoes despite the chilly evening.

'Do you have a mobile?'

'Sure.'

Flood recited Laura's mobile number. 'Call it now.' When she answered on the first ring, 'Ponytail' held the phone next to Flood's ear who now needed both hands to restrain the fast-recovering Vinnie.

'Laura, where are you?'

'We're at Jessica's house. We couldn't let you go there without backup, you bloody fool. Once we heard gunshots we decided to go in. When we saw what had happened, we called the Armed Response Team, Harvey and two ambulances. They'll be here soon.'

Flood sighed with relief.

'Thanks, Laura. Who's *we*?'

'Me and Martin Cahill. I'll explain later. Jessica told me that you chased after Vinnie. Where are you now?'

'I've got him. We're down on the towpath which runs behind the houses, about two hundred yards from you. Can you come?'

'I'm on my way'

Flood nodded at 'Ponytail'. 'Stay until my colleagues arrive then you can go back to your boat.'

Vinnie had recovered from his near-drowning experience sufficiently enough to shout, 'Get off me, you filth!'

Flood spat out, 'You're lucky I didn't drown you. I still could if you don't behave.'

'Fuck off!' Vinnie shouted. Flood responded by pushing Vinnie's arm even further up behind his back. Three minutes later, Flood heard Laura's footsteps as she sprinted towards them.

'Bit late for a dip isn't it?' Laura said, as she knelt down beside them.

'But look what I caught,' replied Flood, yanking Vinnie's head off the ground by his hair.

Laura handcuffed Vinnie's wrists behind his back and dragged him to his feet. She stood face to face with him.

'Vincent Lidgate, I'm arresting you on suspicion of kidnapping and assault occasioning grievous bodily harm—' Before she could complete the caution, he spat in her face.

Flood grabbed the front of Vinnie's soaking T-shirt with both hands and thrust a knee vigorously into his groin. He yelped in pain as he doubled over.

After Laura had completed the caution, Flood, finding it hard to maintain his self-control, pushed his face close to Vinnie. 'You can add to those charges drug-running, possession and use of a firearm, attempted murder and murder. That should ensure you'll be banged up forever, you sadistic little bastard!'

Vinnie spat at Flood, who, expecting it, moved his head out of the way. Flood repeated his groin treatment. 'You'll have no balls left if you carry on like this,' he snarled, as Vinnie doubled over again.

The trio retraced their steps back up the towpath towards Jessica's house. Flood's shoes squelched as he walked. He held Vinnie close to him, grasping the back of his shirt.

Laura asked, 'Who shot Lidgate?'

'Jessica. She had good reasons to hate him. The feeling was mutual. When Lidgate reached for his gun, she had no choice. She shot him in self-defence.'

Vinnie turned his head to them with difficulty. 'Like fuck, it was!'

'Shut up!' Flood yanked Vinnie's shirt backwards.

'Lidgate's in a bad way,' Laura said. 'He's lost a lot of blood. I applied a tourniquet to his leg, otherwise I didn't think he'd survive.'

'I hope he does. I want to see him go down for a long time.'

'At least your girls' ordeal is over, thank God.'

'Can you believe that these bastards were about to torture Pippa?' He jerked Vinnie's shirt back for the third time, holding it so tightly, it momentarily choked off his air supply. He coughed and spluttered.

They reached the gate, marched through the rear garden and entered the back door of the house. When they arrived in the hallway, Laura barked at Vinnie, 'Lay face down on the floor.'

'Fuck off.'

Laura kicked Vinnie's legs from underneath him, taking him by surprise. He landed heavily on his back, unable to use his handcuffed hands to break his fall. She used her boot to roll him onto his front and stood with it firmly on his neck, pinning him to the floor.

'Any more from you and I'll press my foot down so hard you'll be begging me to stop.'

Leaving Laura in the hallway, Flood, still dripping with water, turned into the living room. He saw Jessica sitting in a chair cradling her baby. His daughters sat opposite, staring at them with a vacant look in their eyes. Pippa's leg was elevated onto a chair. A damp towel lay over her ankle.

He rushed towards the girls. They barely acknowledged

him. Their haunted expressions confirmed Flood's worst fear; they'd been severely traumatised. Despite his damp clothes he sat between them, put his arms around both girls and pulled them close to him.

'What happened to your ankle, Pippa?'

'It really hurts, Daddy. As I ran upstairs, I tripped and fell awkwardly. The lady helped me down and put this wet towel over it.' She nodded in Jessica's direction.

'Let me look at it.' He carefully unwrapped the towel. Pippa's swollen ankle had already turned blue. Flood guessed it was broken. Unwisely, he gently prodded. Pippa flinched.

'Ouch!'

'Sorry, Pippa. The ambulance will be here soon.'

Flood glanced over at Jessica. She rocked her baby gently in her arms, singing nursery rhymes in a barely audible voice. Stillness surrounded her. The contrast between her bursting into the basement and angrily firing two shots from her pistol couldn't have been greater, thought Flood.

'Thanks for helping the girls, Jessica.'

He wondered what had happened to her pistol. Peering around the room, he noticed it on the table. 'Is Lidgate still in the basement?' he asked.

Jessica's stillness evaporated. 'Yeah. One of yours is in there, making sure the bastard can't escape. With his busted leg and shoulder, he ain't going nowhere.'

'I'd better go and look.' Flood gingerly kissed the top of each girl's bald head.

Entering the hallway, he nodded at Laura who maintained her foot on Vinnie's neck.

'You OK?'

Laura replied, 'No problem,' as she pushed her foot a little harder on Vinnie's neck.

Flood opened the door to the basement and saw Martin Cahill sitting in one of the garden chairs with his gun pointed at Lidgate. His gun lay on Cahill's lap.

Lidgate, constantly whimpering with pain, sat on the concrete floor with his back against a wall. The tourniquet Laura had applied to his thigh seemed to have worked. His good arm held a towel over his knee. Laura had also tied in place another towel over the wound to his shoulder.

He groaned, 'For Christ's sake, get the medics here! That bitch has fucked me up.'

Cahill, ignoring him, turned to face Flood. 'Did you get the other bastard?'

'Yes. Laura's got him in the hallway. What are you doing here? You were supposed to let Laura know if the girls had been moved.'

'I know. Sorry I let you down. There's a good reason why I couldn't call you.'

'Tell me about it before the boys in blue arrive.'

CHAPTER TWENTY-SIX

Saturday 17th March 2001

'When the BMW left the lodge this morning, I followed it. I took a chance, not knowing if the girls were inside or not. I kept the car in sight for a good part of the journey. Then a 4x4 shot out of a side road at speed and smashed into me on the driver's side. I don't know whether it was an accident or the gang had spotted me and set me up.'

'Go on.'

'The next thing I know, I'm opening my eyes in St Bart's Hospital. Apparently I'd been badly concussed, knocked out for a good half-hour. When I came round, it took me a couple of hours to recover enough memory to remember what I was supposed be doing. The medics wanted me to stay in overnight for observation but I discharged myself. I tried calling you but you didn't reply, so I called Laura.'

Flood remembered his mobile vibrating in his pocket shortly after Lidgate had arrived at Jessica's house.

'She picked me up from the hospital, told me your girls had been moved to Jessica's house. She said she'd decided to back you up. I told her I wanted to come too. Add some muscle.' He waved his gun in the air.

Cahill turned back to face Lidgate. 'It's a bloody shame Laura called the cops. Be good to give this arsehole some of his own medicine, don't you think?'

Flood realised that if Laura hadn't called the police, Cahill would have probably relished putting Lidgate out of his misery. 'I think Jenny would approve,' he said, staring down at the moaning Lidgate.

Flood heard the blaring of police and ambulance sirens in the distance. He walked into the hallway in his still-wet clothes, stepping over the prone Vinnie.

'The Cavalry's arriving, Laura'. Flood opened the front door. Within seconds, two police cars, two black Mercedes vans and two ambulances, all with flashing blue lights, drew up outside.

The Armed Response Team rushed in, toting their Glock pistols. Once they'd ascertained there was no firearms risk, they waved in the paramedics. Flood directed them to the basement and the living room.

DI Harvey swaggered into the hallway flanked by a male and a female detective. Three male uniformed officers made up the response team. Harvey nodded at Laura who stood with her boot still firmly pressed on Vinnie's neck and shot a brief glance at Flood. He looked back at Laura.

'What have we got here, DS Miles?'

She nodded down at Vinnie. 'This charming git is Vincent Lidgate. I've cautioned him for kidnapping and GBH with more serious charges to follow.' As she spoke, she dragged Vinnie to his feet. He tried to shrug her off.

'Get your fucking hands off me!'

Harvey turned to one of the response team. 'Find him a blanket. Wrap him up, take him to Southwark Station.' The officer frog-marched him to one of the vans.

Vinnie shouted over his shoulder, 'You'll be fucking sorry you did this.'

Harvey asked Laura, 'Who else is here?'

'Tommy Lidgate, leader of The Goshawks gang. He's in the basement.' She nodded towards the door. 'He's been shot in a leg and shoulder. He'll need to go to the hospital. Martin Cahill is in there with him. He has the situation under control.'

Harvey looked puzzled. 'Cahill? He's suspended, isn't he? What's he doing here?'

'We couldn't have sorted this out without him,' Flood fired back.

'Oh, really?' He turned back to Laura and flicked his head in Flood's direction. 'Interesting company you keep. One copper suspended and one too stressed to remain in the Force.' Flood resisted the urge to punch him.

Harvey continued: 'I'm surprised at you, DS Miles. Why didn't you follow the rules? You obviously knew about this little get-together. Why didn't you go by the book? Talk to

Foxy. Talk to me. We could have come up with a tactical approach for getting these girls freed.'

'I have my reasons.'

Harvey shrugged. 'We'll deal with that later. Who else is here?'

'The owner of the house Jessica Lidgate, Tommy Lidgate's daughter-in-law. Vinnie's her son. She's in the living room with Andy Flood's two girls. They're pretty shaken up. One in particular. We think she's broken her ankle.'

Harvey, unmoved, turned to one of his DCs. 'Round up everybody. We'll need statements from all of them. Take them to the station. Keep them separated. I want to know every last detail of what happened here.'

Flood remonstrated, 'What about my girls? They've been through hell. They need urgent medical treatment.'

'I'll speak to the paramedics.'

Laure interjected, 'There's one other person in the house.'

'Who?'

'A baby boy. He's with his mother Jessica.'

Flood cut in. 'Her sister lives nearby. I'm sure she'll look after him while you interview Jessica. There's something else you should know. Vinnie Lidgate fired his gun at me. Twice. The second time we ended up in the canal, as you can see.' Flood gestured towards his wet clothes. 'He had the gun in his hand as we hit the water. It'll be at the bottom of the canal. You'll need to get divers to retrieve it.'

Harvey responded, thick with sarcasm. 'Thanks for the advice. Sounds like you could have got yourself killed. You shouldn't get involved in *police* matters.'

He turned to one of his uniformed officers who'd been covering the front door. 'Go with Mr Flood. He'll point you in the direction of a firearm relevant to this investigation. Take PC Davies with you to secure the area. We'll get the divers here as soon as possible.'

He turned back to Flood. 'As soon as you come back, I'll have you driven to Southwark Police Station. You can make your statement there.'

'I'm not going anywhere without a change of clothes.'

Laura butted in. 'I assume Barlow's clothes are upstairs. I'm sure Jessica won't mind if you borrow them. I'll tell her.' She headed for the living room.

Harvey brushed past Flood and stepped into the doorway of the basement. Flood heard him exchange words with one of the paramedics working on getting Lidgate comfortable enough to transfer him to A&E. An officer had relieved Cahill and another had taken him out to one of the police cars.

Flood went to the living room and put his arms around Pippa as they silently watched a paramedic inspecting her ankle. Laura followed Flood into the room and put her arm around Gemma whose body had begun to tremble.

Harvey joined them. He asked the paramedic, 'What's the situation?'

'Looks like a nasty fracture. We'll have to take her to Whittington Hospital, get the ankle X-rayed. That's not my main worry, though. Clearly both girls are traumatised. They'll need to be assessed at the hospital. We'll be leaving in a few minutes.'

Flood said, 'After I've shown you the location of Vinnie's gun, I'm going with them. They need me. I have to know that they're going to be alright.'

The firmness of Flood's resolve led Harvey to mutter, 'OK. Make sure you come to the station immediately after the hospital visit. I don't care what time it is.' Harvey left the room to check on securing the crime scene.

Pippa glanced up at her father. She offered up a faint smile. Gemma's face remained expressionless. The paramedic threw a blanket over her shoulders.

A SOCO and a photographer who'd just arrived, entered the room. They ignored everybody and walked directly to the table and Jessica's gun. The photographer took two photos of it in situ. The SOCO picked it up with a gloved hand and carefully placed it in a plastic evidence bag and wrote a note on it. They left the room without a word. Flood assumed Harvey had seen the gun and told the officer to collect it.

The female detective entered. She approached Jessica who cuddled her baby so tightly, Flood thought she'd suffocate him.

'You'll need to come to Southwark Police Station for an interview, Jessica. I understand your sister lives nearby. It's best if she looks after your baby. I'll call her. What's the number?' Jessica remained silent, staring down at her baby.

The detective urged, 'Jessica, this is important. You have to come to the station.' Jessica slowly drew her eyes away from her baby and looked at Flood and Laura, defiantly at first. Getting no response, her expression changed, not sure what she should do.

Flood said, 'I think it's best to get this mess sorted out. You've been through a lot, Jessica. Give the detective what she needs.' She hesitated for moment before muttering the number.

Flood changed into Robbie Barlow's clothes which fitted reasonably well. He led the two PCs, one carrying a large torch, to the spot where he and Vinnie had crashed into the canal. One of them marked out an area of the bank with crime tape, then stayed to guard it.

By the time the other officer and Flood had returned to the house, everyone had left except for the SOCOs conducting a forensic search of the premises and the photographer who snapped away repeatedly. A PC guarded the front entrance.

*

One of the other PCs drove Flood the three miles to the brightly-lit, yellow brick and glass Whittington Hospital on Highgate Hill in silence. Flood's emotions fluctuated between elation and concern; elation that the girls were safe but concern about the long-term effects on their mental state.

The smell of antiseptic and cleaning fluid filled his nostrils as he entered the A&E waiting room. He immediately thought of his mother's predicament and realised that if he hadn't been in this hospital he'd be at Southampton General. He decided it was too late to ring Julie. He'd call first thing in the morning.

Sitting closest to the door, Flood was surprised to see Gemma curled up in a fitful sleep, half on, half off Laura's lap.

Laura's arm rested on top of her in a protective gesture. The sight of Gemma's bald head brought home to Flood what she'd been through.

Flood sat next to them. 'How are they?' he whispered. 'I got here as soon as I could.'

Laura looked up. 'Pippa's upset. She didn't want to be separated from Gemma. She wouldn't let go of her hand when we came in.'

'Where is she?'

'She's having her ankle X-rayed.'

'I could kill those bastards! Why are you here, Laura? Shouldn't you be at the station?'

'I told Harvey. You can't just dump the girls at the hospital. He wanted to send a Family Liaison Officer. I told him I've acted as a FLO many times. I said they needed to be with someone who knew what they'd been through. At least until you arrive. Even Harvey could see how distressed they were.' As she spoke, she stroked Gemma's back.

Flood ran his hand over Gemma's smooth head. 'Thanks, Laura. I'm so glad you changed your mind about getting involved.'

'I still think you're bloody insane. But I thought about what you've been through. It brought back memories of what happened to my daughter. I wish I'd done more to prevent it. I thought I'd dealt with it, put it behind me. Obviously I haven't.' She looked away. Flood suspected her eyes had welled up.

He put an arm around her shoulder and hugged her. 'Are you alright?' Laura brushed her eyes with the back of her hand. She turned back to face him.

'Yes, I'm fine. Did you speak to Cahill?'

'Yes. He told me what happened.'

'Did he tell you that he called me from the hospital?'

'Yes, he did.'

'He said that although he felt groggy, he still wanted to help get Jenny's killers. I thought he'd be useful as backup so I picked him up.'

'What made you decide to follow me?'

'After you'd left for Jessica's house, I realised Lidgate and Vinnie were entirely capable of killing your girls if they found themselves surrounded by the Met. I just couldn't let you go there on your own.'

'You'll have some explaining to do. Foxy'll say you should have reported the incident, let *him* decide the level of response. He's bound to get Professional Standards involved.'

'Don't worry about me. It's your poor Pippa and Gemma you should be concerned about. They've been through so much.' She stroked Gemma's back again.

An earnest young man wearing a white coat approached them and addressed Flood. 'I'm Doctor Smythe. I'm glad you're here. DS Miles has explained what happened to your girls. Quite appalling. The ankle is broken, I'm afraid. We'll need to operate. We've arranged to do it tomorrow when the swelling's gone down. We've given her something to kill the pain.'

'Thanks, Doctor.'

'Frankly, we're more interested in both your daughters' psychological state. Understandably, they're confused and disorientated. We've taken advice from the paediatric mental health team. They recommend that they both stay here tonight. Fortunately, we have beds available. After they've had some rest we'll assess them tomorrow when we have a consultant child psychologist here.'

'You think that's best?'

'That's what the mental health team have advised.' Flood desperately wanted to take the girls home, fuss over them and tell them how much he loved them.

'Can I stay here with them?'

'Of course. We've got a fold-up bed you can use but frankly, there's not a lot you can do for them. They'll both be given something to help them sleep. They're in good hands, believe me.'

'Can I see Pippa?'

'Of course. She's in the paediatric ward up on the fourth floor. We'll take Gemma up there now. You can help settle them in.'

Flood gently shook Gemma. 'C'mon, Gem, time for bed.'

She sat up and looked around the waiting room, wide-eyed. Flood and Laura helped her to her feet. Laura stayed in the waiting room as Flood, the doctor and Gemma took the lift.

Flood put his arms around Gemma. 'You're safe now. It's all over.' He kissed the top of her head. She remained distant and silent.

Pippa lay asleep in a bed in a cubicle at the far corner of the ward. A nurse approached. 'Here's your bed, Gemma. Right next to your sister. We'll be looking after you tonight. I've left a gown on the bed for you. I'll bring you a glass of water. OK?' Gemma didn't reply.

The nurse pulled the curtains around them. After she left, Flood helped Gemma change out of her clothes and get into bed. The nurse returned with the water and some pills.

'Here, take these. They'll help you sleep.'

Flood stayed for another half-hour, by which time Gemma was dozing fitfully. He kissed both girls' heads as he always did at night and made his way back to the waiting room to meet Laura. She drove Flood to Southwark Police Station to make their statements. As they got closer, Flood turned to Laura.

'Do you think the girls will ever get over this? You know, mentally?'

'I don't honestly know what goes through their minds after they experience such a dreadful situation. They'll obviously need a lot of help to get over it.'

'Do you think it's my fault that they've ended up like this?'

'I don't think any of us believed how ruthless Lidgate could be. When you went there to rescue them on your own, I was so angry with you. You took a huge risk. You and the girls could have been killed. Then I realised that there was no guarantee the Met could get your girls out alive either. At least we did.'

'Yes, we did, didn't we?' Flood wanted to add, *but at what cost?*

As Laura stopped the car at traffic lights, he said, 'Jessica shouldn't go down for shooting Lidgate. She had every right to feel aggrieved. He screwed up her son and murdered the father of her child. When he reached for his gun, she acted in self-defence. That's what I'll say in my statement. Thank God Jessica came back to the house when she did.'

CHAPTER TWENTY-SEVEN

Sunday 18th March 2001

Harvey's team took Flood and Laura to separate rooms to be interviewed and to make their statements through the early hours of the morning.

Flood left the police station at 9.30 am. He ambled, zombie-like, over London Bridge, gulping in breaths of air freshened by a breeze wafting across the River Thames. His head thumped due to lack of sleep and having to concentrate on accurately explaining the nightmarish events of the previous evening. He lost count of the number of black coffees he'd consumed.

He tried using his mobile again. Its soggy trip into the murky water of Regent's Canal still rendered it useless. Before catching the tube to Islington to collect his car, he found a payphone close by Southwark tube station.

His first call was to Whittington Hospital. A pleasant-sounding nurse told him that both girls had a good night and that Pippa's surgery would take place around mid-morning. She told him someone from the mental health team would be carrying out psychological assessments over the next two days.

'Can I come and see them?'

'Of course. But we're preparing Pippa for surgery and Gemma's still disorientated. Why don't you visit them this afternoon after the operation?' Flood reluctantly agreed.

Next, he called Julie who sounded slightly less stressed than before. 'Mum's out of Intensive Care, thank God. They want to keep her in for a day or two. What's the latest news on the girls?'

Flood briefly explained the events of the previous night, adding, 'I'm seeing the girls this afternoon. Tell Mum I'll try and come down to see her this evening. I'll explain more then.'

Julie's tone softened. 'Good. She's so worried about them.'

*

When Flood arrived home, he climbed the stairs and lay down fully-clothed on his bed. He woke at 2.30 pm and immediately called Whittington Hospital again. A different nurse checked the girls' notes and told him the operation had gone well and that Pippa was comfortable. Flood asked to speak to the consultant child psychiatrist. A confident voice attempted to put his mind at rest.

'We need more time to assess them both. What they've been through is quite shocking. We'll keep them in for observation for another night. It's important for them to be together at this stage. It might add to their trauma if they go home too early. I'm sure we'll have a better idea of a prognosis tomorrow.'

Flood immediately showered, got dressed and arrived at the hospital just after 4.00 pm.

He packed a holdall with some of the girls' clothes, pyjamas and toothbrushes. He added a box of craft materials for Gemma and a handful of books by Roald Dahl which Pippa loved. On the way, he purchased a giant bar of Galaxy and a box of Maltesers, their favourite chocolates.

When Flood arrived, the girls greeted him with tepid smiles, so different from their usual welcome. Pippa lay on top of her bed with her plastered leg elevated on a soft pillow. She sat quietly gazing at it. Gemma lay on her bed staring at the ceiling. He tried to raise their spirits by waving the chocolates at them. This usually brought whoops of joy. Not this time.

'Hasn't anyone written on your plaster yet, Pippa? I expect all your friends at school will want to write something.'

She looked tearful as she said, 'How can we go to school like this?' She raised her eyes upwards, referring to her bald head.

Flood didn't know what to say. Instead, he turned to Gemma. 'Do you want to write something?'

She shook her head. 'I don't want to.'

'That's alright.' He turned back to Pippa. 'I expect one of your friends is bound to write something like, *enjoy your break!*' She looked at him blankly.

Neither of the girls initiated a conversation. During one period of silence, Flood said, 'Look girls, I know that you've both been through a lot. A doctor will want to talk to you tomorrow about what happened. You must tell him everything. Don't leave anything out. It will help you. Do you understand?' They both nodded.

The afternoon carried on in much the same way. Flood realised that a light had gone out inside their heads. He hoped that they were still in shock and prayed that it was temporary.

After the girls had picked at their tea, watercress sandwiches and a slice of Victoria sponge, Flood kissed them goodbye and, with a heavy heart, made the two-hour journey to Southampton General Hospital. He followed the signs to the High Dependency Unit where he found Julie sitting beside their mother's bed, holding her hand.

To his immense relief, Flood's mother looked better than the last time he'd seen her. She and Julie were desperate to hear about the girls. He spared them most of the gory details but some, he couldn't hide. Like Pippa's broken ankle and their bald heads. He played down his fears about their psychological state.

His mother cried at first but recovered well enough to say, 'Oh well, at least their hair will grow back again. And young bones heal quickly, don't they?'

As he left, Flood asked the Ward Sister about his mother's prognosis. 'She's doing well. If her recovery continues at this rate, she'll be able to return home in the next few days.'

Greatly relieved, Flood drove back to London, his mind constantly turning over the potential long-term effects of the girls' experience. He wondered too, how the investigation was progressing. He called Laura for an update from his car.

'Given the number of serious offences, Harvey's applied to the magistrates to give him more time to question Lidgate, Vinnie and McBride. They'll need it. There are Barlow's tapes and pocketbooks to go through for starters. There's also the corruption issue. Swanson's been temporarily suspended. The Met are searching his place as we speak. Lidgate's under police guard in St Thomas's Hospital.'

'And Jessica?'

'Still being interviewed at the station. She's a suspect *and* a witness so it'll be interesting to see what Harvey does. I heard he's considering charging her with GBH and possession of a firearm with intent to endanger life. He's also looking at a deal if she'll testify against the gang. It's complicated by her relationship with her son and Barlow. We'll have to wait and see.'

'Harvey's *got* to do a deal with her. Offer her a Witness Protection Programme at least. Her evidence is crucial.'

'There's no telling with him.'

'What about Cahill?'

'He's made his witness statement and left. He's going to be interviewed by Professional Standards for helping us.'

'And what about you, Laura? Have the Met said what they're going to do?'

'I'm suspended. They're holding a misconduct hearing in the next few weeks.'

'I'm so sorry, Laura. I feel responsible.'

'Don't be. I'm looking forward to spending more time with my granddaughter. Ruby's growing up so quickly. How are Pippa and Gemma?'

Flood explained the situation.

'I do hope they'll be alright. Give them my love.'

*

Two days later, Laura rang Flood at home. 'Sorry I didn't call before. I thought you'd need time with your family. Anyway, I'm sure you'd like to know who's been charged with what. The custody sergeant's a friend. He told me.'

'And?'

'You'll be pleased to know that Lidgate, Vinnie and McBride have all been charged with Georgina's murder.'

Flood puffed out his cheeks and flopped on a chair. 'Good.

Let's hope they can make it stick.'

'Their charge sheets run to two pages: three murders, kidnapping, drug-running and GBH. Vinnie's also been charged with attempted murder. Good news, eh?'

'Fantastic!'

'I've saved the best bit untill last. McBride's turned Queen's Evidence. He's prepared to tell all. Apparently, he resented Vinnie being Lidgate's favourite. Oh, and Jessica's agreed to be a key witness against The Goshawks. It'll be difficult for her to testify against her son.'

'She lost him years ago. Is she being charged?'

'No. Harvey sounded out the CPS. They've accepted that she fired in self-defence at Tommy Lidgate. She'll be offered witness protection if she agrees not to sue the Met for being used by Barlow to infiltrate The Goshawks gang.'

'Thank God someone's talking sense. They're obviously shit-scared of the public's reaction. What about Barlow's handler Swanson?'

'They've finalised the search of his flat and he's been interviewed. I heard that the Met have accepted that he passed on all Barlow's reports to his superior officers. He's been reinstated.'

'Perhaps Barlow was paranoid about him after all.'

'I also heard that the CPS strategy is to get a successful result on these charges rather than extend them to all the other stuff the gang have done. The hope is that once Lidgate's banged up, other witnesses will feel less intimidated and come forward.'

'I can't wait to see those evil bastards in the dock.'

'Me too. How are things at home?'

'As good as can be expected. Mum's out of hospital, staying at Julie's – she can't bear the thought of living here anymore. The girls are back at home, still in shock. They've been assessed and will be having counselling. The psychiatrist warned me not to expect too much too soon. She said they'll never completely get over the incident. There's no magic tablet. It'll be a long time before they'll be back to anything approaching normal.'

'I'm so sorry to hear that.'

'I Just hope that Mum and the girls won't have to attend the trial. It would set them back months.'

*

In the following weeks, Flood thought long and hard about what he should do with his family. He knew they couldn't continue living in the same house. It held too many raw memories. His mother insisted that she'd never feel safe there. Julie agreed that their Mum could live with her for as long as she wanted.

The girls didn't want to stay either. Every time the doorbell rang, they refused to answer it. They flinched every time they heard a sound outside the house that they didn't recognise.

Flood decided to sell his houses in London and Southampton. The latter also held bad memories; it's where they lived when Vinnie killed Georgina. He came up with the ideal solution; move to Winchester.

He explained his plan to the girls and his mother. 'It's a fresh start. New house, new school and we'd be close to Auntie Julie.' For the first time since the incident, he sensed a frisson of excitement from them.

Flood was pleased with the valuations of his houses, especially the one in London. It meant he could sell both homes, buy one in Winchester and not work for a year, at least; time he knew he'll need to devote to mending his broken family. He vowed that from now on, he'd put his family first.

He explained his plan to Laura. 'What a brilliant idea!' she said. 'That's got to be the best move for your family.'

'There is a downside. I won't be able to see so much of you.'

'I know, but what you're doing is good for the girls.'

'What happened at your misconduct hearing?'

'I'm back in uniform. Foxy's found me an admin job. He warned me; if I stepped out of line again, I'd be finished at the Met.'

'You don't deserve that, Laura.'

'There is one advantage. I'll be able to have most weekends off. We can see each other then. That's OK isn't it?'

'Better than OK. I'd like nothing better. The girls think the world of you. They'd love to see you.'

*

Four weeks later, Laura called Flood to tell him that following the charges, the Plea and Case Management hearing was taking place the following day.

'I'm sure you'd like to know the outcome. Harvey will talk to the CPS after the hearing and get the lowdown. He's bound to let his team know what happened. DC Tyler will tell me everything. I used to mentor him.'

*

She called Flood the following evening. 'First, the good news. McBride's pleaded guilty to all charges, leaving him free to spill the beans. Lidgate and Vinnie pleaded not guilty to everything, despite the evidence and testimonies lined up against them.'

'So McBride's officially a supergrass? His testimony could prove decisive.'

'Don't get too excited. There's a problem.'

'Which is?'

'Tommy and Vinnie's defence teams put up a robust argument to have Robbie Barlow's tapes excluded. They said they needed more clarity about the authorisation given to Barlow to carry out covert surveillance. These days, the Commissioner has to approve it. They don't give it easily, given some of the cock-ups in the past. The judge has to consider upholding the poor criminal's human rights these days. The prosecution couldn't provide the court with sufficient proof that Barlow had operated within the law.'

'Bloody Hell! If the judge doesn't admit Barlow's evidence, we're stuffed. Who is the judge?'

'The Honourable Mr Justice Brennan from the High Court.'

Flood wrote down his name.

'Who's acting for the Lidgates?'

'Samantha Cornelius, QC for Tommy, and Roger Whitney, QC for Vinnie.' Flood added their names to his note.

Laura continued: 'The judge adjourned the hearing for a week. He'll make a ruling then. His decision may well force the CPS to reconsider the charges.'

'I can't believe it! That's all we need.' He yelled down the phone, 'What have we got to do to get justice in this bloody country?'

As soon as Flood put down the phone, he googled the judge and discovered that Michael Brennan had studied criminology at Oxford. He was called to the bar, becoming a QC in 1986 and appointed to the High Court ten years later, aged forty-six. Despite his youth, he'd already presided over high profile murder cases. He'd also become an advocate of improving the efficiency of court procedures. Flood hoped he hadn't lost his touch.

Next, he googled the barristers. They'd both had over twenty years' experience at the bar. Samantha Cornelius, in particular, had gained a reputation for winning appeals against the conviction of eminent criminals. Flood realised that this would be a battle between super-heavyweights. His mind rocked with the possibility of Lidgate and Vinnie getting off all or some of the charges.

CHAPTER TWENTY-EIGHT

Spring/Summer 2001

Flood busied himself by starting the process of selling his houses and searching for a new one. He involved the girls as much as possible, asking their opinions about the houses they viewed, discussing the colours of their bedrooms and the rooms they liked best. He hoped that by including them in the process, it might aid their recovery. They were still far from their bubbly best.

*

Laura called Flood immediately the reconvened Plea and Case Management hearing had concluded. 'DC Tyler's briefed me about the judge's ruling on the admission of Barlow's tapes. Apparently, the Commissioner first gave the authorisation for Barlow's surveillance two years ago. The prosecution provided proof that it had been renewed every month, as required. Unfortunately, there's some disagreement about the wording of the authorisation. The prosecution argued that it covered *everything* to do with working undercover in The Goshawks gang. The defence argued that it should have been more precise, that the authorisation should have been specifically issued for each trip to Marseilles when Barlow set up the tape recordings.'

'Christ, you'd assume the bloody Commissioner would get that right. Can the tapes be admitted in court or not?'

'He'll admit them provided they can be authenticated as being originals.'

'Thank God.'

'There's more good news. The judge ruled that neither your mother nor the girls need attend the trial in person to give their evidence. The prosecution will rely on their statements being read out in court. The judge also agreed that if additional

218

information or clarification is required, they'd be cross-examined via video link to the courtroom.'

Flood breathed a huge sigh of relief. 'Good. It was bad enough when they had to make their statements a couple of days after their ordeal. I wouldn't want them to go through all that again. It would put their recovery back weeks. Did the judge give a date for the trial?'

'Yes. It's at the Old Bailey, Monday 17th September. He's allowed eight weeks.'

Flood pursed his lips. 'Sounds about right. Do you know what's happened to Jessica?'

'Harvey's agreed a deal with her. She's somewhere safe with her baby in the Witness Protection Programme.'

'That's probably best for her. She'll hate it, though. She won't be allowed to get in touch with her friends or family and even the Met can't guarantee her safety. Just hope she hasn't relapsed, become a user again. We need her testimony.'

'It must be so hard for her to see what Vinnie had become.'

'She'd disowned him years ago. You can see why she hated Lidgate. Have you heard from Cahill?'

'No. I'll be seeing him soon, though. I've been called as a witness at the inquest into Katie Brunswick's death. It's next Wednesday at Chelmsford Coroner's Court. I can't believe it's nearly five months since she died.'

'Coroner's inquests take forever. Think I'll come along, too. Should be interesting. How are you getting on working in uniform?'

'Admin is definitely not my thing. It's doing my head in. I'm seriously thinking about quitting.'

'I can't say I'm surprised, Laura. The Met isn't what it used to be.'

*

The following Wednesday, Flood left early for the three-hour drive from Winchester to Chelmsford. The inquest was due to start at 9.30 am. As he drove in bright sunshine, he thought about Katie, recalling her frost-covered body lying face down and handcuffed to a large branch of a fallen tree in Epping Forest.

A dozen people were already seated inside the courtroom by the time Flood arrived. There were separate areas for general and police witnesses, family members, media and members of the public. Laura was already seated with the other police witness, DI Fuller. As Flood took a seat in the public area, he nodded an acknowledgement to them.

Martin Cahill's bulky frame sat in the general witness area. He looked suitably morose. Noticing Flood, he caught his eye and nodded too, adding a faint smile.

A grey-haired, well-dressed corpulent man sat in the family section. Flood assumed it was Katie's father, the Conservative MP, Michael Brunswick.

Spot on time, the coroner, Keith Rogers, entered. Like most young barristers Flood knew, Rogers carried himself well, acted in a confident manner without being overbearing. He wore nerdy, over-size glasses with thick black frames.

After welcoming everyone, he said, 'I thought I would explain to those of you who are not familiar with a Coroner's Court why we are here. It is to ascertain how the deceased, Katie Brunswick, came by her death. We are not here to decide who is to blame. We will deal only in the facts. I have called together witnesses who have made statements. I will question them. There will be an opportunity for family witnesses, if they wish, to also ask questions.

'The proceedings are informal. We don't wear wigs or gowns. The only formality is that I ask witnesses to swear an oath to speak the truth.'

He called Katie's father first. He tearfully, took the stand and confirmed that his daughter had a borderline personality disorder resulting in unstable and erratic behaviour.

'She never seemed to be able to hold down a relationship for long. She possessed a fierce, jealous streak. She'd love someone one minute and hate them the next. She was often depressed about that.' He gave more examples to support her condition.

The coroner called DI Fuller and asked him to explain the

circumstances surrounding the discovery of Katie's body. Fuller described, in detail, the search in Epping Forest.

He added, 'Following an extensive search, an empty bottle of *Grey Goose* vodka was found in the forest and four packets of *Paracetamol* tablets, three of them empty, were found in her car.' A spark shot across Flood's mind. Something wasn't right. He scribbled a note in his pocketbook.

The coroner asked Fuller about the handcuffs. 'They were locked around the branch of a large fallen tree. No keys were found. The handcuffs were issued to a police officer, Martin Cahill, who was subsequently questioned about them under caution. No charges were made.'

The coroner then called Laura who told the court about the interviews with Cahill and confirmed the numerous texts sent by Katie to Cahill's mobile phone threatening to commit suicide.

The pathologist followed Laura into the witness stand. He confirmed that Katie had consumed a large amount of alcohol and *Paracetamol* tablets before she died. He reiterated his findings regarding the date and timing of her death. He said that that he'd also considered other possible causes of death, including hyperthermia but concluded that she died as a result of liver failure following a drugs overdose.

Finally, the coroner called Martin Cahill who explained to the court everything he'd told Flood and Laura in their interviews. How he'd had a tempestuous, sexual affair. How he'd reasoned with her about the break-up of the relationship. How, after three hours, he thought she'd accepted it. And how she'd given him a hug before he'd driven off leaving her in her car.

He broke down several times. The coroner said, 'Take your time, Mr Cahill. We understand how you must be feeling.'

After all the witnesses had been heard and questioned, the coroner asked whether Katie's father wanted to ask any questions. He shook his head. The coroner adjourned the hearing, saying that he'd deliver his verdict after lunch when they returned at 2.00 pm.

Flood, Laura and Fuller found a pub a few doors down

from the court. They chatted over beers and sandwiches before returning.

The coroner entered precisely at 2.00 pm, clearly a stickler for good timekeeping. He read from a prepared statement. 'The evidence overwhelmingly points to a young woman with a mental health issue. Her medical records, the threats to commit suicide made on Mr Cahill's mobile phone, her father's personal knowledge of her behaviour, all support a verdict of suicide whilst the balance of her mind was disturbed.

'I am confident that Katie used Martin Cahill's handcuffs to frame him after he'd rejected her. Such was her state of mind at the time. She was clearly a very troubled person.'

Flood watched Cahill carefully as the verdict was announced. He looked down, stared at the floor then to the ceiling as if to say, *thank God this is over.*

The coroner thanked the witnesses and closed the hearing. Everybody left the court room in a sober, dignified manner.

As soon as they got outside, Laura turned to Flood. 'I don't think we believed it would be any other verdict, did we?'

'No. But something Fuller said is bugging me. It's to do with the vodka bottle found at the scene. I need to think about it.'

'OK, Andy. See you soon.' They hugged each other and got into their cars for their respective drives home.

On the way, Flood revisited in his mind everything regarding the investigation of Katie's death. Then he remembered taking photos of a drawer in the Cahill's bedroom but couldn't remember where the camera was. He realised he hadn't used it since his resignation.

As he got closer to home, he eventually recalled dumping it in a box containing chargers, cables and miscellaneous electrical items and stored them in the garage with several other boxes. Flood hated throwing things away on the basis that they'd be useful one day. Georgina had often chided him about it.

Now he had an idea where the camera was, he couldn't wait to get home. He pushed the accelerator pedal harder to the floor every time he had the opportunity to speed. As soon as he arrived on his driveway and before entering his house, he raised the garage door and entered. He searched through a pile of boxes, pulling them out until he found one marked, 'electrical items'.

He scrabbled inside until he found the camera lying underneath a jumble of cables. He yanked out the charger and the camera, took them to the house and plugged them into a socket in the kitchen.

He left them on charge for half-an-hour before turning on the camera. Flood's heart rate thumped up a notch as it sprung into life. He thumbed through to the gallery, stopping at the photo he wanted to see. Amongst Cahill's freshly-ironed shirts lay a three-quarter empty bottle of *Grey Goose* vodka next to three silver foil blister packs with the words, *500mg Paracetamol* printed across them. An empty plastic box of *tictacs* lay next to the packs.

Flood stared at the photo for a full minute, questioning why he hadn't made the connection before. The Senior Investigating Officer, DI Fuller, hadn't mentioned finding an empty bottle of vodka at the crime scene when Flood visited it with Laura. It must have been discovered later after a more extensive search. By then, Flood had resigned from the Force.

Early the next morning, he walked to Boots in Winchester High Street, as they were opening. He purchased two packets of *Paracetamol* each containing sixteen tablets, the maximum you were allowed to buy from a pharmacy in one trip.

Striding down to Lloyds Pharmacy, he repeated the purchase. On the following day, with mounting excitement, he went to a different till in each pharmacy and bought the same quantity. Now he had enough to prove his point.

He popped into a sweet shop and bought a box of *tictacs* before hurrying home, anxious to try out his experiment.

When he finished, he called Laura and explained his theory. 'I'm pretty sure I know what happened to Katie and Cahill in Epping Forest. I need you to check out a few things without going through the usual channels. Can you do that?'

'Sure. May take me a couple of days. I'll call you then.'

Forty-eight hours later, she called back.

'I've checked out everything you asked. You were spot on.'

*

'Hi, Martin.' Flood and Laura stood under the porch at Cahill's house in Lewisham the following morning.

Cahill smiled. 'This is a surprise. Come in. Tea, coffee, something stronger?'

Flood held up a hand. 'No, we're fine thanks.'

Cahill invited them to sit at the same glass table they'd sat around on their last visit.

Flood continued: 'We wanted to talk to you about the outcome of the coroner's inquest. It must have been hard for you.'

'Very hard. I'm glad it's over.'

'I'll come straight to the point, Martin. We know exactly what happened when you met Katie in Epping Forest for the last time.'

Cahill smiled. 'Do you?'

'Yes we do. In our interviews you told us that you realised you'd made a mistake and wanted to end your affair with Katie. You said that you realised how much you loved Jenny and that you wanted to be with her. You had one problem.'

'Which was?'

'Katie Brunswick. She stood in your way. She would have made your life hell, ruined your reputation and scuppered the fresh start you said you wanted with Jenny. You told us Katie would have no qualms about carrying out her threat to send the sex tapes to Jenny and to your mother. So you *had* to prevent her from doing so.'

Cahill smirked. 'Carry on. This is interesting.'

'It must have been galling for you. You dealt with Katie only to discover that someone had murdered your wife on the same day.'

'What do you mean, "dealt with"? You know full-well the Met carried out a thorough investigation. It took forever. I spent hours with them. They couldn't find anything to charge me with. And the coroner's confirmed that Katie committed suicide.'

Flood felt in his coat pocket and retrieved a pack of *Paracetamol* tablets.

'Recognise these?'

'Should I?'

Flood took out a blister pack holding eight tablets and handed it to Cahill. 'Here. Open one.'

Cahill glanced at Laura who returned a fixed, unsmiling stare. 'What are you getting at, Flood? I don't want to play your stupid games.' Cahill threw the blister pack back in Flood's direction.

'Why not? You know what's in the pack don't you?'

'I've no idea what you're talking about.'

Flood picked up the pack. 'I'll open it, shall I?' Flood expertly popped out one of the tablets with his thumb. He placed the tablet in his mouth. After a few seconds, he said, 'Oh, this isn't a *Paracetamol*. No. I'd say it's a *tictac*.'

'What are you saying?'

'I'm saying that you lied to us about your last meeting with Katie. Everyone knew that she was vulnerable, unstable and often threatened to kill herself. We believe that at an earlier meeting, you'd convinced her to enter into a suicide pact with you. That's why you met at Epping Forest on that fateful morning. You encouraged or assisted a suicide contrary to Section Two of the Suicide Act 1961. That carries a maximum sentence of fourteen years. If the CPS is convinced that you handcuffed Katie so that she couldn't escape, it's possible you could be charged with murder.'

Cahill spat out, 'I've never heard anything so stupid.'

'Let's see, shall we? I'm suggesting that on that morning, you took with you two bottles of *Grey Goose* vodka, except you'd replaced one of them with water. You also took six packs of *Paracetamol*. In two of the packs, you'd replaced the tablets with *tictacs* and re-sealed them. It's not difficult. I've done it myself with a razor.'

Cahill sat back in his chair, smiled and folded his arms.

Flood continued: 'You sat together in her car. You egged

her on, you drinking water from the vodka bottle and popping *tictacs*, while Katie downed the best part of a bottle of *Grey Goose* and fifty *Paracetamol*. You kept going until she almost passed out. All you'd get is a sugar rush and a pain in your guts.'

Cahill stood, turned away from the table and looked out of the window. He turned back to face Flood. 'You can't prove any of this. It's pure hypothesis.'

'Maybe, but when we searched your house, I took some photos. One is a shot of the contents of a drawer in your bedroom dresser. It clearly shows a *Grey Goose* vodka bottle, blister packs of *Paracetamol* and a box of *tictacs*. You dumped them there, not thinking your house would be searched. When I guessed what you'd done, I used my camera to zoom in on the blister pack. You need to magnify the photo to see that they'd been tampered with. I could show you if you like.'

Cahill walked to the sink, poured himself a glass of water, swirled it once and swallowed it with a flourish. He slammed the glass back on the table.

'I've never heard such tosh!'

'I asked DS Miles to get one of the Met's analysts to check CCTV at every supermarket and off-licence within a three-mile radius of your house on the day before your meeting with Katie. Tell him what you found, Laura.'

'We got lucky.' Laura consulted her notebook. 'You were seen leaving Sainsbury's in the High Street, Lewisham at three fifteen pm carrying a plastic bag. We checked Sainsbury's records of liquor sales around that date and time. Hey Presto; they recorded the purchase of two bottles of *Grey Goose* vodka plus food items with your Sainsburys credit card at nine minutes past three.'

Flood cut in. 'Guess who the credit card belonged to?'

Cahill sat down at the table, his ruddy complexion turning redder. He raised his eyes to the ceiling and shook his head.

Flood pressed home his point. 'You dragged her from the car, barely conscious, and helped her walk over the frozen ground to a remote part of the forest before handcuffing her to a large branch of a tree with *your* handcuffs. That became her last resting place.'

'Why the bloody hell would I be stupid enough to do something like that?'

'Because you wanted the police to think that Katie, in her delusional state of mind, did it to frame you. The coroner's view was that it would have been entirely within her character to do so. In reality, it ensured that she couldn't escape from a certain death.'

Flood added, 'It's too clever, by half. You left her there, confident she'd die from a combination of the alcohol, the tablets and the freezing conditions. Precisely what you wanted. It solved your problem.'

'You're out of your mind. I don't think I've ever heard such bollocks.'

'Do you admit that you assisted Katie to commit suicide and that you handcuffed her to a tree?'

Cahill leant forward. He shouted, 'Of course not. Anyway, she'd already decided to end her life.'

'That's hardly a convincing defence is it? I'm sure a jury would be very interested to hear your motive.'

After a short silence, Cahill softened his tone. 'Look Flood, we're in the same boat, you and me. Kindred spirits and all that. We suffered the same fate with our wives — both killed by gangs bent on revenge.'

'Except I didn't make sure someone died to save my marriage.'

Cahill whined, 'Why are you doing this? I helped save your kids. If I hadn't seen them being abducted, you'd still be searching for them. Worse still, they could be dead.'

'That doesn't make us equal. You shouldn't be allowed to get away with what you did.' Flood nodded to Laura. She arrested Cahill and read him the caution.

CHAPTER TWENTY-NINE

September/October 2001

A month before the Lidgates' trial, Flood received a letter from the CPS. As a key witness involved in the charges laid against the defendants, the letter warned him that he'd be required to give evidence for at least three days and to make suitable arrangements.

The following weekend, Flood invited Laura, her daughter, Liz and grand-daughter, Ruby to his home. Pippa and Gemma loved the four-year-old. They made a great fuss of her, playing with her for hours until she became overexcited. Liz put her to bed to catch up on some much-needed sleep and spent the evening watching TV in the lounge. After the girls went to bed, Flood and Laura sat in the kitchen, sipping coffee.

'I can't believe we're almost there,' he said. 'I've hated these last few months. I'm used to being in the thick of investigations, not a bloody spectator. I haven't got a clue how well Harvey's prepared for the trial.'

'You'll find out soon enough. I'm sorry I couldn't have been more useful. How do you feel about giving evidence?'

'Can't wait, Laura. The only thing bugging me is that we can't be in court to hear all the evidence until we've completed our testimonies. I want to see Tommy and Vinnie Lidgate's reactions, get a feeling for how the trial's progressing.'

'At least, you'll be able to hear the closing arguments and the judge's summing up. And the case is bound to be high profile. The media will be all over it. Do you want to stay at my place when you're in court?'

'That would be great. Mum can stay at my house with the girls.'

*

A week before the trial, Flood received another call from the

CPS. 'My name's John Parry-Jones, QC. You probably know that I'm the lead prosecutor in the Lidgates' trial. As you're our key witness, I'd like to meet you before it starts.'

'I'd like that. When?'

'Are you free tomorrow? We could meet at my chambers in Lincoln's Inn. Say five pm? We can't discuss evidence but I can tell you about the way the case is going to be handled.'

Flood arrived at the chambers on time. A junior showed him into a tiny wood-panelled room on the first floor. Flood's feet sunk into the thick pile of a pattered rug as gold-framed portraits of former heads of chambers stared down at him.

When Parry-Jones entered, Flood's first impression was that he exuded none of the formal attributes of the room. Quite the opposite. He carried a thick file under one arm and reached out the other to Flood. Speaking with a cut-glass voice, he said, 'Mr Flood. Good to see you. Thanks for coming in. Please sit down.' He waved at a chair.

'First, may I say that having read all the statements, I deeply sympathise with you and your family. You've been through so much.' Parry-Jones ran the long fingers of one of his hands through his thick mane of snowy-white hair.

'Let me explain the running order. The judge will hear the murder cases first in chronological order: Georgina, Jenny Cahill and Barlow. Then he'll hear the evidence regarding the kidnapping of your daughters, the drug-running and, finally, the attempt on your life by Vincent Lidgate.'

Flood imagined Parry-Jones in court. His enthusiastic delivery combined with piercing blue eyes would unsettle the toughest of witnesses, he thought.

'You're going to be in the witness box for a long time. It's going to be hard for you. Do you have any questions?'

'Who else are you calling as witnesses?'

'Obviously, forensics and firearms specialists.' He opened his file and read from it. 'We'll also be calling DS Miles, DI Harvey for the police, plus Jessica Lidgate and McBride.'

'No Martin Cahill?'

'No. As you know the prosecution have to disclose any convictions or cautions to the defence prior to the trial. They'll know that Cahill's been arrested in connection with the Katie Brunswick case. The defence will have access to the taped interviews you had with him. They clearly showed that he lied to you about his alibi. They'll crucify him on the stand. That's why we don't want to call him.'

Flood raised his voice. 'Surely that weakens our case? Cahill witnessed the abduction, kept watch on the lodge, saw what happened at Jessica's. And what about McBride? He's got convictions as long as your arm and a history with The Goshawks gang. But you're calling him.'

'I agree. It's a gamble putting McBride in the dock. The defence will love it. They'll say his testimony can't be relied upon and that he'll say anything to implicate Tommy and Vinnie Lidgate in the hope that he'll get a lighter sentence. It's entirely possible that if the judge believes that to be the case, he could even exclude his testimony.'

Flood found himself tensing up. 'But McBride's evidence is crucial.'

Parry-Jones lowered his voice. 'I agree. That's why it's a risk we have to take. With his testimony and the physical evidence, we believe that we've got enough to secure the convictions. You'll have to trust me.'

Flood left the chambers feeling decidedly dejected.

*

In the week leading up to the trial, Flood read the crime reports in all the major newspapers to judge who gave the best coverage. He knew that this would be the only way of keeping up to speed until he was called to give evidence himself.

He settled on Alison Wright of the *Daily Life*. He discovered that she'd been writing for the paper for ten years and reported on many high profile murder cases. Flood arranged to have the newspaper delivered to Laura's flat for the duration of the trial.

He spent the days immediately before the trial in his study running through the statements he'd made. He carefully considered the questions he might be asked. He didn't want to leave anything to chance. He wasn't required to attend court until after the judge had heard the opening arguments from the prosecution and defence teams. He felt like a greyhound in the starting traps, itching to chase the hare.

*

On the morning of the second day of the trial, Flood woke early. Leaving Laura in bed, he pulled on his dressing gown and anxiously ran down the communal stairs to pick up the *Daily Life*. He returned, taking the stairs two at a time. After flicking on the coffee machine, he sat at the kitchen table and thumbed through the paper to read Alison Wright's report of the opening day of the trial. This became his daily ritual.

He read the headline:

GRANDFATHER AND GRANDSON ACCUSED OF TRIPLE MURDER, KIDNAPPING, TORTURE AND DRUG-RUNNING

Alison Wright laid out all the charges made against Thomas and Vincent Lidgate, saying that they'd pleaded not guilty to all of them. She reported that due to the possibility of fear and intimidation, the prosecution had successfully applied for the anonymity of the jury.

She added that in his opening speech, the prosecution lead QC, John Parry-Jones, told the court that he'd present compelling evidence including forensics, CCTV, recorded confessions and witness testimony to support each charge for each defendant. She quoted him:

> *These offences were meticulously planned and driven by a vicious gang with an obsession for revenge. When it looked likely that their offences would come to light, they took brutal action, murdering anyone who got in their way. They abducted and threatened to torture two young girls to ensure their grisly crimes would never be revealed.'*

Laura entered the kitchen wearing a Japanese Kimono, which she used as a dressing gown. He stood, kissed her on the cheek and said, 'Look at this.' As she took his seat, he poured her a cup of coffee. She took a sip as she read the report.

When she finished, she said, 'So… it's finally started.'

'Yes. I'm keen to hear what the defence counsel has to say tomorrow. They can't get away with all this, can they?' Flood waved a hand over the press report.

'I've learnt never to guess the outcome of a trial. I've been disappointed so many times. All we can do is give our evidence and hope Harvey's got everything he needs from McBride and Jessica. Then it's down to the jury.'

Laura took another sip of her coffee and looked up at Flood. 'Hey, I've got an idea. Why don't we get out of London for the day? If we don't, we'll only sit here and drive ourselves nuts discussing the trial. Be a good way to take our minds off the case. You've thought of nothing else for the past seven months.'

'Where do you want to go?'

'It's a nice day. What about Brighton?'

He shrugged. 'Brighton? OK.'

'Good. I'll call in sick. One rule though. No talking about the case.'

'It's a deal.'

Flood realised Laura had been right to get him out of the flat. They toured the Lanes and he bought her a matching set of earrings and bracelet from an antique jeweller which thrilled her. She wore them over lunch at Casalingo, an authentic Italian restaurant. Occasionally she fiddled with the bracelet, staring at it with a smile on her face. Other diners could have never guessed that an extraordinary drama affecting them was unfolding in a courtroom less than sixty miles away.

*

The following morning, the day of his first court appearance, Flood got up early. He scanned the *Daily Life* for the press report. He read:

GRANDFATHER AND GRANDSON DENY ALL CHARGES

Alison Wright reported that Thomas Lidgate's lead defence counsel, Samantha Cornelius, QC, would present cast-iron alibis for each of the three murders, adding that her client denies personally kidnapping the two young girls. Nor did he sanction the threat to torture them, his counsel stated, although he admits to witnessing it.

Lead counsel for Vincent Lidgate, Roger Whitney, QC, said that he would provide evidence proving that many of the charges levied against the defendant were malicious. Alison Wright quoted him:

'Every one of the prosecution witnesses has a grudge to settle with him.'

Flood stood and yelled, 'Laura. Come and read this load of tosh.'

She emerged from the bathroom, this time fully dressed and made up. He stood and gestured for Laura to take his seat. After reading the report, she turned and looked up at him standing behind her.

'Oh, you know how it is. Opening speeches are always designed to get the jury thinking. How many times have I thought after the prosecutors' opening argument, what are we doing here? The defendant is obviously guilty. And then when I hear the defence argument, I think, it's obvious that they are innocent.'

Flood let out a gasp of frustration. 'I know. But isn't this typical of Lidgate? Trying to wriggle out of the charges. He's already distancing himself from the action. I bet he'll blame everything on Vinnie.'

'Are you surprised?' She nodded at the clock on the kitchen wall. 'You'd better get ready. You're due in court at ten o'clock.'

She hugged him tightly and kissed him on his cheek. 'I'd better get going as well. The Met's admin won't do itself, you know.'

233

CHAPTER THIRTY

19th September to 14th November 2001

The aroma of musty books, reminding him of the library at his school, hit Flood as he entered the windowless Court Twelve. Unlike other Crown Courts in which he'd given evidence, Flood always felt the Old Bailey exuded a theatrical, almost regal ambiance. Words resonated across the courtroom, rebounding off the walnut panels, making them sound more significant.

When called to the elevated witness box, he felt the eyes of everyone in the court boring into him. Each with differing emotions, he thought. He glanced at the judge, the Honourable Mr Justice Brennan, resplendent in his cream wig and red robes which threatened to envelope him.

From his position in the witness box, Flood had a clear view of the defendants. Tommy Lidgate sat in a wheelchair. Flood had been told that Lidgate would never walk again unaided. He still couldn't use crutches due to the damage done by the bullet which had shattered his shoulder.

Vinnie wore a badly fitting suit and tie like his grandfather, presumably in an effort to impress the jury. Two burly dock officers sat between them. Vinnie stared around the courtroom biting his nails, appearing disinterested in the proceedings. Flood couldn't decide whether his demeanour represented bravado or disguised genuine fear.

After Flood gave his name and swore on the bible, Mr Parry-Jones, QC, rose to his feet. Flood felt a palpable sense of anticipation from the jury. The hare had been let loose. And now the greyhound starting trap was released.

Parry-Jones's easy, confident charm shone through as first, he set out Flood's credibility as a prosecution witness. He asked him to confirm his years of service, his experience as a senior police officer, his impeccable record, including successfully putting away a notorious gang leader. He prompted Flood to tell the court about his two Chief Constables' Commendations.

He went through Flood's statement meticulously, highlighting the horrors that he and his family had suffered, starting with Georgina's murder and ending with the kidnapping and threats to torture his daughters. Each time Flood glanced at the dock, Lidgate glared back at him in a bold attempt at intimidation.

'After you arrived home to discover that your seventy-three-year-old mother had been trussed up and bundled into a cupboard, can you tell the court what happened next?'

Flood, as he had been trained, directed his reply to the jury. 'I've never seen such terror in my mother's eyes. She had a heart attack shortly afterwards and has never got over what happened. It hurts me to see her now. She's like a beaten dog.'

Parry-Jones continued: 'I imagine you felt the same when you discovered that your daughters had been abducted, first to the cellar at the lodge and then to Jessica Lidgate's basement. Can you describe the conditions?'

'My girls were seriously distressed. They'd been tied up and had their heads shaved. Vincent Lidgate was about to apply a vice to my daughter's hand. I don't know how anyone could do that to such young girls.'

Samantha Cornelius, QC, Tommy Lidgate's defence counsel, stood to make an objection. Mr Justice Brennan, anticipating her, put up a hand, leant forward, and directed his comment towards Flood. 'I recognise that you and your family have suffered a great deal but we don't need to hear your opinions, Mr Flood. Just stick to the facts please.'

Flood nodded an acknowledgement. Parry-Jones picked up where he left off. 'Can you tell the court how you all escaped from Jessica Lidgate's house?'

Flood recounted the events, reliving his feelings of helplessness until Jessica's intervention. He added, 'My girls were badly affected by the gunfire in such an enclosed area. If Jessica hadn't returned to her house when she did, I believe our lives would have been in danger.' He directed the last sentence towards the defendants. Thomas Lidgate stared back even more defiantly. Vinnie sat, unmoved, a vacant expression on his face.

Flood carried on. 'This happened to my girls on top of them losing their mother four years earlier in the revenge hit-and-run attack. They were only three and five years old.' Flood paused to let that fact sink in to the jury's minds.

He continued: 'Since their abduction, every noise, every shadow that passes our house makes them jump. When you put it all together, it's had a devastating effect on them. They've had a tough time.'

He noticed several members exchange glances with each other and shake their heads.

*

It had taken two-and-a-half days for Parry-Jones to complete his examination. As he finished, Flood scanned the jury members' faces seeking clues about their feelings. He knew that predicting their mood was a mug's game. From their expressions, he hoped that he'd at least gained their sympathy at the halfway stage of his examination.

Flood soon realised how Samantha Cornelius, QC, had earned her reputation. She possessed none of Parry-Jones' charm. Not helped by her appearance. Her eyes appeared to be constantly squinting. Her sullen expression gave her an aura of a woman not to be messed with. She challenged every aspect of Flood's testimony as if *she* was the one being accused.

He noticed that she had a habit of looking away from him at the start of a question, addressing no one in particular. Then she'd swivel her head back to eyeball him as she reached the end of the question, like a darts player aiming at the bull's-eye.

*

Towards the end of her two-day interrogation of every detail of his statement, she said, 'You have a reputation for cutting corners, don't you, Mr Flood?'

'I have no idea what you're talking about.'

'Let me give you some examples. Is it true to say that you've spent most of your spare time investigating the murder of your wife since she died four years ago?'

'Yes I have.'

'Would you say that you've been *obsessed* with trying to find the perpetrators?'

'I think anyone in the same position would do the same.'

'The police investigated the case thoroughly. Nothing pointed them in the direction of the defendants. I suggest that once the undercover officer, Robbie Barlow, put it into your mind that a member of The Goshawks gang *may* have been responsible, you *assumed* that they were guilty.'

'I believe the tapes confirmed their involvement.'

'We'll discuss the tapes later. Let's look at your relationship with Robbie Barlow. You've admitted that you colluded with one of your criminal contacts to get Barlow fake passports and driving licences. You also admitted that you planned to hand them over in return for Barlow getting proof of the identity of the person who murdered your wife. Rather than go through normal police channels you decided to work with Barlow alone. Is that correct?'

'Yes it is. The Met had relegated my wife's murder to cold case status. This was my only way of getting to the truth. I had no choice.'

'And what about dropping Martin Cahill from your list of suspects in the Jenny Cahill murder case? You arrested him on the basis that he appeared to have a strong motive and an unsubstantiated alibi at the time.

'Then you told the court that Robbie Barlow had suggested to you that a member of The Goshawks gang was responsible. So you immediately dropped the Martin Cahill line of enquiry without further investigation. Indeed, Cahill joined you in a plan to get your girls released after they were kidnapped. Why did you cease to investigate Cahill's involvement?'

'Because Martin Cahill finally produced an alibi. That's why we let him go. When I resigned, I handed all the files over to another senior officer. You'll have to ask him why he didn't follow up.'

'I put it to you that you simply *assumed* that a member of The Goshawks gang was responsible. Isn't that true?'

Mr Justice Brennan, who'd been tapping a pencil on his bench, interrupted. 'This is all very interesting Ms Cornelius but where is this line of questioning taking us?'

Cornelius looked aggrieved. She patiently said, 'M'lord, I'm nearly there.'

She looked down and thumbed over a page in her file. 'Here's yet another example. You told the court that when you learnt from Jessica Lidgate that Barlow had secreted the tapes in a Transit van parked in a lockup on a trading estate in Finsbury, you, together with DS Miles, didn't inform the police. You visited the site, gained entry and searched the building in complete disregard of any potential forensic findings. Can you confirm this is true?'

'You know that is the case. But Jessica had faith in me. That's why she gave me the keys to the lockup and the van. She didn't have faith in the Met.'

'So you admit that you cut corners.'

'I did what I thought was best.'

Cornelius glanced down at her file again. 'Why did you go to Jessica Lidgate's home to rescue your daughters without involving the Metropolitan Police?'

'I thought I could reason with Tommy Lidgate. He said that if I got the Met involved, his gang would harm my daughters. I believed him.'

Mr Justice Brennan appeared to lose patience. He barked, 'I've asked you before, Ms Cornelius. What is your objective, here?'

'M'lord, I'm questioning this witness's credibility and whether his testimony can be relied upon. I'm suggesting that he developed an obsessive vendetta against The Goshawks gang and Thomas Lidgate in particular. He became personally involved. He didn't seek help from the police. He's cut corners purely in order to pursue only the defendants.'

'You've made your point, Ms Cornelius.'

'Thank you, M'lord. I have no more questions for this witness.'

The judge nodded at Vinnie's barrister, Roger Whitney, QC. He defied the appearance of a stereotypical lawyer. Despite his twenty-five years' experience, he looked younger, more athletic and fresher-faced than his opposite numbers.

He addressed the judge. 'To avoid duplication and further delay, M'lord, the defence case brought by my learned friend in respect of this witness, applies equally to the defendant. I would only add the following points.'

He turned to Flood. 'With regard to the shooting of Jenny Cahill, we've heard from the firearms expert who testified that it would have taken a crack shot to have fired the fatal bullet from a hand gun from a moving car. He said, either that, or the shooter got lucky.

'The prosecution have provided no evidence whatsoever to prove that Vincent Lidgate is a good shot. For example, you told the court that the defendant fired a shot at you twice from close quarters in and around the basement where your daughters were being held. If he's such a *good shot*, surely he'd have been more successful?'

'Fortunately for me, he wasn't.'

'Then, apart from being lucky, the *most likely* explanation for the fatal shooting of Jenny Cahill is that it must have been a proficient sharpshooter. Which rules out Vincent Lidgate. Do you agree?'

Flood forced himself to remain calm despite his body wanting to explode. 'As I said in my statement, Vincent Lidgate fired his gun at me twice. I don't know how he missed.'

'As my learned friend has suggested, you never investigated Martin Cahill to the point where you could rule out his involvement, did you?'

'I interviewed him several times. We finally established that he had a cast-iron alibi so we let him go.'

'But you can see where I'm coming from. Couldn't Martin Cahill, given his motive, have hired a sharpshooter to kill his wife?'

'My team checked his emails, phone records, and movements. We found no evidence to support the possibility of a third party being involved.'

'Thank you. I have no further questions, M'lord.'

The judge turned to Flood. 'Thank you for your testimony. You are free to go.' He turned to the jury. 'We'll adjourn now until tomorrow morning, ten am sharp.'

As he stepped down, Flood looked across at Lidgate and Vinnie. For the first time since he'd been in the witness box, Flood detected faint smiles creasing their faces.

*

Flood had lost all sense of reality during the trial. The case had completely consumed him. As he walked the mile-and-a-half to Laura's flat, he thought about his girls and his mother. He'd call them tonight, tell them how much he loved them and express the hope that their tormentors would be put away for a very long time.

As he opened the door, Laura rushed to hug him. She planted a kiss fully on his lips. Drawing back, she asked, 'You look shattered. How did it go?'

Flood slumped down on the sofa. He shook his head. 'Tough. Cornelius has got the knack of making complete bullshit sound plausible. It's not looking good, Laura.'

'I'll get you a glass of wine.' She opened the fridge and retrieved a bottle of Sancerre. As she poured generous measures into two glasses, she said, 'I got a call from the CPS an hour ago. They want me in court tomorrow. You're done, I assume? Tell me all about it.'

When Flood finished, he took a sip of wine and said, 'I'll come with you tomorrow. I want to hear the rest of the evidence. Just hope it's enough to get the convictions.'

*

When they arrived at the Old Bailey, Laura entered via the main entrance and Flood made his way to the stairs to the visitors' gallery. He climbed up to the third floor, passed through security and sat in one of the few remaining seats.

Parry-Jones took Laura through her statement covering her role in the Jenny Cahill case, the link with Barlow and assisting Flood in the plan to rescue his girls after their abduction.

Flood felt pride in the way she handled her evidence. She was confident and forthright. Several members of the jury nodded as she explained her part in the investigations. Especially when she told them how she'd comforted Pippa and Gemma after their ordeal.

Flood felt himself growing increasingly angry as Cornelius's cross-examination turned personal towards the end of her questioning.

'It's clear to the court that you developed a relationship with former DCI Flood. I suggest that you became sucked into his fixation of blaming Thomas Lidgate for his wife's murder. It led you to hold back vital information from the police, didn't it?'

'I believed it was the right thing to do at the time.'

'The records show that you ignored police procedures on several occasions. Let me list some of them.' Cornelius read from her file:

- 'Not declaring the fact that you knew that DCI Flood had made contact with an undercover officer, Robbie Barlow.
- 'Not filing in police records a copy of the tape recording taken at the time.
- 'Entering a crime scene, namely the lockup where the Transit van was parked, without back up and forensic support. I could go on. What do you have to say to that?'

'I genuinely thought that not involving the Met gave us the best chance of putting away the despicable men who are accused of these crimes.' Laura looked directly at the dock.

'The Metropolitan Police obviously didn't agree with you, did they?'

'No.'

'It's certainly not the behaviour they would expect from an

experienced detective sergeant. That's why they demoted you. Put you back in uniform. Took you off front line duties. Isn't that true?'

Laura's eyes blazed back at her inquisitor.

'Yes. But you're taking this out of context. The Met were getting nowhere on the Jenny Cahill case. As far as the kidnapping was concerned, the threat to Andy Flood's girls was real. Dealing with Barlow the way we did resulted in successfully rescuing the girls from a life-threatening situation.'

Cornelius's eyes squinted at Laura harder than ever. 'You're missing my point, *Constable* Miles. You deceived the Metropolitan Police. I hope your statement and testimony is not deceiving the jury. No more questions, M'lord.' She returned to her seat, a satisfied look on her face.

The judge addressed Vinnie's barrister. 'Do you have any questions, Mr Whitney?'

'No, M'lord. My learned friend has covered all the points I wanted to raise.'

The judge said to Laura, 'Thank you. You may stand down.' He turned to the jury. 'We'll take a lunch break now. We'll reconvene at two pm.'

Laura looked relieved. She glanced up at Flood as she stepped out of the witness box and slowly walked out of the courtroom. He smiled at her before leaving the public gallery ahead of anyone else. Bounding down the stairs, he met her at the main exit with a hug.

'Well done, Laura. You did well.'

As they separated, she said, 'I see what you mean about Cornelius. What a bitch!'

'What can I say. I'm sorry I got you involved. I had no idea it would come to this.'

*

They went to the Greek cafe over the road for a sandwich and a cup of tea. An hour later, they returned to the courtroom and sat together in the still-crowded gallery as McBride began his testimony via a video link from Belmarsh prison. He was being held there awaiting sentencing after pleading guilty to all the charges.

Flood felt the already tense atmosphere in the courtroom heighten as McBride's face appeared on the screen for the first time. He looked slimmer, probably the effects of prison food, he thought.

He watched Vinnie and Tommy Lidgate both glaring towards the screen, signalling pure hatred at the man whose testimony could seal their fate. Tommy mouthed the words, *fucking snitch!*

McBride stated that Vinnie was the driver and he was the passenger in the hit-and-run attack on Flood's wife. He also admitted that he was the driver when Vinnie shot and killed Jenny Cahill. He told the court about his role in the gang's drug-running and the torture and murder of Robbie Barlow.

When Parry-Jones questioned him about the kidnapping of the girls, McBride's tone grew edgy. 'I didn't agree with that. It went too far. I told Tommy. He accused me of going soft.'

'But you still went ahead with it though, didn't you?'

'You don't know what it was like. Tommy Lidgate threatened to kill me if I didn't go along with what he wanted. He's the boss. He ordered Vinnie and me to do all the things we did.'

Parry-Jones turned to the jury and repeated the sentence. '*He ordered Vinnie and me to do all the things we did.*' Flood inwardly cheered.

'I have no more questions, M'lord.'

Cornelius began by asking McBride, 'Why did you pleaded guilty to all the charges?'

'My lawyer advised me to. They said the evidence against me was so strong.'

'Your alleged partners-in-crime were advised to plead not guilty to the same charges. Do you expect to receive a more lenient sentence by pleading guilty and pointing your finger at your former associates?'

'No.'

'Why have you decided to act as a witness for the

prosecution?'

'Because I didn't agree with the kidnapping of kids.'

'But you went along with everything else the gang did. It seems odd that you *suddenly* developed a conscience. I put it to you that you turned Queen's Evidence in the *expectation* of getting your sentence reduced. I'd go so far as to say that you have the motivation to pile on as much of the blame as you can onto the defendants on the basis that the more dirt you dish on them, the more lenient your sentence. Isn't that right?'

Parry-Jones' face looked about to burst. He jumped to his feet. 'M'lord. My learned friend has absolutely no evidence that this is the case. It is, as the court knows, a criminal offence for anyone to offer such inducements.'

'I agree, Mr Parry-Jones. Ms Cornelius, please contain your comments to the facts.'

'Thank you, M'lord. No more questions.'

Vinnie's barrister, Roger Whitney, stood, pulled up the right-hand side of his gown, which had slipped off his shoulder and addressed the jury.

'M'lord has authorised, in the interests of justice, the release of this witness's criminal record.' He turned over several pages of his lever-arch file, colour-coded with Post it stickers attached. Stopping at one, he read out a list giving the dates of twelve convictions for violent behaviour, possession and supply of drugs and carrying offensive weapons. 'You've spent three of the last six years in jail. You don't appear to have learnt anything from your time inside. Why should the jury believe your testimony against your co-defendants?'

'Because it's true,' McBride mumbled.

'No more questions for this witness, M'lord.'

Flood recognised a clear pattern emerging in the defence teams' strategy. They'd realised that they couldn't successfully challenge the evidence, so they'd rely on discrediting every prosecution witness; question their motives, put up enough of a smokescreen to create doubt in the minds of the jury.

CHAPTER THIRTY-ONE

November 2001

Following a short break, Jessica's testimony was beamed into the courtroom via a video link. Flood hardly recognised her without her trade-mark thick eye make-up. Her skin looked pasty and pinched and the spark had disappeared from her eyes.

Parry-Jones took her carefully through her relationship with Barlow, ending with their plans to start a new life together away from the criminal fraternity.

Then he asked, 'In your statement, you said that you *hated* Thomas Lidgate. Will you tell the court why?'

Jessica's eyes narrowed. 'Yeah. First, he took my Vinnie away from me. He'd never have done 'alf the things he did if Tommy hadn't groomed him.' Flood noticed Lidgate's lips turn into a snarl.

'What do you mean by *groomed him?*'

'He wormed 'is way into Vinnie's brain when he was fourteen. Took advantage of the fact that his father spent most of his time in prison. Vinnie's impressionable, easily led. He idolises Tommy.'

'What did Tommy Lidgate actually *do*?'

'Showed him how to deal in drugs, use a knife to torture people. Even showed him how to use a gun. There was nothing Vinnie wouldn't do to please Tommy. He always wanted to prove himself to him.'

'Is there another reason why you hate Tommy Lidgate?'

'Yeah. When he found out about Robbie being an undercover cop, I'm sure he got Vinnie to torture him, then kill him when he didn't tell him what he'd done with the tapes.'

Tommy Lidgate yelled from the dock, causing everyone in the courtroom to flinch. 'That's absolute bollocks!' He pointed at Parry-Jones. 'You should be asking her about trying to kill *me!*'

Mr Justice Brennan glared at him. 'If you interrupt again, you'll be sent down to the cells. I won't have it in my court.' Turning back to Jessica, he said, 'You've just expressed your opinion. Please stick to the facts, Mrs Lidgate.'

Parry-Jones lowered his voice as he addressed Jessica again. 'I know this is difficult for you. Can you tell the court what you witnessed in the basement of your home?'

Jessica made a point of turning to the judge and said, 'I'll give you a *fact*. I saw *my* son about to torture a kid, holding her fingers in a vice. I couldn't believe me eyes. He'd never have done that unless Tommy told him to. Just proves the influence he has on him.'

'Did you also witness your son shooting at Mr Flood?'

Keeping her eyes on the judge, she said, 'Here's another *fact*. Yeah. I was stood at the bottom of the stairs. I saw him, clear as day, point a gun at him and shoot. Tommy Lidgate's turned my son into a monster.'

'Thank you, Mrs Lidgate. No more questions M'lord.'

Samantha Cornelius, who'd been looking closely at her notes during Jessica's examination, stood and asked, 'How long have you been married, Mrs Lidgate?' She repeated her dart thrower's technique of turning back to face the witness at the last moment.

'What's that got to do with anything?'

'Just answer the question, please.'

'Twenty-three years.'

'So you've been involved with this criminal family for almost a quarter of a century. It's become a way of life for you, hasn't it? Your husband has served several prison sentences during your marriage. He's currently serving twenty years for a vicious attack on another gang member isn't he?'

'Yeah.'

'Is it any surprise, then, that your son simply followed in the family tradition? He wouldn't need a mentor or someone to groom him, telling him what to do. His criminality is part of his DNA, isn't it?'

Before answering, Jessica looked around the courtroom

looking for someone to give her the right answer. Eventually, she said, 'That's your opinion.'

Cornelius responded, 'It seems to me that you're blaming Tommy Lidgate for turning your son into a criminal when all the evidence points to Vincent simply following in his father's footsteps.'

Flood wanted to scream at Cornelius, *you can't put all the blame on Vinnie!*

Mr Justice Brennan interjected. 'Ms Cornelius, as you well know, the crime of grooming in this context doesn't exist. Please explain where you're going with this argument?'

'The point I'm making, M'lord, is that if this witness *believes* that Thomas Lidgate groomed her son *and* ordered him to commit the crimes he's accused of, her testimony may be tainted.'

'You've made your point. Please move on.'

'I have no more questions, M'lord.'

The judge asked Roger Whitney, 'Do you have any further questions for this witness?'

'No, M'lord.' The video link was terminated. A blank screen replaced Jessica's care-worn face as Parry-Jones stood and called his expert witnesses.

The forensic experts presented overwhelming evidence linking Vinnie and McBride to the lockup and the disused swimming pool where Barlow had been murdered. Parry-Jones focussed heavily on the fact that fibres from Barlow's clothes were discovered on Vinnie and McBride's coats.

Roger Whitney claimed that there was nothing sinister in this. 'The three of them had spent the best part of four days together in the confines of a Ford Transit van. They'd travelled to Marseilles and back, arriving in the UK a day before the police discovered Barlow's body. Cross-contamination of fibres would be expected.'

The firearms expert testified that striations from the gun used in the killing of Jenny Cahill were identical to a gun later used by Vinnie in the attempted murder of Flood. 'These striations are the unique marks a bullet makes as it passes through the barrel. There can be no doubt about it. It is the same gun.'

Whitney countered: 'Vincent Lidgate admits to owning the gun. But in his statement he said that he often lent it to other members of the gang. It's quite common. Unfortunately, he can't remember which member had it at the time of Jenny Cahill's murder.'

Flood's confidence in nailing Vinnie grew. It went off the scale when he heard the testimony from the manager of a bodyshop in London which carried out repairs to the BMW used to mow down his wife.

Parry-Jones stood and replaced several stray strands of his white hair underneath his wig. He reminded the court that in McBride's police interview after he'd agreed to turn Queen's Evidence, he'd told them where the BMW Estate car had been taken for repair. Flood recalled that the police had trawled over a hundred and fifty bodyshops within a ten-mile radius of Southampton without success, unaware that the car had been driven to London for repair.

The prosecution called Peter Wiggins. After he'd sworn the oath, Parry-Jones asked, 'Please tell the court your occupation.'

'I am the bodyshop manager for Mitchell Crash Repairs.'

'I know it's over four years ago but can you confirm that on Monday 4th March 1997, your firm carried out repairs to a 1996 black BMW Estate, registration number, P737XRO?'

'Yes.'

'Can you tell the court the nature of those repairs?'

'The front grill was badly dented, the paintwork damaged and one of the headlamps had been smashed.'

Flood's mind immediately flashed back to the time when he first learned about the hit-and-run. Much of the pain of that moment remained.

'Would you recognise the person who brought the car into your bodyshop?'

'Yes. I would.'

'Is he in this courtroom?'

'Yes he is.'

'Can you point him out?'

Wiggins pointed at the dock, straight at Vinnie. 'He's sitting on the left.'

Flood noticed Vinnie shrug his shoulders.

'You raised an invoice for the work, didn't you? There's a copy of it in the bundle in front of you. Can you read out the name of the customer?' Wiggins flicked through the bundle and stopped at a document and said, 'V. Lidgate.'

'How did he pay you?'

'In cash.'

'Did he ask you any questions about the repair?'

'I remember him asking if I could keep the car in storage for a while. I said I couldn't. I didn't have the space. He drove it away.'

'Thank you, Mr Wiggins. I have no more questions, M'lord.'

Roger Whitney declined the offer from the judge to examine Wiggins further.

Parry-Jones called his final witness, a police officer from the Met's traffic unit, Sergeant John Taylor. 'You impounded a BMW Estate car after it was used to drive to the safe deposit company and carried out a full inspection. Can you tell the court your findings?'

Taylor stiffened to attention in the witness box as he replied, 'We carried out a comprehensive inspection of the car including the underside and chassis. A shard of a reflective lens from a bicycle pedal had become tightly wedged between a rubber bush and the car's sub-frame. We compared it to other pieces of lens from the bicycle pedal which had been collected and retained from the crime scene involving a fatal hit-and-run attack in February 1997. It was a perfect match.'

'Thank you, Sergeant Taylor.' Parry-Jones turned to the jury. 'You will see photographic evidence of this complete match in your bundles. I have no more questions, M'lord.'

Flood felt sick at the confirmation that he'd been a passenger in the same car used to kill Georgina.

Almost before the judge had time to ask Whitney whether he had any questions, he jumped to his feet, anxious to defend Vinnie.

'The defendant has never denied that he took the car to have it repaired. He doesn't recall asking the manager about storing the car. There is no record of that conversation. All that has been established here is that this particular BMW collided with Georgina Flood's bicycle resulting in her death. There is no concrete evidence of who drove the car apart from the testimony from someone who has turned Queen's Evidence. It's his word against the defendant's.' He paused momentarily before saying, 'I have no questions for this witness, M'lord.'

Parry-Jones stood and faced the judge. 'That completes the case for the Crown, M'lord.'

'Thank you, Mr Parry-Jones. Ms Cornelius, Mr Whitney, do either of your defendants wish to give evidence in person regarding their defence?'

Cornelius stood and said, 'No, M'lord. I will not be calling Thomas Lidgate.'

As she sat, Whitney got to his feet. 'No, M'lord. I will not be calling Vincent Lidgate either. However, I would like to bring to the jury's attention that the prosecution case against my client is partly based on Thomas Lidgate's version of events. He puts all the blame on him. Vincent Lidgate strongly refutes this.'

The judge thanked him and said to both barristers, 'Have you both advised your defendants that if they choose not to give evidence, an adverse inference can be drawn from their failure to do so?'

They both replied, 'Yes, M'lord.'

Flood had witnessed this scenario countless times. He knew that by not giving evidence in person, a defendant cannot be cross-examined by the prosecution. The Crown would not have the opportunity to exploit any inconsistencies between what they said when questioned by the police and what they say in court. Barristers had told him that it was one of the toughest decisions they ever had to make.

In this case, Flood suspected both barristers considered that an *adverse inference* was preferable to taking the risk of the defendants coming across badly under cross-examination. The judge and jury would have to rely only on the defendants' statements and a record of their police interviews contained in their bundles.

Before the judge asked the barristers to begin their closing arguments, Samantha Cornelius stood and said, 'M'lord. I have one other issue regarding possible undisclosed evidence concerning the main prosecution witness, Mr Flood. It has only recently been brought to my attention. I intend to make an informal request to my learned friend for the prosecution. He may need time to consider the matter.'

Parry-Jones looked up from his notes. A puzzled expression crossed his face.

Mr Justice Brennan grunted. Flood realised that he hated anything which slowed down the progress of the case.

'In that case, in view of the time, it's now three pm, I'll adjourn for the day. I'll start tomorrow at two pm prompt. That should give you time to explore the disclosure, Ms Cornelius.'

Parry-Jones looked up at the public gallery and, on seeing Flood, pointed a finger towards the front of the building where there was a meeting area. He mouthed, *meet me there.*

Flood and Laura made their way down the stairs to the public exit from the gallery and across the road to the Greek cafe. Flood found her a seat.

'What's that all about, do you think?' Laura asked.

'I've no idea. Wait for me here. I'll come back for you after I've seen Parry-Jones.'

*

Flood sat on a bench in the general waiting area, trying to guess the nature of the undisclosed evidence. He felt he'd scrupulously stuck to his statement while giving his testimony.

Fifteen minutes later, Parry-Jones entered, looking flustered. Flood stood to meet him as he said, 'This is most unusual. The defence have questioned whether we have disclosed *everything* regarding your resignation from the Metropolitan Police Force.'

251

CHAPTER THIRTY-TWO

November 2001

As Parry-Jones moved towards several vacant chairs in a quiet corner of the waiting room, Flood's hands turned clammy, his mouth furred up and a knot grew in his stomach.

His brain worked overtime: had the police cover-up been detected? What did Lidgate know? What had he told his barrister?

Parry-Jones sat down opposite Flood, took off his wig, laid it in his lap and straightened his hair with both hands. 'Is there anything else you can tell me about your resignation that wasn't in your statement?' His intense blue eyes scanned Flood's face.

'Nothing. The Met said I was showing signs of stress, thought I might be having a nervous breakdown. They agreed it was best if I resigned.'

Parry-Jones frowned. 'If there is another reason that you've not disclosed and they discover it later, believe me, that is not going to be good for you.'

Not good? More like total disaster, thought Flood. He replied emphatically, 'There isn't.'

'OK. I'll inform the defence that we have disclosed everything. It's highly possible that they will ask the judge to call you back to the witness box.'

*

Flood arrived back at the cafe and met up with Laura. She stood as she saw him approach.

'My God! You look awful. What happened?'

Flood blurted, 'I think bloody Lidgate's found out the real reason for my resignation.'

'What?' She put a hand to her mouth then took it away. 'How could he possibly have discovered that? You told me that only a handful of people know what really happened.'

'I'm sure Lidgate's tentacles reach deeply into the Met. The defence will cross-examine me tomorrow. I've got to make the stress argument stick. If I don't, it's game over for me.'

*

Samantha Cornelius wasted no time in cross-examining Flood again. 'Can you explain to the court why, at a critical stage of your investigation, you suddenly resigned from the Metropolitan Police Force?' He knew that barristers, like detectives interviewing suspects, mostly asked questions to which they already knew the answers.

He'd never known a courtroom so silent. He took a deep breath. 'I resigned because I found the job too stressful to continue. I was on the brink of having a nervous breakdown. It's a tough job being a London detective.'

'Were you examined by a Metropolitan Police medical expert? We don't seem to have a record of that.'

'No. It was a mutual decision agreed with my Borough Commander.'

Cornelius looked down at her notes. 'Stress wasn't the real reason, was it?'

Flood felt the now familiar clamminess around the back of his neck and hands. He fought hard not to look or sound nervous. A thought flashed through his mind. *Was this going to be where his life effectively ended?*

He said, with as much conviction he could muster, 'There was no other reason.'

'The timing of your resignation is interesting. It came shortly after you'd met Barlow. You told the court that he'd told you that he had a good idea of who murdered your wife and Jenny Cahill. Doesn't that strike you as odd?'

'Stress can occur at any time.'

'That's interesting because following your resignation, you didn't appear to be too *stressed* to continue the investigation as a private investigator. Not too *stressed* to enlist the help of Martin Cahill and DS Miles to rescue your daughters. I can't think of anything more *stressful* than having to deal with their kidnapping and watching them having their heads shaved.' She swivelled her head towards him yet again and asked, 'Do you still maintain that you resigned because of stress?'

'Yes. I've told you. I had no choice.'

'We've accessed your medical records. There is no previous evidence of stress whatsoever. Quite the opposite, in fact. You seem to have enjoyed excellent health throughout your exemplary twenty-five years in the Police Force. That is the case, isn't it?' Her eyes bore into Flood.

Parry-Jones jumped to his feet. 'M'lord. The witness has told my learned friend that he resigned on grounds of stress three times and that the Metropolitan Police confirmed that was the case.'

Mr Justice Brennan peered down from his bench. 'Ms Cornelius?'

'M'lord. I'm making the case that, since resigning, Mr Flood seems to have been involved in further stressful situations. I'm suggesting that, perhaps, he wasn't stressed. In which case, there may be another reason for his resignation which has a bearing on this case.'

'Unless you can provide it, Ms Cornelius, the court will have to accept that another reason doesn't exist.'

'Thank you, M'lord. That completes the case for the defence.'

The judge asked Roger Whitney whether he had any questions. 'No, M'lord. That completes the case for my defendant, too.'

Flood tried not to show any emotion as he stepped out of the witness box. His rapid heartbeat, which had threatened to overcome him earlier, gradually returned to normal. He'd never before sensed such a powerful feeling of relief.

He made his way back to Laura's flat. She'd had to work her regular shift that day and wasn't there when Flood arrived. He poured himself a large glass of wine and walked around the living room like a caged panther, asking himself, repeatedly, *If Lidgate knew the real reason for my resignation, why didn't Cornelius bring it to the jury's attention?*

Laura arrived an hour later. After they'd embraced, she took off her coat and asked, 'Dying to know what happened in your cross-examination. I've been thinking about you all day.'

'I stuck to the story. That I resigned because of stress. Cornelius suggested that there was another reason. The judge didn't buy it. He told her to put up or shut up.'

Laura looked puzzled. 'So Lidgate can't know the truth. Otherwise, he'd have told her.'

'I think he knows something. Or it's a bluff. Or the Met covered it up. I don't know.'

*

The closing arguments from the barristers on the next day followed passionate claims and counter claims from the prosecution and the defence. Flood's emotions swung from one end of the scale to the other. The judge's summing up, beginning the following day, would provide a more balanced view of the major issues for the jury to consider, he hoped.

Early the next morning Flood and Laura fought their way past the phalanx of reporters and photographers hanging outside the Old Bailey. The case had attracted an increasing amount of press coverage as the weeks progressed.

After the usual security checks, they climbed the stuffy stairwell to the crowded public gallery. The barristers and their teams were already at their tables, chatting informally in hushed whispers to each other.

A court official wheeled Lidgate into the dock, followed by Vinnie and the two dock officers who stood between them. Flood had noticed that for the entire period he was in court, he'd never seen Vinnie and his grandfather speak to each other while in the dock. Not even an acknowledgement.

Mr Justice Brennan entered the courtroom as the usher called out, 'All rise.' The judge peered into his laptop, using it as an autocue. As he spoke, his eyes constantly switched between the jury and his script. Flood concentrated hard, anxious to hear the judge's view of the strengths and weaknesses of the evidence.

'Members of the jury, I will address only those essential matters which bear directly on the issues you have to determine for each defendant. I will start with the charges against Vincent Lidgate.

'With regard to the murder of Georgina Flood, you heard extracts from tape recordings taken by the undercover officer, Robert Barlow, between the defendant and Jack McBride. You will have to decide whether Vincent Lidgate did carry out the fatal hit-and-run attack or that he simply bragged to Barlow that he was responsible in order to impress him. I would remind you that McBride, a witness for the prosecution, alleges that he sat next to Vincent Lidgate and witnessed the collision.

'You must also consider the relevance of Vincent Lidgate's role in arranging for the repairs to the damaged BMW. Were his actions those of a guilty man or of someone simply seeking to restore the car to its former condition?'

'I turn now to the murder of Jenny Cahill, a former Metropolitan Police firearms officer. Vincent Lidgate admits to owning the gun used to kill her but at the time of the shooting, he claims that he'd lent it to another member of the gang although he can't remember who. McBride testified that he drove the car and witnessed Vincent Lidgate fire the fatal shots. You will have to consider the following points:

- do you accept the testimony from the firearms expert who linked the gun used to kill Jenny Cahill with a gun owned by Vincent Lidgate?
- is it possible that someone other than Vincent Lidgate fired the fatal shots?'

He paused and looked at the jury, allowing the questions to sink into their minds.

'In respect of the charges of torturing and murdering Robert Barlow, the Crown presented overwhelming DNA evidence implicating both Vincent Lidgate and Jack McBride. The defence argue that cross-contamination was to be expected as they'd spent several days together in a Transit van. You must decide whether this is a plausible explanation.

'The alleged kidnapping and torturing of young children is bound to stir your emotions. However, I must ask you to rely only on the evidence presented to you.

'The prosecution claim that the girls were kidnapped by the defendants in order to trade them for the tapes sent to Mr Flood. You've seen a disturbing video sent to him showing the girls' heads being shaved and threats being made.' Flood noticed several members of the jury shaking their heads.

'In addition, the prosecution allege that the girls were about to be tortured in front of Mr Flood by Vincent Lidgate. They claim that he was desperate to get his hands on the tapes as he'd been the one that spilt the beans, and in doing so, lost face in front of his grandfather. The prosecution further maintain that if Jessica Lidgate had not returned when she did, the girls would have suffered a great deal.

'Vincent Lidgate's defence is that it was not his intention to harm the girls; just to put enough pressure on Mr Flood to give up the tapes. You will have to decide whether that is the case.

'I turn now, to the charge of the attempted murder of Andrew Flood. The prosecution claim that Vincent Lidgate tried to kill him, shooting at him on two occasions with the same gun used to murder Jenny Cahill. Defence counsel claim that the shots fired were only a warning, designed to stop Flood chasing the defendant. You must decide whether the charge of attempted murder is proven. Members of the jury, I realise this is a lot for you to take in. We'll take a break now. I'll adjourn proceedings for one hour.'

*

Flood and Laura walked down the stairs to the exit. He shepherded her across the road to the now familiar Greek cafe. He guided her to a table away from the other customers and went to the counter to buy coffees.

Laura spoke first as Flood, his mind racing, stirred his drink. 'Penny for your thoughts?'

Flood shook his head. 'I can't believe that the jury won't see what a little shit Vinnie is. Surely there's enough evidence to find him guilty?'

Laura replied, 'That's the trouble with juries. You never know what they're thinking until you get the verdict.'

*

Flood and Laura returned to Court Twelve moments before the judge entered. He sat, straightened his laptop and peered at the screen again.

'Members of the jury, I will now deal with the charges against Thomas Lidgate. With regard to the fatal hit-and-run attack on Georgina Flood, you heard Vincent Lidgate say in the tape recording that he was working on his grandfather's orders. You also heard from Jack McBride who testified that it was Thomas Lidgate who ordered the attack. His defence counsel strongly refutes this. They provided an alibi for the time of the murder and insist that he had no motive for the killing.'

Flood shot Laura a look of incredulity and mouthed, 'What?'

'Regarding the murder of Jenny Cahill, you heard Vincent Lidgate say on the tapes that he was working on his grandfather's orders. Jack McBride made the same allegation. However, Thomas Lidgate, once again, produced an alibi and says that he knew nothing about Vincent Lidgate and Jack McBride's plans. You must decide who to believe.

'In respect of the torturing and killing of Robert Barlow at the lockup and the disused swimming pool, once more, the prosecution rely on testimony from Vincent Lidgate and Jack McBride that they were acting on Thomas Lidgate's instructions. They both insist that he wanted Barlow eliminated if he didn't reveal the whereabouts of the tapes.

'Thomas Lidgate's defence is that there is nothing whatsoever linking him to this crime. No DNA, no CCTV, no witnesses, only statements from two members of his gang, one of whom has turned Queen's Evidence.

'I refer now to the kidnapping of the two young girls. Thomas Lidgate has since admitted that he planned the kidnapping and provided a new statement to that effect.'

Flood turned to Laura and mouthed, *Good*.

Mr Justice Brennan continued: 'He also admitted to making calls to Mr Flood and sending him a video of the girls' heads being shaved. In his statement, he said that he didn't want to cause them any harm; just to shock Mr Flood into swapping the tapes for the girls.

'When they were being held in the basement of Jessica Lidgate's house, the prosecution allege that Thomas Lidgate ordered Vincent Lidgate to torture them. His counsel argues that he didn't. That it was Vincent Lidgate's idea. You will have to decide who is telling the truth.'

This time, Flood shook his head. He restrained himself from shouting *No!* at the judge who spoke about the other charges of illegally importing, producing and supplying Class A drugs. McBride's testimony and Barlow's tapes and pocketbooks provide convincing evidence, he said.

He reminded the jury that Thomas Lidgate admitted ownership of the paint factories but not the importation and supplying of drugs. The judge said that according to Lidgate's statement, he employed Vinnie and McBride to collect and deliver barrels of paint from France as part of his legitimate importation business.

The judge continued: 'You must decide whether Vincent Lidgate and Jack McBride acted alone in this venture or whether the operation was masterminded by Thomas Lidgate.

'There are two further points for you to consider. Thomas Lidgate's defence in respect of the murders of Georgina Flood, Jenny Cahill and Robert Barlow rely largely on the fact that he wasn't present at the time of each of the offences. This does not mean he may not be responsible.

'The question you must ask is: did Thomas Lidgate groom and order his grandson to commit the crimes as his mother has testified, or did Vincent Lidgate carry out these murders with Jack McBride's help in an effort to impress his grandfather?

'The final point to be considered is this: both defendants' defence counsels questioned the credibility of the prosecution witnesses. They raised it again in their closing arguments, making damaging assessments of their motives. It is a fact that they have all suffered to a degree from the alleged crimes of the defendants. Both defence counsels made the point that therefore, their testimony is unreliable, serving only their embittered self-interest.

'You must decide whether this challenging of the witnesses' credibility is a smokescreen, putting doubts in your minds or whether there is truth in the defence's allegation. I can't direct you here. Witness credibility is a matter for you, the jury, to decide.

'The defendants elected not to give evidence but relied upon the explanations given in their statements and police interviews. They have every right, in law, not to give evidence and you should only draw adverse inferences from that if you are sure that there is a case for them to answer and that there is no reasonable explanation for not giving evidence.'

The Honourable Mr Justice Brennan ceremoniously closed down the lid of his laptop and looked directly at the jury.

'The Crown has the burden of proving the guilt of the defendants. That burden never shifts. The defence, at no stage in this case, has to prove anything whatever to you. If you are sure of their guilt, you convict them, if you are not sure, you acquit them. The defendants are only guilty if the prosecution evidence is so overwhelming that it allows no other explanation.

'That is all I have to say about the facts of this case and the law. Please remember verdicts have to be separate verdicts as there are different evidential considerations for each of them. Choose one of your number to say what your verdicts are. If you need help, please refer to the jury bailiff who'll escort you to the jury room.'

He added that in view of the lateness of the day, 4.00 pm, the jury would be allowed home. He reminded them not to work on the case until they return the next day, nor to discuss it with anyone except a fellow member of the jury.

He stood and made his way to his chambers as the bailiff shouted, 'All rise.'

CHAPTER THIRTY-THREE

November 2001

'So, that's it. We have to sit and wait until tomorrow,' Laura said, as they passed through the exit from the public gallery onto the street.

Flood, who'd not uttered a word since the judge dismissed the jury, spat out, 'Fucking Lidgate! Vinnie's had it. He's going to cop everything. Lidgate's defence is spot on apart from the kidnapping. There's no evidence putting him anywhere near the crime scenes.'

Laura shook her head. 'We know he's a slippery character.'

'Slippery is not the word. Narcissistic psychopath, more like. I don't know what I'll do if Lidgate gets off. Even the drug-running will be down to Vinnie and McBride. The only mistake Lidgate made was sending me the video of the girls.'

Before Laura could answer, he continued: 'I don't know about you, Laura, I'm bloody shattered. These last few weeks have caught up with me. Now I *do* feel stressed.'

Laura replied, 'C'mon, let's go for a drink. We deserve it. There's a pub round the corner.'

Once they'd settled in the bar, Flood, his mind still buzzing, asked Laura. 'Do you believe in evil?'

'I do now.'

'I always have. Evil people don't think like us. They're disturbingly immoral and wicked. They're only out for themselves.' He shook his head. 'I don't get it.'

*

Flood woke first in the morning, his head slightly fuzzy. One drink had led to another and although not getting rip-roaringly drunk, they'd had enough to dull their pessimistic feelings about the jury's verdict. He collected his newspaper and read a report of the judge's summing up in the *Daily Life* which highlighted his comments about the credibility of the witnesses. They added to Flood's discomfort. He tried to take his mind off the case by thinking of his girls, imagining them safely at school, trying to impress their teachers.

Despite Laura urging him to eat something, he breakfasted on cups of tea; he couldn't face any food as doubts about getting justice drifted back into his consciousness.

They arrived at the Old Bailey at ten am to be informed that the jury were deliberating. They waited in the small waiting room outside Court Twelve as Flood's stomach continued to turn somersaults.

At ten minutes to twelve, the usher put his head around the door to say the court would be sitting in the next ten minutes. Flood exhaled and turned to Laura saying, 'Here we go.'

He looked down from the public gallery towards the dock and watched Lidgate fidget in his wheelchair. Vinnie looked more uncomfortable, as if it had finally dawned on him that Lidgate had planted all the nasty stuff on his shoulders. He shot his grandfather several plaintive glances for the first time, as if to say, *why have you done this?* Tommy Lidgate ignored him.

The judge entered followed by the jury who filed into the same seats they'd occupied for almost two months. Each of them looked serious and sombre, giving no clue about the verdicts.

When they'd settled, the judge nodded to the clerk of the court who said, 'Foreman of the jury, have you reached a verdict on which you are all agreed?'

The foreman stood up. 'Yes, we have.'

The clerk read out the charges one by one and asked for the jury's verdict. Laura reached over towards Flood, held his hand and squeezed it increasingly tightly as the foreman said, 'Guilty': five times for Lidgate, six for Vinnie, including the attempted murder charge.

Flood wanted to pick up Laura and hug her until she begged to be put down. He'd dreamt of this day, every day, for the last four-and-a-half years. Now, he felt as if a reservoir in his eyes had been breached. Tears ran down his cheeks. He brushed them away with the sleeve of his jacket. Laura reached over and put her arm around his shoulder.

Refocusing his eyes on the dock, he watched Lidgate glaring at the jury one by one as if memorising their faces. Rocking in his wheelchair, he yelled at them. 'You'll all fucking die, mark my words.'

The judge, unfazed, barked at one of the dock officers, 'Take him down.' Vinnie's pathetic, skinny face with the sticky-out ears looked utterly bemused.

Mr Justice Brennan set a date for sentencing in a week's time. Thanking the jury, he picked up his laptop and headed for his chambers. Flood stood with the rest of the court. He regained his composure and nodded at Parry-Jones as the other dock officer led Vinnie down to the cells. Flood imagined Georgina's face smiling down on him.

As soon as he left the court, he called his mother and the girls at Julie's house. He wanted them to be the first to know that these evil men couldn't harm them anymore, that they'd be put away for a long time. He hoped it would prove to be an important step towards their recovery.

*

Flood attended the Old Bailey with Laura again a week later to hear the sentencing. The judge began by describing Lidgate and Vinnie as two of the most evil men he had come across in over twenty years in the legal profession.

'It's a sad fact that organised crime is a brutal and savage industry. It lies only just below the surface of our civilised society which needs protection from the criminals responsible, especially ones as despicable as you two.'

He handed down three whole-life sentences to Tommy Lidgate for the murders. He added ten years for the kidnapping, a further ten years for grievous bodily harm and fourteen years for drug production and dealing. He ended by saying, 'You will die in jail.'

Lidgate, leaning forward in his wheelchair, yelled back, 'You and your family will die soon, too. I promise.'

Mr Justice Brennan, undeterred, said to the dock officer, 'Take the prisoner to the cells immediately.'

Lidgate yelled over his shoulder as he was being wheeled out of the court, 'You haven't heard the last of me.'

The judge addressed Vinnie. 'I've taken into account your age and that you were under the control of your grandfather when you were young. However, I've concluded that once you became an adult, you had a choice; to follow his murderous instructions or to disobey them. You chose the former and showed a callous disregard for the rule of law.'

He handed down the same sentences, adding a further fifteen years for the attempted murder of Flood. 'You too will spend the rest of your life in jail. London is now a safer place.'

Vinnie hung his head down towards the ground and kept it there as the dock officer led him down to the cells.

The judge sentenced McBride to a minimum term of twenty-two years, reduced because he'd pleaded guilty. It would not be a pleasant experience given his status as a supergrass, thought Flood.

He'd revelled in the verdicts a week earlier. Now he experienced a surge of elation at the sentences. He fought back a temptation to punch the air.

Laura turned to him. 'At last, you've got justice for Georgina. Now you can get on with your life.'

*

The next day, Flood received a call from his old boss, Detective Superintendent Fox. 'Good result, Andy. The Borough Commander's very pleased. Glad it turned out alright for you, too. Sorry you're not still in the job. The Met need more people like you.'

'Thanks. I'm just glad it's over. I don't ever want to see the inside of a courtroom again. I assume you heard about the defence questioning my resignation? They implied there was another reason. Do you know anything about that?'

Fox paused before replying, 'You remember Barlow's handler, Swanson?'

'Yes. Of course I do. Barlow never trusted him.'

'We believe Tommy Lidgate got word to him to get something on you. Something that would destroy your credibility as a witness. Intel said they discovered that Swanson was investigating your background. The Hartley case back in September last year was the most recent high profile investigation you worked on. Swanson started there. We've been watching him. We know he paid a visit to Hartley in jail. He'd have told him that he was framed. Then Swanson visited the forensics manager, the one who discovered your fall from grace, asking about the forensics. He informed the Borough Commander. You'll remember, the BC and the manager are great pals.'

Flood's heart rate doubled. 'Christ! What did the forensics manager tell Swanson?'

'Don't worry, Andy. He gave nothing away. That courtroom shenanigans by Lidgate's barrister was obviously a bluff, hoping you'd crack.'

'Can't you arrest Swanson?'

'We've got nothing on him that will stick... so far. He's somehow covered himself over the Barlow tapes. I've no idea how. Don't worry. We'll take care of things. Swanson's on round-the-clock surveillance. It's as important for the Met to keep a lid on this as it is for you.'

*

After the trial, Laura visited Flood every weekend. He watched with pleasure how she interacted with his girls. She chatted to them constantly, showing great interest in their new school and the friends they'd made. Flood realised from the way the girls spoke to him about Laura that they'd grown to love her.

On one such weekend, after the girls had gone to bed, Flood and Laura sat at the dining table enjoying dinner. Laura asked how the girls were.

'Still not right. They're sleeping better, although sometimes one or both of them will wake up from a nightmare, screaming. Pippa, especially. She'll burst into tears at the slightest reminder of her ordeal. Both sleep with the light on at night.'

'Did the psychiatrist say whether they'll ever get back to normal?'

'She says it depends to a large extent on me. They need to be convinced that I'll always put them first. They're the most important thing in my life, so of course I will. I'm determined to help them get over this.'

'And your mother?'

'She's OK. Needs to take things easy. Julie's fantastic with her. Having the girls close by is a great help. I'd say, given everything that's happened, we're coping well.'

Laura raised her wine glass and said, 'Here's to coping well.'

Flood picked up his glass and clinked it against hers. 'I'll drink to that.'

As she placed her wine on the table, she asked, 'Have you heard how Jessica's getting on?'

'I assume she's still in the Witness Protection Programme. I liked Jessica. She showed great bravery at the trial. Barlow was brave too. He could have got out of the Met on his own but he gave his life for his new family. What's the latest on Martin Cahill?'

'You won't believe this. He's on the Met's wanted list. He skipped police bail after he was charged with assisting Katie Brunswick to commit suicide. He's vanished.'

'Bloody typical,' said Flood.

'And you, Andy. Are you OK?'

'Yes… yes. Except if the truth about my resignation comes out, I'm screwed. Foxy says he's got it covered. I hope he's right. All I want to do is to get on with my life.'

He paused for a moment before saying, 'On that subject, I've been thinking. Why don't you leave the Met? We could start up a private investigation business together. We make a bloody good team.'

'What, you mean like Holmes and Watson?'

'I'm serious. Anyway a deerstalker hat doesn't suit me. I

don't like smoking pipes, either. You could come and live with us.'

Laura smiled. She cocked her head to one side. 'I don't know which of the three aspects of your proposition appeals to me most: leaving the Met, living with you or working with you.'

He adopted Sean Connery's James Bond accent. 'I appreciate it's a difficult choice.' Flood smoothed his hair back with one hand and then the other in an exaggerated manner. 'Think about it; you'll be doing all three. I promise I won't call you Miss Moneypenny.'

Laura smiled. 'It's tempting. Since the trial, you've made me feel so happy.'

Flood looked deeply into her eyes. 'I want to be with you, Laura. I never imagined anyone on this earth could help me recover from a broken heart. But you have.'

He walked round to her side of the table. Laura stood up. Drawing her into his arms, he kissed her on the lips. Laura responded and hugged him close to her.

Flood stepped back. 'I love you, Laura. The girls love you. My sister loves you. Even my mother approves! We'd have a great life together. Will you think about it?'

Laura beamed back at Flood. 'I will.'

THE END